AN IRISH

FOLKLORE

TREASURY

A selection of **OLD STORIES, WAYS** and **WISDOM**
from the **SCHOOLS' COLLECTION**

JOHN CREEDON

Gill Books

Gill Books
Hume Avenue
Park West
Dublin 12
www.gillbooks.ie

Gill Books is an imprint of M.H. Gill and Co.

Main introduction and all chapter introductions
© John Creedon, 2022
Chapter opening artworks © Brian Gallagher 2022

9780717194223

Design origination by Graham Thew
Designed and typeset by Bartek Janczak
Printed and bound by Printer Trento, Italy
This book is typeset in 11.5 on 14pt, Mrs Eaves.

For permission to reproduce photographs, the author and
publisher gratefully acknowledge the following:
© iStock/Getty Premium: 22, 24, 30, 36, 48, 59, 69, 79, 93,
94, 99, 105, 113, 115, 118, 120, 122, 134, 137, 139, 140, 149,
162, 166, 172, 179, 182, 187, 191, 205, 208, 211, 215, 227,
234, 236, 246, 252, 277, 289, 292, 305, 308, 314;
© Shutterstock: 54, 267.

The author and publisher have made every effort to trace
all copyright holders, but if any have been inadvertently
overlooked we would be pleased to make the necessary
arrangement at the first opportunity.

*The paper used in this book comes from the wood pulp of sustainably
managed forests.*

A CIP catalogue record for this book is available from the
British Library.

5 4 3

About the Schools' Collection

The Schools' Collection is part of the National Folklore Collection now located in the archives of UCD. The National Folklore Collection came to be as a result of the Irish Folklore Commission being set up in 1935 by the Irish Government to study and collect information on the folklore and traditions of Ireland. It contains approximately 2 million manuscript pages, 500,000 index cards, 12,000 hours of sound recording, 80,000 photographs and 1,000 hours of video material collected from across the 32 counties of Ireland.

The Schools' Collection section of the archive, from which the stories in this book are taken, was compiled between 1937 and 1939 by pupils from 5,000 primary schools. It depended heavily on the cooperation of the Department of Education and the Irish National Teachers' Organisation.

More than 50,000 schoolchildren from across the 26 counties of the Irish Free State were enlisted to collect folklore in their home districts. This included oral history, topographical information, folktales and legends, riddles and proverbs, games and pastimes, and trades and crafts. The children gathered this material from their parents, grandparents and neighbours, resulting in over 500,000 manuscript pages. Over 20,000 of the children's original copybooks containing the stories they gathered are still stored as part of the National Folklore Collection.

The Dúchas project was later set up to digitise the National Folklore Collection and the full Schools' Collection can now be accessed there: www.duchas.ie.

About the illustrator

Brian Gallagher studied Illustration at Bristol Polytechnic. Since then he has enjoyed a successful career as a professional illustrator and fine artist, winning a World Illustration Award in 2016 and the Royal Ulster Academy of Arts Print Prize in 2019. His clients include Harper Collins, Penguin Random House, the Office of Public Works and the National Trust. See more of his work at www.bdgart.com.

We were all children once, so I dedicate this book to my eleven siblings: Norah, Carol Ann, Constance, Geraldine, Vourneen, Don, Rosaleen, Marie-Thérèse, Eugenia, Cónal and Blake.

Contents

INTRODUCTION

'Thousands of old people dictated their own first-hand experiences from the 1800s and the traditions that dated back centuries further. With every story we're introduced to a little boy or girl, with their own personality and turn of phrase. In some you can almost hear the melody of the local canúint. I trust many of these accounts will spark memories of your own childhood and the people who coloured it. I know they did for me.'

**EVELATION OCCURS WHEN** you least expect it.

My father and I agreed on most things: never outstay your welcome, never boo a fellow human being, and never tire of the road. From the age of fifteen, Connie Patrick Creedon had been driving Model T trucks for his father. He hauled lorry-loads of turf for CIÉ Road Freight during the Emergency and then drove Expressway buses until he retired to run the little shop that helped feed and educate his twelve children. In his old age, freed from the seven-day-a-week grind of a late-night cornershop, he picked up where he left off, packed up his little bag and hit the road.

He loved to sing in the car and most of his songs were songs of the road. Songs like 'I'm a rambler, I'm a gambler' or 'The Jolly Beggar Man', which captured many of the joys of the open road:

... of all the trades a' goin', sure beggin' is the best,
for when a man is tired, he can sit and take a rest.

These were songs of cowboys, hobos and drifters, all of them rollin' along with the tumbleweed.

On a stopover during one of the road trips that lit up his final years — a journey he and I took to Mayo in July 1998 — he stayed up singing and playing the harmonica till early morning. After a few hours' shut-eye, we were heading out of Westport just ahead of the sheriff and his posse. I asked if he had ever climbed Croagh Patrick, given that it was named Patrick after him.

'Christ, my climbing days are well over, but c'mon so, we'll take one quick belt out the road to make sure 'tis still there.'

Having ensured the Reek was still standing, I suggested we drive over to Murrisk to view John Behan's National Famine Memorial, which had been unveiled by President Mary Robinson the previous year.

'God forgive me my sins, but you're worse than your sisters for d'oul art. Do you expect me to drag my poor oul bag of bones out of the car again?' he groaned.

I did, and he did.

The large bronze installation depicts a coffin ship with skeletal figures. Set against the backdrop of Clew Bay and pointed westwards to America, the memorial is a dramatic reminder of the millions of people who died or were displaced during the Great Famine of 1845–49. My father was silenced by the power of the piece. With his two hands clasped behind his back, he limped slowly around the memorial, issuing the occasional tut or sigh to himself.

He hardly spoke all the way to Ballinrobe. I glanced once or twice to check if he had fallen asleep.

'What's going on in your head?' I asked.

'Yerra, those poor people in the Famine, God be good to them, they suffered something awful.'

'I know ... awful. Do you think they'd be proud or disappointed with the way Ireland is today?'

For the most part, my father never theorised much about anything. It was always a narrative, always a story to illustrate his understanding of a subject. I once asked him if he believed in angels: 'Mother of God, I don't know anything about that, but did I ever tell you about the time your grandfather thought he saw a ghost out towards Graigue?' On this occasion, I pressed him for an opinion.

'Do you think the people who suffered in the Famine would be happy or disappointed with us? You know what I mean, winning independence and the Celtic Tiger and all the rest of it?'

'I have no idea about that, but I used to know a man who was in the Famine,' he said, staring straight ahead.

'In the Famine?' I chuckled. 'How could you possibly have known a man who was in the Famine? Sure, the Famine was 150 years ago.'

'Well, I'm telling you now, I *did* know a man who was in the Famine.'

'Go on, so — tell me.'

'From the time I was five or six years of age, I used go out with Denis Lucey in my father's truck to deliver meal around Bantry. Denis used call to an old man, named Sullivan I think, who grew up in Glengarriff and who lived well into his 90s. That man told us, not once, but several times, that when he was a small boy, the Famine was raging back West along. He said there was a man who would come out from Bantry Workhouse in a pony and wicker cart, known as the 'ambulance', to collect the dead and dying. One day, the driver stopped in Glengarriff and tied the horse outside where the hotel is now.

'Sullivan said "I was with some other children, and we ran up to see the bodies inside the ambulance. I had a little sally rod that I pushed in through the weave of the wicker and poked a dead man in the shoulder. But the man managed to raise a hand and push the rod away. Clearly, he was still alive, but he was on his way to the workhouse nonetheless, God help us. And although

I was only a small *boyín* at the time and didn't know any better, it's to my immortal shame that I did such a terrible thing."'

Now it was my turn to be silenced.

I struggled with the maths. The Famine raged from 1845 to 1849. My father was born in 1919 and would have met Mr Sullivan in the mid-1920s. If, as old Mr Sullivan said, he was only a 'small *boyín*' during the Famine and went on to live to be over 90, then he could easily have been recalling his eyewitness account right into the 1930s, not to mind telling my father a decade earlier. So there was indeed ample time for each man's life to have overlapped the next.

Floored by this revelation, I turned to my father and said, 'How come you never told me this before?'

'Because you never asked me,' he replied, trying to pin the blame on me. In truth, he had forgotten all about it, until John Behan's memorial sparked the memory and then, suddenly, there I was, listening to a man recall a first-hand account of the Great Famine.

Little did I know that my compadre was going to ride off into the sunset himself the following January.

The great lesson I took from that trip is … ask! That's precisely what the Irish Folklore Commission did when they set up the Schools' Folklore Collection in 1937. They asked. They asked schoolchildren to ask their parents and grandparents for their recollections. There was no time to lose. Here was a people whose culture and ways had been driven underground for centuries. Now there would be a drive to secure their stories in a national memory bank.

Remember, just fifteen years earlier, in June 1922, during the Irish Civil War, the Four Courts came under heavy shelling from Free State troops. The subsequent fire at the adjoining Public Records Office destroyed a wealth of information on births, deaths and burials. These priceless written records were erased forever, but now this oral history project would attempt to gather a social history from the memory of the living.

The scale and significance of the project cannot be underestimated. The Deparment of Education responded to the Irish Folklore Commission's call with enthusiasm. With the support of the Irish National Teachers' Organisation, they enlisted 50,000 schoolchildren in the 26 counties of the then Irish Free State. They would write over half a million pages of manuscript. *Bailiúchán na Scol*, or the Schools' Collection, is the result.

Today, whether we like it or not, virtually every detail of our existence is recorded on CCTV, phones and online databases. It's unlikely that our story will fall through the cracks ever again. But in these pages, amidst the chalk-dust classrooms and cleared-away kitchen tables of 1930s Ireland, we meet little boys and girls documenting, in their best handwriting, the 'story of us'. Many of their elderly sources had little education and could neither read nor write themselves. But the Irish word for folklore is *béaloideas*, literally meaning 'mouth education' or 'instruction', and that's exactly what happened. Thousands of old people dictated their own first-hand experiences from the 1800s and the traditions that dated back centuries further. With every story we're introduced to a little boy or girl, with their own personality and turn of phrase. In some you can almost hear the melody of the local *canúint*. I trust many of these accounts will spark memories of your own childhood and the people who coloured it. I know they did for me.

I am so grateful for those long car journeys where my father told and retold his stories. I have also come to recognise the huge debt of gratitude we all owe to the thousands of Irish schoolchildren who formed the great folklore *meitheal* of 1937. This golden harvest is their great legacy to us.

I

SUPERNATURAL BEINGS

'The threshold between this life and whatever lies beyond has occupied the human mind since Adam and Eve were babies. Like most cultures, when we don't know, we're forced to invent. The Celtic mind was particularly fertile.'

 **NEVER HAD A** first-hand encounter with the banshee myself. However, on the night my grand-uncle Jeremiah was waked in Inchigeelagh, all the dogs in the village spent the night howling and wailing. They began their ológoning shortly after my father and I arrived from Cork. By the time the priest arrived, the blood-curdling keening had grown to the volume and pitch of an air-raid siren. There might have been a rational explanation. Perhaps it was ignited by the murmur of so many people gathering in the dimly lit village at an hour when Inchigeelagh and its dogs would normally be settled for the night. I remember the old men making sense of it all:

'I s'pose they're lonely after him. God knows, poor ol' Jeremiah had a great ol' *grá* for the dogs.'

'Erra, he had … and they were fond of him.'

A dog is a great thing. Apart from their acute sense of hearing − the first line of household defence − their powers of perception seem to reach into that liminal space between this world and the next: a facility denied to all but the most intuitive of humans. When a snoozing dog suddenly cocks its head and points its ears, you can be sure that those little antennae have picked up something you have missed. An elderly widow, Nan Casey, and her sweetheart of a collie lived up the hill from us in Cork. If the collie ever growled at a caller to the door, Nan always closed it.

The threshold between this life and whatever lies beyond has occupied the human mind since Adam and Eve were babies. Like most cultures, when we don't know, we're forced to invent. The Celtic mind was particularly fertile. Even J.R.R. Tolkien, creator of *The Lord of the Rings* and *The Hobbit*, bemoaned the lack of an English mythology to match what he encountered on his trips to the West of Ireland.

The banshee was one of the busiest and most feared of Irish supernatural beings, for she was the mystical harbinger of an imminent death. 'Banshee' is a compound of the Irish words *bean* (woman) and *sí* (fairy). She was described by those who claimed to have seen her as a witch-like woman of not more than a metre in height who wore a cloak. She would swoop over a household, issuing a spine-chilling wail to herald the imminent death of some poor misfortunate within.

Another female supernatural being who also features prominently in our folklore is the mermaid. Unsurprising, I suppose, given that we are an island nation and share in a global tradition of tall tales from the sea. Remember, the Vikings settled here, and their sagas would also have been shared with the *seanchaí* around the open fire. Irish fishermen travelled deep into the Atlantic Ocean to the rich fish stocks off the coast of Newfoundland, curiously referred to as *Talamh an Éisc*, meaning 'Land of the Fish'. Even without the benefit of a degree in marine science, fishermen could still clearly observe that whales, dolphins and mermaids occupy that middle ground between fish and us. After all, they are mammals, and the females give birth and suckle their young. The water-horse also occupies this space between the water and the land and that liminal space that connects our world with another (as Gaeilge *idir-eatharthú*, meaning 'betwixt and between'). It is here that the imagination is free to roam.

The protective power of iron against evil forces is a recurring theme in these stories. The iron tongs were used to ward off the banshee, and in water-horse tales, horseshoes are considered an amulet against evil powers. I have one knocking around my garden for years. I have never actually found a place to hang it, yet despite numerous clear-outs, it has never gone into a skip.

The Irish word for 'hare' is *giorria* from *gearr-fhia* (literally, 'short deer'). It's a beautiful description of the animal, and I'm delighted to include here a fine example from the 'witch-hare' genre, in which an old lady shapeshifts into a hare and back again. I've even heard it said that you should never eat a hare in case it's your grandmother! In this tale, there's a dramatic 'chase scene', with a nod to Christianity overcoming the old magic and a reminder of the cruel 'othering' of people who are different from the norm.

While researching a television programme about the Hag of Beara, I was reminded of how elderly single women have often been dismissed as crones, witches and hags — and the fear of strange women exhibited in these otherworldly tales is plain to see. This is not exclusive to the Ireland of the past, as the term 'crazy cat-lady' is now liberally applied to older women displaying any signs of eccentricity. Military propaganda dehumanises the enemy by name-calling, referring to them as 'Krauts', 'Yanks', 'Commies' and so on. In Christian culture, the snake and cloven-hooved goat have been ascribed devilish characteristics. Is this the same motivation that drives our need to demonise the object of our pursuit, such as the hare?

But there is one figure that seemingly always evades capture. In the court of Irish mythology, the leprechaun is the jester and the rogue. I love leprechauns. Always have, always will, world without end, amen. The very first verse I ever learned by heart was William Allingham's 'Fairies', which created the image of a leprechaun in my young mind. It was taught to me by my mother during a few rare days that I was off school with chickenpox, when we had each other's undivided attention.

> Up the airy mountain,
> Down the rushy glen,
> We daren't go a-hunting
> For fear of little men;
> Wee folk, good folk,
> Trooping all together;
> Green jacket, red cap,
> And white owl's feather!

I wanted a leprechaun and, encouraged by my dad, I rummaged in every ditch and *sceach*, like a Jack Russell after a rabbit. There's a spot on the old road from Cork to Killarney, at a bridge just west of Ballyvourney, where on the day I sat the entrance exam for secondary school, my father showed me where he had once sighted a leprechaun. It was the only time he had ever caught a glimpse of the little *manín*. But where there's a sighting, there's hope. To this day, if I spy a rainbow when driving along the motorway, I'm impulsively drawn to investigate ... or at least pull in at the next filling station forecourt to buy a lottery ticket.

Reported sightings of leprechauns are so rare these days, I fear they may be near extinction. We all have a duty to maintain the wild places in the Irish countryside and maintain a landscape where the wee folk can get on with their own mischief. Otherwise, it may fall to future generations to try to reintroduce leprechauns to the wild.

She raised the death cry

SCHOOL: *Ballynarry, Co. Cavan*
TEACHER: *E. Mac Gabhann*
COLLECTOR: *Hugh Sheridan*

Some years ago there dwelt in one of the midland counties of Ireland a rich farmer, who was never married, and his only domestics were a boy and an old housekeeper named Moya. This farmer was well educated and was constantly jeering old Moya, who was extremely superstitious and pretended to know much about witchcraft and fairy world.

One November morning this farmer arose before daylight and was surprised, on entering the kitchen, to find old Moya sitting over the fire and smoking her pipe in a very serious mood. The farmer asked in wonder why was she up so early and the old woman said, 'I am heart-scalded to have it to say, but there is something bad coming over us, for the banshee was about the house all night and she has almost frightened my life out with her bawling.' This farmer was always aware of the banshee having haunted his family, but as it was some years since she had last visited the house, he was not prepared for old Moya's announcement. He asked old Moya about the banshee's appearance and when he heard all, he ordered her to prepare his breakfast, for he said he had to go to Maryborough that day and he wanted to be home before night.

The old lady advised him not to go that day and she said, 'I would give my oath that something unlucky will happen to you.' But the man was not one to take advice; after taking his breakfast he arose to depart. It was very cold and, the man having finished his business, he went to a public house to get some drink, and to feed his horse. There he met an old friend and glass, and they did not find time pass.

When old Moya found the horse at the stable door without his rider and the saddle covered with blood, she raised the death cry and a party of horsemen set out to seek him, and at the fatal spot he was found stretched on his back and his head almost in pieces with shots. On examining him it was found that his money was gone and a gold watch taken from his pocket.

'Give me back my comb'

SCHOOL: *The Rower, Co. Kilkenny*
TEACHER: *Labhaoise Nic Liam*
INFORMANT: *Mrs. Brennan, around 50 years old*

About one hundred years ago, there lived in a house not far from the church of the Rower a farmer and his wife who were famous for giving charity and lodging to the travelling poor. They kept a servant girl who was a bit gay and reckless. She was in the habit of going out at night to take a ramble. One night when returning, she took a short-cut in through the orchard. The path led in by the gable end of the house. In the end there were two windows, one a couple of feet from the ground and one at the top of the house.

When the girl was passing by the window she saw a woman dressed all in white sitting on the window sill combing her hair. The girl, thinking it was her mistress who was trying to frighten her, snatched the comb and ran in. She had scarcely reached the door when she heard three weird unearthly cries. The girl fainted and the people of the house didn't know what to do. The woman in white continued to cry out, 'Give me back my comb, give me back my comb.'

Next night there came a poor travelling man looking for lodging. The mistress made him welcome, and gave him his supper, and put him to rest on the settle. After a while he noticed that the girl who used to be so gay seemed very dull. He asked the cause, and was told of her adventure of the night before. He told her she was very foolish, and never to meddle with anything that did not meddle with her, that woman was the banshee, and that she was sure to come again to look for her comb. Shortly after they heard the cries again, 'Give me back my comb.'

The travelling man told the girl to redden the tongs in the fire and catch the comb with it and put it out through the end window. She did so, and it was well for her that she didn't put out her hand with it because the banshee was so mad she bent the tongs with the grab she made at it.

The caoining

SCHOOL: *Drumlusty, Co. Monaghan*
TEACHER: *Seán Ó Maoláin*
INFORMANT: *Edward Jones, age 60, Rahans, Co. Monaghan*

'The Banshee' is supposed to cry for certain people. Therefore when some families hear the Banshee crying, they know that someone is dying belonging to them.

About a half mile from Drumlusty N.S. in the direction of Inniskeen, there are ruins of a dwelling house. A man named Walshe and his family lived there the time of the '98 Rebellion. His wife died following the 'CAOINING' of the Banshee, and soon afterwards two of his children became ill and died, each death being preceded by the 'caoineadh' of the banshee. Soon afterwards another of his children became ill; late at night the door of the house was opened, and a brown hooded figure glided in and commenced caoining over the sick child. The man, becoming exasperated, seized the tongs and threw them at the 'Banshee'. It disappeared at once, the child got well, and despite deaths in the family afterwards, the 'Banshee' was never heard 'caoining' them afterwards.

CAOINING, *caoineadh: keening, crying.*

A most unearthly cry

SCHOOL: *Corracloona, Co. Leitrim*
TEACHER: *Pádraig Ó Caomháin*
INFORMANT: *Mrs. B. McMorrow*

The old people around this district firmly believed in the banshee. I often heard my mother say that there were certain families that were always 'cried'. These families were the McGowans, the Gallaghers, the Keanys, the Meehans and the O'Briens. I heard my father say that he and an uncle of his heard the banshee crying one night just before an old Keany woman died. A McGowan man lived beside us. He had a sister married down near Derrygonnelly, Co. Femanagh. Before this sister died the story goes that they heard the banshee. I also heard other people saying that they heard the banshee and it always foretold the death of some person.

I had a strange personal experience in this connection. On the night of the 14th of March 1919 (the time of the big flu epidemic) my sister and I went out at 10 o'clock to get some turf to 'rake the fire'. Suddenly we heard a most unearthly cry. It started about a mile away from us and ran along the ground for about half a mile. Then it began to ascend and went up, up, up, getting fainter as it went, until it died away in the sky. We never heard anything so weird and concluded that it must be the banshee. We went home and told our people that we heard a banshee. They laughed at us. It happened that our next door neighbour, Mrs. D—, whose maiden name was Gallagher, took the flu that night and was dead that day week.

The white hare

SCHOOL: *Clifden, Co. Galway*
TEACHER: *An Br. Angelo Mac Shámhais*
COLLECTOR: *Connie McGrath, Clifden*
INFORMANT: *Mrs. J. Lysaght, Clifden*

Long ago there was a student from Ballynahinch in France studying for the priesthood, and a year before his ordination he was home at his native place. He was always a keen sportsman and his people were ever proud to have a fine hound.

About this time there was a lot of talk about a white hare that was often seen on the slopes of the Twelve Pins in the direction of Maam Valley. It was said that this hare used to suck the cows and many times the cows belonging to the poor people of the district would come home in the evening and would have not a drop of milk. Some women also complained that the milk would produce no butter and they said that the white hare was surely a witch. The student heard all this talk and he said that he would chase the white hare. Some old people in the place said that it was often chased but got safely away from all hounds, and said that there was no hound to kill that hare except an all-black hound. The student enquired around the neighbourhood and at last discovered an all-black hound near Oughterard.

It was a fine May morning when this lively young man set out with his all-black hound to chase and kill the white hare on the hillside near Ballynahinch. After a short time up gets the hare in a RUSHY CURRAGH, and headed for a valley in the mountains.

The chase was very thrilling but the student had a very good view and had high hopes that the black hound would succeed. Among the rocks and round the lakes the hare kept her distance, and for over an hour it seemed as though the hound would be baffled, but still the hare was not able to get out into the open mountains. The student saw that the hare was ever trying to escape in one direction, and he kept on that side.

At long last the hare headed for a small stream that tumbled down the rugged slopes, and the hound, still in good running form, came in close pursuit. The student saw a little hut or cabin in the distance and in a few moments the hound, hare and huntsman were just beside the hut. After a few clever turns the hound was within biting distance of the hare, and just as the hound was springing to bite, the hare made one jump in a little opening that acted as a window.

The student rushed to the door, which was small, and stuffed with heather tied in a bundle, and to his great surprise saw an old woman sitting at a spinning wheel and working away as if nothing had happened. He questioned her sternly as to whether she saw a hare coming in and she denied that that was so. He looked around the cabin, which was made of bog sods, and could see no place where the hare could hide. At last, a little vexed, he walked over to the woman and pulled her off the stool, thinking that she might have the hare hidden beside her. To his great amazement he saw a pool of blood on the floor and at once it struck him that the woman was bleeding; she seemed to be out of breath.

After a few threats she admitted that she was bleeding and that she had been bitten by the hound and that she was the white hare that used to suck the cows. She promised to give up her evil ways and she did.

This woman was well known before this event. She lived alone in the hut and was never suspected of doing anything wrong.

RUSHY CURRAGH: *a fen covered in rushes.*

An caipín bréaghach

SCHOOL: *Dromclough, Kilcarra Beg, Co. Kerry*
COLLECTOR: *Bridie Flaherty*
INFORMANT: *Mrs. Ellen Foley, 74, Mountcoal, Co. Kerry*

A fisherman went down to the seashore one morning to see if any seaweed was in after the night's tide, and saw a beautiful young girl sitting on a rock combing her hair. He said to himself, 'This must be the mermaid I hear all the people talking about.'

She did not see him at all as her back was turned to him. He stooped and took off his shoes, and tip-toed out to the rock. He heard it always said that if you could steal her cap she would follow you. He saw the cap on the rock beside her, and he took it, and went off with it, and she followed him on. He ran for home, and she ran after him roaring for her 'CAIPÍN BRÉAGHACH'.

He took the house of her, and there was a loft where a CLEEVE of turf could be put up. He threw the cap up there. She went into the house and asked for the cap that she could not go back to her home in the sea without it. 'No,' said he, 'I want a housekeeper, and I'll keep you now as I got you; I have no one in the house with me.'

So she sat down; he began to cook his dinner, and she got up and helped him. All the neighbours gathered in to see the mermaid. She was there for a week, and he sent for the priest and they got married. She forgot all about the sea until one day in due time a baby boy was born to them, and after five or six years they had four children.

In them old times everyone's home was filled with canvas sheets made from flax. In that time they never washed them during the three months of winter. According as they would get soiled they would pack them up in the loft until the Spring. Then they would be washed and put out to bleach.

When the Spring came he said to the mermaid he would take a few bags of corn to the market to sell it. He went off, and she said to herself it was time to wash the sheets. She was never known to laugh during the while she was there. She put down the water and threw down the sheets. When she had last of the sheets thrown down, she found her little cap.

She made three hearty laughs that rang in the air. She then turned and kissed the little children, and put on her cap, and made for the Cashen where she saw a few fishing boats. The men tried to catch her, for they knew what had happened. She was too clever for them and made a terrible jump into the sea, and was never heard of or seen since.

When the man came home he asked where she was, and they said they did not know. The eldest boy told what happened. He saw all the clothes, and he thought of the 'caipín bréaghach'. He searched for it, but it was gone. Day after day he went to the rock, but she did not appear anymore.

CAIPÍN BRÉAGHACH: *this could mean 'false cap'*
or 'deceiving cap'.
CLEEVE: *a wicker basket.*

The magic mantle

SCHOOL: *Enniscrone, Co. Sligo*
TEACHER: *Bean de Búrca*
COLLECTOR: *Emily O'Connor*
INFORMANT: *Nora Whyte*

Many stories are told about mermaids in this district. They are like human beings, except that from their waist down is similar to a fish. Mermaids have beautiful hair. Their hobby is combing their hair.

The only family that were connected with mermaids in this district were the O'Dowds, who lived in the old castle in the Castle Field. One day Chieftain O'Dowd was shooting in Scurmore Wood. He saw a mermaid sitting on a rock combing her hair. He brought her home and married her. They had seven children, and after some time the mermaid became lonely for her sea friends. Knowing this, Chieftain O'Dowd hid her mantle, but his youngest daughter saw him hiding it; the child told her mother. The mermaid was delighted; now that she had the magic mantle, she could go back to the sea; without the mantle, she would have to stay ashore. That night, taking her seven children with her, the mermaid stole from the castle. She brought them to a field near Scurmore; there she changed six of them into rocks, and took the youngest child, who told her where the mantle was hidden, with her into the sea. And the mermaid nor the child were never seen or heard of again. But the six rocks are still to be seen in the summer where the waves of the bar lap and wash over them at times. It is said that these rocks bleed every six years. If you touch each rock, you will dream of fairies that night.

The lake of the knife

SCHOOL: *Carrowbeg, Co. Donegal*
TEACHER: *Rachel Nic an Ridire*
COLLECTOR: *Robert Mc Eldowney, Ballymagaraghy, Co. Donegal*
INFORMANT: *Pat Mc Colgan, age 87, Ballymagaraghy, Co. Donegal*

In ancient times, so the people relate, there lived in Lough Skean a beautiful mermaid. Every morning, at sunrise, she used to rise from the lake and sit on a rock about three hundred yards from the shore and sing a weird 'caoineadh' which could be heard for miles around.

The man from whom I heard this told me that his grandfather, who had seen the mermaid, described her as the most beautiful creature ever a human being laid eyes on. Her fair golden hair fell in ripples down below her waist, while her skin was as white as snow, and her features as clearly cut as those of a marble statue. Her body from the waist downwards was covered with large greenish scales, and very much resembled that of a fish.

It is related in the district that a youth named Sean O'Connor fell in love with her but the mermaid, hearing this, knew she could never live on dry land. One morning Sean went as usual to the lake, expecting to see his love emerge and sit on the rock. For hours he waited but poor Sean, having given up hope of ever seeing her again, drew up a large knife and plunged it through his heart.

Ever since the lake has been called Lough Skian or the lake of the knife. The mermaid was often seen sitting on the rock after that but on still nights her weird caoining can be heard for miles around. It is said that she is mourning Sean O'Connor, the boy who gave up his young life for the love of her.

A beautiful mermaid

SCHOOL: *Lissadill, Co. Sligo*
TEACHER: *Gleadra Ní Fhiachraigh, A.E. Ní Chraoibhín*

A man was fishing off the coast of Raughley, about four miles from Lissadell. He saw what he thought was a fine fish and struck it with a harpoon. He did not succeed in catching it and both fish and harpoon were lost to him.

Some weeks later he was working in a field close to the shore when a very finely dressed gentleman rode on a beautiful horse to him. He talked to the man and asked him to go with him. The fisherman at first declined but was so pressed by the gentleman to go with him that he said he would if the gentleman would leave him back again. After a moment's thought the gentleman promised to do so.

They both rode off on the horse. The horse went down to the shore and plunged into the sea and swam some yards and then descended into a cave. There on a rocky bed was lying a beautiful mermaid with the harpoon in her side. Her husband (the rider) asked the fisherman to pull out the harpoon and explained that it was necessary to bring the man who stuck the harpoon into the mermaid to remove it again; otherwise the mermaid would die.

The fisherman removed the harpoon and was then brought back to the field again. The rider explained that only for he had given a promise to bring him back again he could not have allowed him return to earth.

She can talk, sing and cry

SCHOOL: *Carrowbeg, Co. Donegal*
TEACHER: *Rachel Nic an Ridire*
COLLECTOR: *Robert Mc Eldowney, Ballymagaraghy, Co. Donegal*
INFORMANT: *Pat Mc Colgan, age 87, Ballymagaraghy, Co. Donegal*

There were supposed to be mermaids in the district long ago. There was once a man in Buttach who got married to one of them and one day when he hid her tail in the barn, he went to the town, but while one of the children was playing, he found it and brought it to her, and she put it on at once and off she went to the sea again. The children used to go down to the beach every morning to get their hair combed with her own comb and their faces washed in the salt water and it was always their own mother came up to the surface to do it for them. They were often heard crying when leaving her.

Half of the mermaid is a woman and the other a fish. She has lovely, curly, golden or yellow hair. She can talk, sing and cry. When fishermen hear her cry, they do not like to go to sea as it is supposed to be a sign of a storm. This one that I mentioned in the story is the only one I ever heard tell of coming ashore. When she is seen she is usually sitting on a rock singing or combing her beautiful hair. She uses no mirror as she can see herself in the water. There were some local families connected with mermaids in the past. When there was going to be a death in the family the mermaid came and cried outside the house. Fairies do the same thing in certain families but when they cry, they are known as the 'banshee'.

The water-horse

SCHOOL: *Annagh More, Co. Mayo*
TEACHER: *Mártain Ó Braonáin (also the collector)*

One time a man went down to the sea and he got a water-horse and brought him home to do his work. When he had the horse a while he got a set of shoes on him. The man kept the water-horse until he had all his work done. Then he sent his son down to the sea with the horse, but the horse could not go out into the water on account of the shoes being made out of iron and the iron is blessed. The boy brought the horse to his father again and he took the shoes off him and put the boy riding on him again and they went off to the sea. When the boy was near the sea he tried to halt the horse but he could not. The horse started to gallop and he ran out in the sea with the boy on his back. When he got under the water he ate the boy and there was no more about him.

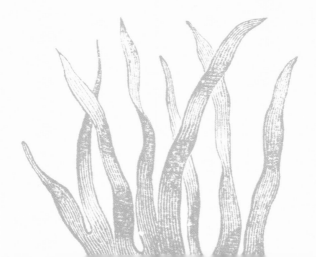

Our hero the leprechaun

SCHOOL: *Parteen, Co. Clare*
TEACHER: *Ciarán Ó Ceallaigh*

Leprechauns are small little men living in a moat or commonly called a fort and they wear a tiny cap on top of their heads, a tiny coat of green and a pair of buckled shoes. Some people say that they have a crock of gold stored away in inland places.

The oldest fairy is always the cobbler and he mends the other fairies' shoes. He always sits under an oak tree at this work during the hot weather and he is always found here either in early morning or else in late evening. If you wish to find a leprechaun you must go very, very easy by the ditches and listen very attentively till you hear the ticks of his little hammer, and if you are in luck to find him you must be very careful to keep your eyes on him, because if you look away behind you he will disappear.

A young man was once lucky enough to catch one coming from behind; he stole on tip-toe and grabbed him by the jacket and lifted him off the ground and demanded his purse of gold.

'She has it,' says the imp.

'Who?' says the young man.

'That lady behind you,' says the imp.

With that the young man let go his hold and turned round quickly to catch the young lady, as he thought, but she was nowhere to be seen, and turning again, our hero the leprechaun was a hundred yards away bursting his sides laughing at the fool.

A fairy cobbler

SCHOOL: *Curraghcloney, Co. Tipperary*
TEACHER: *Máire, Bean Uí Fhloinn*
INFORMANT: *Mrs. James Dalton, 42, Boolahalla, Co. Tipperary*

There was once a man named Jack Reilly who set out one moonlight night to set snares for rabbits. He came home when he had them set and at about 11 o'clock he went out to see if there was anything in the snares. In one of the snares there was a hare and on the fence near the snare stood a fairy cobbler. The man was thinking if he could catch the leprechaun and get the gold from him it would be better for him than all the rabbits in the world. He made a run at the little man but he was too quick for him and ran down the hill. The man threw the dead hare after him, hoping to knock him, but when the hare struck the fairy it became alive, and up on his back jumped the fairy and left the man staring open-mouthed after him up the hillside.

A pot of withered leaves

SCHOOL: *Abbeytown Convent N.S., Boyle, Co. Roscommon*
TEACHER: *Sr. M. Columbanus*
COLLECTOR: *Marjorie Carney, Easter-Snow, Co. Roscommon*
INFORMANT: *Mr. Martin Gaffney, Ballyfarnon, Co. Roscommon*

In ancient times, the people of our district used to tell quite a number of old tales connected with the fairy folk, especially leipreachauns, but most of the old inhabitants of the district have died long since, bringing most of those old stories to the grave with them. Some of those old stories are still told by the old inhabitants, but there is one in particular told about the fairy cobbler of Lough End.

Once upon a time there lived on the shores of Lough End, which is situated about two miles east of Ballyfarnon, a poor widow and her son, Padraig Mulvany. Padraig was a very lazy fellow, and every time he got a chance he used to steal away to the fairy LIOS behind the house, and dream the day away, hoping against hope that a leipreachaun or fairy might appear and give him a pot of gold.

One day, he was sitting in the usual spot at the top of the lios when a fairy leipreachaun appeared. As quick as lightning Padraig seized him by the scruff of the neck and demanded a pot of gold. The leipreachaun, remaining quite cool, told Padraig to follow him to a hollow tree, in which the gold was hidden. Padraig seized the pot of gold quickly, but the leipreachaun, taking out his gold snuff-box, asked Padraig to take a pinch.

Padraig stretched out his hand, but the leipreachaun threw the box of snuff into his face. When he had stopped sneezing poor Padraig looked round for his pot of gold, but all he could see was a pot of withered leaves.

LIOS: an enclosure or ringfort

A small, funny-looking little man

SCHOOL: Banagher, Co. Offaly
TEACHER: Séamus Ó Maoilchéire
INFORMANT: Tom Rogers, 78, labourer, Banagher, Offaly

The leipreachaun is a small, funny-looking little man. He is a fairy cobbler and he repairs shoes for the fairies. Every night he sits on a fairy mushroom with his last and his other implements in front of him on another mushroom and, with his hammer in his hand, he mends the shoes. He has ears like an ass and a long crooked nose, but he is supposed to have a box of gold.

There is a man living in Banagher by the name of Mr. Tom Rogers who caught a leipreachaun. One moonlight night he was coming home from a gamble. It was after midnight so he took a short-cut that led by the side of an old RATH OR LIS.

He was just going past it when he heard a tapping. Crawling to the edge of the lis, he saw a leipreachaun mending shoes in the centre of it. Tom stole up behind him and caught hold of him.

'What do you want of me?' said the leipreachaun.

'Where have you the gold?' said Tom, and he making sure to keep his eye on him, for it is said that if you look away at all he will vanish.

'Look at the big dog behind you,' said the fairy.

'You can't trick me, me boyo,' said Tom, and he caught the poor fairy by the throat. 'Tell me where is the gold or I will choke you.'

'It's down under my feet,' said the leipreachaun.

Tom looked down and when he looked up again the leipreachaun had vanished. 'I know where the gold is, anyway,' said Tom, and he marked the spot with a thistle and went home.

The next morning he went to the fort again with the spade. The night before there was only one thistle in the lis; now the whole place was covered with them. Tom had to go home again because he didn't know which thistle marked the spot.

There was a poor farmer and his wife who also caught a leipreachaun. They locked him up in a chest. One night they were sitting by the fire when the leipreachaun said, 'It's a fine night for sowing beans.'

'Begorra,' said the farmer, 'there is something in that,' and he went out and sowed the beans. He then let the leipreachaun go.

At this time Saint Patrick was travelling around Ireland. He came to the place where the farmer lived and asked for a drink. 'That is a fine crop of beans you have,' said the saint. 'Would you sell it?'

'It's only stalks, sir,' said the farmer. He did not know the saint.

Saint Patrick bought the stalks, which were wattles of gold. He gave the farmer hundreds of pounds for them. It is said that it was with this gold he built all his churches and schools.

RATH OR LIS: *both words refer to an enclosure or ringfort.*

The stocking of gold

SCHOOL: *Bekan, Co. Mayo*
TEACHER: *P.S. Mac Donnchadha*
COLLECTOR: *Patrick Kelly, Lissaniskea, Co. Mayo*

The leipreachaun is a small man supposed to be living in the old forts and in the woods. He dresses in a little green jacket, red cap and tiny little shoes. The chief trade he has is shoemaking for the fairies.

There is a story told about an old man named Tom Tighe who lived near a big fort in Lissaniskea. This man used to be out very late at night. As he was a poor man, he had not much money to buy food with, so he used to set traps for rabbits and birds.

One night, as he was coming home, what should he see but a leipreachaun caught in one of his traps. As soon as the leipreachaun saw the man coming he tried his best to get free, but he knew he was caught. The man took hold of him and told him to give up his gold. The leipreachaun said he had none and begged of the man to let him free. After a while the man saw the stocking of gold stuck into a little shoe. He took it out and put it into his pocket, saying to the leipreachaun, 'If you had not told me a lie I would only keep half of the gold, but now I have it all and I'll keep it.'

The man hurried home then, proud of his good fortune. He said he would not have to go bird-catching anymore. Then he let go the birds that were caught, for he had made up his mind that at sunrise he would go to town and buy some good food. When he arrived home he went to bed and brought the gold with him for fear it would be stolen.

The cock was crowing when he got up and he began to open the stocking. There was a very hard knot on the end of it and, try as he would, he could not open the stocking. He tried to make a hole in the stocking with his knife but he broke the blade. He sat down to think, and after a while he came to the conclusion that it was best to return the gold to the leipreachaun and catch a rabbit for breakfast.

He found the leipreachaun in the place where he had caught him the night before, cold and nearly starved with hunger. The man gave the money back to him and let him go. After thanking him, the leipreachaun asked the man what gift would he like to have. 'I would like to be a good player on all musical instruments,' he replied.

'Very well,' said the leipreachaun. 'Your wish will be granted and you will also be able to put the bagpipes playing by itself.' The leipreachaun disappeared then and a rabbit was caught in the trap when he looked at it.

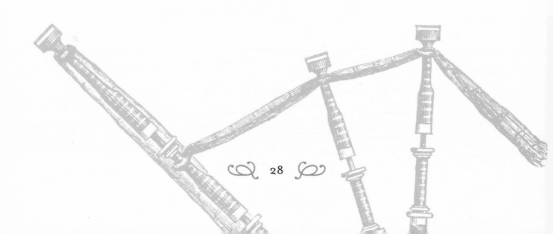

When the man had eaten a good breakfast, he got his old bagpipes and the minute he touched them they began to play reels, jigs and hornpipes. There was a fair in town on this day and he went there with the pipes and soon a crowd of people were gathered around him listening to the wonderful bagpipes.

He got large sums of money from people of various towns after that.

2

MYTHICAL HEROES

'While the narrative might be fanciful at times, we usually find a kernel of truth right at the centre that's as relevant today as it was when first uttered around some ancient campfire.'

For rambling, for roving,
for football and sporting
for drinking black porter
as fast as you'd fill.
In all your days roving
you'll find none so jovial
as the Muskerry Sportsman
The Bold Thady Quill.

IN 1895, when Johnny Tom Gleeson from Rylane, County Cork, wrote these lines, he probably knew he had a hit on his hands. After all, if the Irish love anything, it's a good story. Like a decent Munster hurling final, the story must have a handsome hero who battles bravely against the enemy. We need a large dollop of gory detail, a brilliant and beautiful female lead and a few twists and turns before our gallant hero gets the prize and the baddies get their comeuppance. 'Up our crowd!' we roar. Cúchulainn, Queen Maeve, Christy Ring, Katie Taylor, Paul O'Connell ... We still light up in the glow of their epic battles. These are the tales that will forever be told.

The Schools' Collection reintroduces us, through the wide-open eyes of children, to the incredibly rich cast of characters and incredible drama of our Celtic mythology.

While the narrative might be fanciful at times, we usually find a kernel of truth right at the centre that's as relevant today as it was when first uttered around some ancient campfire. Here is a moral code by which to live. These are universal and timeless truths about honour, honesty and compassion, even in battle.

Many of the great philosophers cross my mind as I read these moral tales. At one point, I was reminded of the folly of war as described by Lao Tzu in his book of ancient Chinese wisdom the *Tao Te Ching*. He tells us that, after conflict, there are no winners. Instead, both sides are faced with the reality of the destruction they've caused. As I scanned school copybooks from Dromsallagh, County Limerick, and again from Aghameen, County Louth, and read of Cúchulainn being duty-bound to fight and kill his lifelong friend Ferdia, I'm reminded of Lao Tzu's assertion that both victor and vanquished will mourn.

In the pages of her copybook young Sheila Rice of Aghameen tells us of Cúchulainn's heartbreak, as the victor 'afterwards regretted his deed'. Cúchulainn carries the dead body of Ferdia from the battlefield and cries, 'What does it matter? The friend I love is dead, noble Ferdia, who was dearer to me than all the world besides.' Like all great truths, this lesson is universal and timeless.

Over the following pages we revisit *Tóraíocht Diarmuid agus Gráinne*. Loved or loathed by a generation of Leaving Cert Irish students, this story has it all: death, destruction, dramatic chase scenes, even a love triangle. We encounter other epic tales that were gathered and first written down in the twelfth-century *Lebor na hUidre* (The Book of the Dun Cow). This is the oldest surviving manuscript written in the Irish language. Last summer, nearly a thousand years later, I was granted the privilege of donning the white gloves and turning its pages. I sat there in the Royal Irish Academy feeling an overwhelming sense of reverence in the presence of beauty, as I examined the work of Mael Muire Mac Célechair and his fellow scribes at Clonmacnoise.

In contrast to *Lebor na hUidre*, this humble book before you features the best efforts of the children of Irish National Schools, as they recount the very same stories in their own words. While they are hardly works of great literature, I feel a similar respect for the schoolchildren's copybooks of the 1930s as I do for the twelfth-century manuscript. These young transcribers recorded our mythology, as it was reported to them by the elderly of their own locality. They, in turn, had received it from the generations before them in an unbroken oral tradition. Unlike Mael Muire Mac Célechair and the monks of old, many of these flame-keepers succeeded without the benefit of being able to read or write. At this remove, many of the essays reverberate to the sounds of an old National School classroom. The language is often quaint and the stories very funny, like the description of the Gobán Saor's young fella drinking tea. In many cases the mythological tales are taken as absolute fact, with dates included!

These stories are brought to life by the quirky details and turns of phrase thrown in by the young collectors. In Clondulane, County Cork, we meet a giant named Liam Harris. A fine name for a giant, although one might expect that, given his size, he would have preferred to be addressed as something more ferocious. I can't imagine myself trembling at the news that Liam was in town.

At Ínse Cloch in Cork, we meet a namesake of mine, schoolmaster Diarmuid Ó Críodáin, who supervised a wonderful essay by young Kitty Sullivan from Dromsullivan ('the ridge of the Sullivans'), who wrote of a time when 'it was the custom of the people to steal each other's wives'. Kitty also puts the dissolution of the Fianna at precisely 284 AD. So now we know!

From Dromclogh, also in Cork, we have the beautifully told story of Fionn and his wife Sadbh. This drama is set at a time when, we're told, the Irish were expecting to be invaded by the Romans 'at any moment'. I can't get the image of an imminent air-strike out of my head.

Read on as young Lizzie Daly from Baranvalla, County Waterford, weaves a cautionary tale about the evils of losing one's temper. She describes, in detail, a murder weapon made by taking a strong man's brains and boiling them until they are as hard as stone. Lizzie then details how Conor MacNessa's anger led to his own horrific death: 'the first man to die for Our Lord'.

You'll never hear me utter a cross word again.

The King's daughter

SCHOOL: *Ardbane, Co. Donegal*
TEACHER: *Briain Ó hEarchaigh*
COLLECTOR: *Nora Mac Shane, 13, Ardbane, Co. Donegal*
INFORMANT: *John Gallagher, 72, farmer, Ardbane*

One day Fionn Mac Cumhaill went in search of the King's daughter. As he was going along the road he saw people disputing at a graveyard what place they would bury a corpse. One crowd would not let the others bury the corpse without paying £5. Fionn thought it a poor thing to see them fighting. He had only five pounds so he gave it to them to let them bury the corpse. He went on his journey and when he had gone a mile he met a man. The man asked him would he take him with him. Fionn said he would but he had no money. The man said he had plenty of money so he went with Fionn.

When they went into the King's house the King's daughter made tea for them. She asked Fionn what did he come here for. He said to marry her. She said he could marry her but he would have three great deeds to do. He told her he would. She told him at one o'clock in the night he would have to take a comb out of her hair and that she would have to be neither in this world nor in the castle.

They read a book until one o'clock in the night. Fionn ate a bit before he would go to look for her. He asked the other man if he knew where she was. He said she was in Hell. At one o'clock in the night the two started off to find the lady. When they reached Hell she was sitting speaking to the Devil at the fire. They stole up the floor and stood behind the chair that she was sitting on. She put over her hand to catch the Devil's hand to leave good-bye and at that moment, the man that was along with Fionn scamped the comb out of her hair and the both went out of the house.

Next morning the lady came in and made ready their breakfast. She was very angry. She said that was a great deed but that they would have to do a greater deed tonight. They would have to take a ring off her finger. They said they would.

Next night at one o'clock the two started off to look for the lady. When they went to Hell she was sitting speaking to the Devil with her two hands up over her head. The man that was along with Fionn pulled the ring off her finger and the both went away. The next morning the lady came in and prepared their breakfast for them and she was twice as angry. She said they had two of the deeds done but that they would have to do a greater one. She said they would have to take off the lip that was speaking to the Devil. They said they would do that.

When the lady went out of the room the two started to look for a scissors. They looked in one box and here there was a big pair of scissors. They took them with them and went to Hell. When they reached Hell she was sitting speaking to the Devil. She was in the middle of telling something to the Devil and the same man snapped the lip off her and went away.

Next morning she came in and prepared their breakfast for them. She said that they had the three deeds done and that she would marry Fionn next Monday. The man that Fionn took with him was going and he called Fionn with him. He told Fionn that he was the man that they were fighting about burying and he gave Fionn a green branch. He told him to JAG this in the lady's head every morning and that it would knock a devil out of her. Fionn thanked the man and he could not be grateful enough to him, and the man went away. Fionn did this every morning and at the end of the week the lady usen't to go to Hell. On the day before the wedding day the lady broke her leg and she died in two hours.

JAG: *to stab, prick or pierce.*

The Enchanter

SCHOOL: *Grianán of Aileach, Co. Donegal*
TEACHER: *Niall S. Mac Aoidh*
COLLECTOR: *Philomena Mac Grath, Castlecooly, Co. Donegal*

Fionn Mac Cumhal had arrived at Tara on the night before Samhain when the feast was just beginning. He was dressed in skins of wild animals and he looked so proud and noble that the guards allowed him to pass in. He walked in to the room and stood before the King.

No one spoke, but everybody in the hall was watching Fionn. 'What is your name?' asked the King.

'I am Fionn, the son of Cumhail.'

'You are the son of a friend,' said the King kindly, and he asked the attendants to find a seat for Fionn. When the feast was over, the King rose and spoke. He reminded them that an Enchanter always came to Tara that night. The King asked was there anyone who would save the royal city from the Enchanter. No one answered until at last Fionn stood up and said, 'Oh King, I will deliver Tara from this Enchanter.'

'If you do, Fionn,' said the King, 'I promise here before the Fianna and nobles of Ireland that you may have any reward that is in my power to grant.' Fionn went out and no sound was to be heard on the roads and fields. Fionn was not afraid, although he did not know yet how he was going to defeat the Enchanter. He heard a quick step behind him and he turned round. There stood an old soldier who had followed him out of the hall. He was holding out a spear and a cloak.

'Noble Fionn,' he said, 'your father was always very kind to me and now I can do something for his son. Take this fairy spear and magic cloak. When you hear the Enchanter's music lean over the spear and hold it fast. Don't be afraid and if you feel no fear you will be able to stay awake. When the music stops spread out this cloak and it will keep the fire from scorching you.'

At last he heard the music. It came nearer, the sweetest music that mortal ears ever heard. The Enchanter was coming. Fionn spread out the magic cloak and not a second too soon. The fiery blast was blown and streaks of fire came through the air. Fionn felt a scorching heat, but no fire came near him. Well covered by the cloak, he ran towards the Enchanter. He hurled the spear at the giant's throat. Down fell the giant and as he fell the ground shook. Fionn took the head to the King and never did Tara live again in fear of Samhain Eve.

'What reward do you claim, Fionn?' said the King.

'Oh, King,' said Fionn, 'I ask the Chief Commander over the Fianna of Ireland.'

'It is granted,' said the King.

That is how Fionn became leader of the Fianna Ireland.

Fionn's Finger Stone

SCHOOL: *Calhame, Co. Donegal*
TEACHER: *Seán Mac Cuinneagáin*
INFORMANT: *P. Mc Closkey, Castletown, Co. Donegal*

Long ago, when Fionn Mc Cool and his companions were hunting the wild deer in Connacht, they came to a little house which was built under the shadow of a high cliff. Being tired and hungry, they thought they would get something to eat in it. Upon knocking at the door, it was opened by an old woman who inquired what they wanted. Upon learning that they were hungry and thirsty she invited them inside and set a fine meal before them. When they had eaten and drunk their fill they returned out again. Great was their surprise to find another group of warriors sitting on the green outside the house. Fionn recognised their leader as his old enemy Goll Mac Morna. At this time there was a truce between them. Both companies saluted one another cordially enough. After they had conversed a while they began some games. Everything went on well for a while.

Now it happened there was a huge stone near by and this stone was supposed to cover the entrance to a fairy dwelling. Goll challenged Fionn to lift the stone from the entrance. Fionn was loth to do so for, as we know, he was tired of the chase before hand. This only caused Goll and his companions to laugh and they taunted Fionn, saying that he was not able to perform this feat. This enraged Fionn, who started up and, getting a good hold of the stone, tried to enforce it out of its place. He found to his sorrow he was unable to do so. This made Goll and his friends laugh, and you may be sure that this did not please Fionn and his heroes.

A battle between the two parties was imminent when the old woman came out of the house and reproached them with causing her so much annoyance. When they told her of the challenge and how Fionn had failed she went into the house again. She came out in a few minutes carrying a ripe yellow apple which she handed to Fionn, telling him at the same time to eat half of it and throw the other half over his left shoulder. When he had done this she told him to lift the stone now. Going over to it the second time, he caught hold of it and with one mighty heave pulled the stone from its bed.

All who witnessed this mighty feat were amazed. Then, lifting it over his head, he gave it a mighty cast over the sea. The stone kept on flying in the air and at last it fell on the top of a hill near the town now known as Killybegs. It bears the tracks of Fionn's fingers even to this day and ever since it has been called Fionn's Finger Stone. It is said that when a person goes up on top of the stone he would feel as if he were sailing through the air.

Another lovely girl

SCHOOL: *Cloneen, Co. Tipperary*
TEACHER: *Éamonn Ó Néill*
COLLECTOR: *Mary O'Meara*

When Fionn Mac Cumhaill and his soldiers were in Ireland, he thought it would be wise for him to get married. There were a lot of girls and women around Slievenamon who wanted to marry Fionn, but he did not know which to take. If he took one special girl it may rise disturbance between him and the other girls.

He tasted the salmon of knowledge and soon thought of a plan. He sat on top of Slievenamon, and all the girls were at the foot of the mountain waiting for the signal to start. Then 'off they went'; some went for a long time but then failed. After a while there were only three left, two young girls, and an old one. Then the fair-haired girl fell and hurt her ankle and there were two left. The old woman kept going and the other girl fell. Fionn thought he would have to marry her, when another lovely girl came up to him, and so he married her and they lived happily together. Nobody knew that Fionn had instructed this girl to go over to Boherboy and she would not have to climb as much as the others.

'You helped one who was weak'

SCHOOL: *Warren Lower, Co. Westmeath*
TEACHER: *Liam Mac Coiligh*
COLLECTOR: *Nellie Murray, Annaghgortagh, Co. Westmeath*
INFORMANT: *Thomas Murray, Annaghgortagh, Co. Westmeath*

One day of long ago a number of boys left their homes to go and join the Fianna. On their way they came to a river. They did not know how to get across. After a while they jumped the river. When they were all on the other side they heard someone call. They looked back and saw a poor old woman. She wished to cross but was unable and asked the boys for help. All hurried on except one. One boy went back and helped her over. When he got over the other side his clothes were soiled and he thought Fionn would not choose him. His companions were gone when he looked. When he arrived at Fionn's tent, Fionn said, 'Why did not you leap the river?' When the boy told Fionn his story he said, 'I choose you, because you helped one who was weak.'

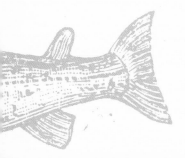

The Tailteann Games

SCHOOL: *Ballyduff, Co. Waterford*
TEACHER: *Brigid Prior*
COLLECTOR: *Chrissie Tobin, Ballyduff, Co. Waterford*
INFORMANT: *Margaret Tobin, 82, Ballyduff, Co. Waterford*

I heard this story told often. Fionn Mac Cumhal was reared by a she wolf, so he was strong and fierce. An old witch had stolen him, and she fed him by putting him under the wolf to drink her milk.

He was tall and powerful and very comely. He became famous at the age of 12. The Tailteann games were being held at Tara. The witch — the foster mother — took him there to take part in the games. He proved himself superior to all the other youths in running and jumping.

The games lasted a week and always finished up with a hurling match. The victors of the various games were chosen to play the hurling match on the last day of the games. Fionn was among the number.

The match began, Fionn was placed by his side in the goal. Each time the ball came to him, he drove it the length of the field out the opposite goal, so Fionn's side was winning every time. The referee began to take the men from Fionn's side, and to put them with the opposite side, till at last every player was on the opposite side, and Fionn left alone to fight them all, and he still continued to win. The crowd thought then he was using witchcraft, and were gathering angrily around him. The witch woman — his foster mother — grasped him, and put him up on her back, and flew through the Irish woods with him, pursued by the soldiers.

She ran towards Ballyinn Lismore, and when she was getting tired, Fionn said to come on his back, and he would carry her home. When he reached the old cabin where they lived, he was leaving her down, but he had only her two shin bones caught in his hand. Her body and clothes had been torn coming through the wood.

A giant named Liam Harris

SCHOOL: *Mainistir Fhearmuighe, Clondulane, Co. Cork*
TEACHER: *Aindrias Ó Scannail*
COLLECTOR: *Tadhg Ó hAilgheanáin, Clondulane, Co. Cork*
INFORMANT: *John Nevin, Gearagh, Co. Cork*

One day as Fionn MacCool was walking along the banks of the Blackwater he met a giant named Liam Harris. This giant was PLAYING A SALMON and whoever would eat this salmon when boiled would be filled with great knowledge.

Now, the giant was playing the salmon for two days and two nights and he was very sleepy. He asked Fionn to play the fish for a bit while he got some sleep, and told him when he had the fish caught to bring him to the cave and boil him. He also said that if he left a blister rise in the salmon he would have his life. And he going away he gave Fionn a ring to put on his finger. When Fionn caught the salmon he brought it to the giant's cave. The giant was asleep. Fionn put it on a SPIKIT and boiled it. After a few minutes' boiling a blister rose, and Fionn did not want to let the giant see it, so he took the salmon off the fire and he put the spikit iron into the giant's eye. There were a lot of deer skins in the cave so Fionn went into one of these and made his exit. Now when the giant woke and found Fionn gone he was very angry. So he went out and called him. Now the ring that Fionn had on his finger was a magic ring and no matter where Fionn went the ring answered the giant's call. At last Fionn threw the ring into the river and when the giant heard the ring answering him in the river he dived in after it and got drowned. Then Fionn made his escape.

PLAYING A SALMON: *fighting a hooked fish*
until it exhausts itself and can be landed.
SPIKIT: *spickit – a rod used as a spit*

He reared him up and called him Oisín

SCHOOL: *Dromclogh, Co. Cork*
TEACHER: *Riobárd Ó Ceallaigh*
INFORMANT: *Pádraig Ó Mathghamhna, 74, farmer, Dromclogh West, Co. Cork*

At about the time the Roman Empire was at its height the Milesians were the ruling power in Ireland. The Romans had conquered practically all of Europe. The Irish people expected to be invaded at any moment and they formed an army of defence in Ireland. The soldiers of this army were called Fianna or Fenians and their leader was Fionn Mac Cumhail. Their business was to guard the harbours and bays of Ireland against invaders.

Fionn had great dogs with which he used to hunt the deer and the wolf. His two most famous dogs were Bran and Sgeolán. These dogs could outstrip and outfight any other dogs in Ireland. One day, as the Fianna were hunting around Killarney, a beautiful deer suddenly started out of the brush-wood. The hounds immediately gave chase, Fionn's dogs leading. They chased the deer until evening. Suddenly, the deer stopped and instead of a deer the huntsmen saw a young lady of exceeding beauty. The dogs gathered round her and began to lick her hands. Fionn soon drew near and asked her who she was and what had caused the transformation. She answered as follows: 'One day as I was going to the well for water I met the chief druid of the Tuatha De Danaans and he said that as my people had conquered his he would turn me into a deer and in that state I should remain until I should meet a great warrior called Fionn Mac Cumhail. At sight of you I am back to myself again.'

Fionn, greatly surprised, asked her to come home with him, which she did, and in due time they were married. They lived a happily married life for some six months. At the end of that period Fionn had to leave home to inspect his army at manoeuvres. He was away from home for some days and when he returned there was no trace or tidings of his fair lady before him. This caused him and his army to search all Ireland, its vales and woods, its caves and crags. He did that seven times and every time took him a year. It was of no avail; no tidings of his fair lady could he find. At length he was told that in the County of Kildare a little boy used to be seen in company with a deer and that the deer used to nurse him. Fionn went towards the place and when the deer saw him coming she fled with great speed out of his sight, leaving the child behind.

Fionn took up the child and questioned him. The child told him that the deer fed him with her milk and that she was very fond of him. He told Fionn that the deer had said that she had been transformed by a druid into a deer and that a great chieftain named Fionn Mac Cumhail had broken the spell and had made her his wife. After being married for six months Fionn had had to inspect his army and while he was away the druid had come and changed her into a deer again and she should remain a deer for ever. Fionn guessed that the boy was his own son. He reared him up and called him Oisín.

The thumb of knowledge

SCHOOL: *Ínse Cloch, Co. Cork*
TEACHER: *Diarmuid Ó Críodáin*
COLLECTOR: *Kitty Sullivan, Dromsullivan South, Co. Cork*
INFORMANT: *Mr. O'Sullivan, 50, Dromsullivan South, Co. Cork*

The Fianna was a party of men who lived in Ireland in the second and third century. They were soldiers paid by the High King to fight for him and to protect the country against invaders. Like their leader, Fionn Mac Cool, they did much hunting and fishing. One of the Fianna named Conán Maol, while hunting with his comrades, threw a rock a distance of two miles. It landed in DONEMARK where it is still to be seen. It is known as CARRAIG-A-ROAN.

Fionn Mac Cool lived for some time with an old druid, who taught him. In the river near the house there was a salmon, known as the 'fish of knowledge', which nobody could catch. Several anxious people tried to, but in vain, and one day the druid succeeded. Full of joy, he brought the fish to Fionn to cook it, but he warned him not to touch it.

Fionn promised, but when he was turning it, it burned his finger. He quickly put the burned finger in his mouth, to soothe it. When the druid heard this, he was very angry because he knew that this deprived him of the knowledge he intended to obtain when he ate the fish. From that time onwards Fionn, when in need of wisdom, had only to put his thumb in his mouth and he obtained it.

The knowledge which he got thus found for him his wife, who was stolen by Diarmuid Ó Duibne, and who was taken by him to a cave in Éoghain Hill, known as 'Leaba Dhiarmuda'. Long ago, it was the custom of the people to steal each other's wives. On one occasion, however, it happened that Diarmuid Ó Duibne stole Fionn's wife, who was supposed to be very beautiful, and then he drew sand in bags from the Bantry sand quay, to a cave situated in the top of Owen Hill, and in this cave they lived.

Now Fionn knew that his wife was somewhere around the coast of Ireland on sand, because whenever he put the 'thumb of knowledge' in his mouth, he knew everything. He went round the coast in search of her, not expecting sand on the hill. The cave or hollow is clearly and plainly to be still seen there. That place is now called Leaba Dhiarmuda, in English 'the bed of Diarmuid and Grainne'.

Another member of the Fianna was named Goll Mac Móirne. He was a very tall man of Herculean strength. It is said that he walked across Bantry Bay to Whiddy, and that the sea on account of his height only reached to his knees. There is a large rock still to be seen in Derryorkane. It is said that it was thrown by Diarmuid from the top of Owen Hill, which is about eight miles distant. The Fianna were all slain in the year two hundred and eighty-four at the Battle of Gabra.

DONEMARK: *a place on the Cork coast, not far from Bantry.*
CARRAIG-A-ROAN: *Carraig na Rón, literally 'rock of the seals'.*

Noble Ferdia

SCHOOL: *Aghameen, Co. Louth*
TEACHER: *Bean Uí Riada*
COLLECTOR: *Sheila Rice*

In the neighbourhood of Dundalk at the present day there can be seen a fort that was once the home of Sualtim, father of the mighty Cuchulain, the hound of the North. Cuchulain was a great warrior who lived in the olden days. Sualtim died when Cuchulain was very young and his mother sent him to some of her friends to be cared for. Cuchulain was always the brightest and cleverest in play or in work than any of his playmates.

One of his great deeds that we read about in Irish history is how he slew the hound of Culann from which he got his name, Cuchulain. When Cuchulain was staying with his [foster] parents he was invited to a banquet nearby which was held in a smith's house. It was late when Cuchulain arrived there and, the smith thinking he had all his guests, he bolted all his doors and let out his wolf dog to prevent anyone coming near the house. When Cuchulain came the dog ran to attack him, but Cuchulain had his hurley ball with him and he put it down the dog's neck, which choked him.

When Maeve's army came to Dundalk to fight there was no one there to meet her but Cuchulain. So it was arranged that one of Maeve's army would fight against Cuchulain. The fight lasted for three days until at length Ferdia fell, pierced by Cuchulain's sword. When Cuchulain had killed Ferdia, he afterwards regretted his deed and he said, 'What does it matter? The friend I love is dead, noble Ferdia, who was dearer to me than all the world besides.'

They could not forget they were friends

SCHOOL: *Clochar na Trócaire, Cappamore, Co. Limerick*
TEACHER: *An tSr. Benin*
COLLECTOR: *Eibhlín Ní Blacball, Dromsallagh, Co. Limerick*

At one time, there was a war between Ulster and Connacht because Maeve wanted to get a bull belonging to Daire, a farmer in Cooley, and he refused to give it to her. There was no one ready in Ulster but Cuchulainn. At that time, battles were decided by single fights between great Champions.

Cuchulainn's greatest fight was with Ferdiad, who had been his friend, whose life he once had saved. Ferdiad did not want to fight his old friend, but Queen Maeve urged him to do so. Even in the fight, they could not forget they were friends. They used fight all day and at night Ferdiad used send food across to Cuchulainn and Cuchulainn used send doctors with medicine to Ferdiad, but the doctors could do little with either of them except to stop the flow of blood.

On the fifth day, they had a terrible fight in the middle of the stream. The noise of their swords meeting was so great that the horses of the Connacht men broke out of their stables with fright and ran away into the woods. Ferdiad got his death blow at last. Cuchulainn took him in his arm and carried him to the bank.

Two strong men

SCHOOL: *Caitrín Naomhtha, Aughrim, Co. Galway*
TEACHER: *Pádraig Ó Ceacháin*
COLLECTOR: *Bertie Mannion, Fairfield, Co. Galway*
INFORMANT: *Martin Mannion, parent, 52, Fairfield, Co. Galway*

My father, Martin Mannion, of Fairfield, about one mile north of Aughrim, told me this story. He is aged about fifty two or three years.

Cuchulain and Ferdiad were two strong men that lived in Ireland long ago. Those two men were married. They were living a short distance away from each other.

Ferdiad's wife did not like Cuchulain at all. She had some grudge or other against him. She was continually asking her husband to give him a sound thrashing, but Ferdiad was afraid of Cuchulain.

At length and at last, he took courage, and set out for his neighbour's house. Cuchulain's wife saw Ferdiad coming. She knew well that this man was able to beat her husband, and he knew it too.

'Here is Ferdiad coming. I wonder what is he looking for. I suppose he is looking for a fight. That wife of his is a holy fright,' said Cuchulain's wife. Cuchulain looked at the door, and at the window, and saw that there were no means of escape.

'Here, jump into the cradle, and I'll put the clothes about you,' said his wife. In he got, and made himself comfortable. Now Cuchulain's wife had a good deal more sense than Cuchulain, and he knew that.

Ferdiad came as far as the door and looked in. 'Is the boss in, ma'am?'

'No, he is not; he won't be back for a couple of days.'

'Sorry, I wanted to see him,' says Ferdiad.

Ferdiad turned round and was going away when Cuchulain's wife called him, and asked him to wait for the dinner. Ferdiad was fast gaining courage. He said to himself it would be no trouble to beat the other fellow, so he walked in and took a chair.

Cuchulain's wife was getting the dinner ready as fast as she could. She had one cake down on the griddle, and was going to make another. The fire was doing very badly, because the wind was on the door. After a while, she said, 'I wish himself was here, and he would turn the house around.'

When Ferdiad heard this, he began to get afraid and he said to himself, that Cuchulain must be a very strong man. He chanced to look into the cradle and saw the child lying fast asleep.

'How old is the child ma'am?' he asked.

'About eighteen months or so.'

'He is a very strong child, God bless him,' said Ferdiad.

When the woman of the house got Ferdiad's back turned, she baked another cake and put the griddle into it. When the two cakes were baked, she gave the cake with the griddle in it to Ferdiad, and gave the other cake to the child in the cradle.

The first bite Ferdiad took out of the cake, he knocked out three or four of his teeth. He looked into the cradle, to see how the child was getting on, and it was getting on all right. At length and at last, he put his finger into the child's mouth to see what sort of teeth it had. As soon as he had did so, the child bit the finger off him. Ferdiad jumped up and said to himself that he had better be clearing out, before the man of the house came in. The child in the cradle was bad enough, but what sort must his father be? 'Well good day, ma'am. I'll call again some other time.'

When he had gone, the child got up and said that that was a narrow shave.

When Ferdiad went home, he told his wife about all he saw and heard. She, too, got a bit scared and said to herself that it was just as well be content with her lot.

A beautiful fairy

SCHOOL: *Caddellbrook, Co. Roscommon*
TEACHER: *Bean Uí Dhocraigh*
COLLECTOR: *Bridie Kelley, 12, Corlis, Co. Roscommon*

Long ago there lived in Ireland a great warrior named Cuchulain. He was strong and brave and fought many a fight. Now Cuchulain had a beautiful wife whose name was Emer and she was living where Rathmoyle House now stands. For a long time they lived very happy together, but at length Cuchulain grew restless for more exciting things than his wife and children and once more he went out to battle.

After he going Emer sat at home and counted the days until he should come back. Week followed week, still no sign of Cuchulain came, and at last Emer began to think that he had forgotten her. Then after a time she heard the sound of horses' hoofs and she knew that someone was coming at last. Then she saw that it was a friend of Cuchulain's. 'What news do you bring me?' she asked, and he said, 'Cuchulain he is under a heavy slumber [from] which no man can wake him.'

Emer lost no time in getting ready and she set off that night with Conall and two men to guard the Chariot. The chariot flew faster and faster till suddenly the horses reared and then stood still, shaking all over. Emer stood up in the chariot to see what was wrong and she saw an old woman standing on the road. Emer thought she was a beggar and was giving her money. 'It is not money I want,' she said, 'but to go with you to Cuchulain. I am a wise woman who might cure him if you fail.' So Emer took her into the chariot, though she felt afraid of her. The old woman wrapped her coat around her and did not speak until they reached the castle. 'Go you in first,' said the old woman to Emer, 'and try to wake him: if you fail you can send for me.'

Then they brought Emer to the room where her husband was. She saw him lying on a couch with his eyes closed. There were people round him singing and playing, trying to wake him, but he did not hear them. Emer told them all to go away and she stood beside the couch and called him and begged him to open his eyes and to look at her, and as she spoke her voice grew louder until it was almost a scream, but Cuchulain did not move, and at last she buried her face in her hands and wept bitterly. When she looked up again she saw the old woman in the doorway. Then she told Emer that Cuchulain must go away. She told her of a place on the seashore where they should meet. At first Emer would not agree, for she did not like to let Cuchulain go, but at last she consented for fear he should die without waking. She then went away, leaving the old woman with Cuchulain.

Now the old woman was really a beautiful fairy whose name was Fand. She took Cuchulain away into the country of the air, and he soon got better, and at last the day came when Cuchulain and Emer were to meet on the seashore. When Emer saw Fand so young and beautiful, she was angry and said she had taken Cuchulain away from her, and she drew her sword, intending to kill Fand. Then a great storm arose and all the sky grew darker and darker, so dark that Emer and Cuchulain could not see one another. But when at last it rolled away Emer and Cuchulain had forgotten all about his sleep and Fand the fairy who had cured him, and they went back to their home together, both very happy. And that was what the fairy wished for: her desire was to see Cuchulain and his wife Emer as happy as possible, for Fand was one of the good fairies.

Queen Maeve and the Enchanted Steed

SCHOOL: *Castlehacket, Co. Galway*
TEACHER: *S. Ó Floinn*
COLLECTOR: *Eddie Kearns, Pollnahallia, Co. Galway*
INFORMANT: *Tim Kearns, 73, Caltragh, Co. Galway*

About the time of Christ there lived in Connaught a queen named Maeve. She had her castle at Cruachan in Co. Roscommon but she had another one on the top of Knock Meadha. She had a white horse called 'The Enchanted Steed' which was able to bring her from Knock Meadha to Cruachan, in twelve minutes. She was very proud of this horse and one night as she was coming home from Cruachan the horse was killed by Maeve's enemy.

The first man to die for Our Lord

SCHOOL: *Ballyduff, Co. Waterford*
TEACHER: *Brigid Prior*
COLLECTOR: *Lizzie Daly, Baranvalla, Co. Waterford*
INFORMANT: *James Daly, 58, Baranvalla, Co. Waterford*

King Conor Mac Nessa was a powerful warrior; he was believed to be invulnerable. Some magician make it known that the only way to kill him was to take out some strong man's brains, boil them as hard as a stone, and put these boiled brains into a sling and get one of the strongest soldiers to aim at Conor Mac Nessa's head with this sling.

The brains were got and the strongest man that could be found got the sling and put the brains into it, and meeting Conor struck him a fierce blow. The ball of brains went into the back of his head.

Mac Nessa went to the most powerful physicians but they could not cure him, only they assured him he would live a long natural life provided he never got into a violent temper.

On the day of Our Lord's death he noticed the darkness in the heavens. He asked his druids what was the cause of the darkness, and he was told that a just man had been put to death that day.

He rushed out and caught his sword, and began hewing down the trees, and with the awful anger in his brain, the brain ball burst in his head and he dropped dead — the first man to die for Our Lord.

The Gobán Saor

SCHOOL: *Breaghwy, Co. Mayo*
TEACHER: *Peadar Ó Catháin*
INFORMANT: *Mr. Pat Brennan, Ballina, Co. Mayo*

The Gobán Saor was the best mason in the world. He had three daughters and he gave one of them in exchange for a son. This boy was very dull and Gobán was always afraid that he would never make his living, unless he would get a good wife.

One day he gave a sheep's hide and he told him to get the hide and the price of it. He could not sell it the first day, or the second. The third day as he saw a lady washing clothes, he asked her to buy the hide, but he said he wanted the price and the hide. She gave him the price of the hide and she took the wool off the hide and kept it. When he went home to the Gobán he was very pleased and he said the girl to whom he sold the hide would have to be his wife. They both got married and lived happily together.

It was the Gobán Saor who built the tower of Killala. One day as he set upon the journey on the road, the Gobán Saor said to his son, 'Shorten the road.'

'How can I shorten the road?' said the boy.

'Very well,' said he, 'it is better for us to turn home.' They made some excuses when they went home.

As they were going the second day, he told the boy to shorten the road, but the boy said he could not shorten the road. They turned back the second day, and when they went in the young boy's wife got astonished. The boy told her that the Gobán Saor told him to shorten the road. 'How could I shorten the road?' said he.

She answered, 'Well you are no good when you could not tell an old yarn, let it be a lie or the truth.'

The third day as they set upon their journey, the Gobán said to the boy, 'Shorten the road.' They told stories to each other until they reached Killala. When the tower was built the owner did not want any tower to be similar to it. One day when he got them up on the top, he took down the ladder as he meant to leave them on the top of the tower until they would die. 'Well,' said he [the Gobán], 'I have an article at home which is needed for the top of this and until it is put on, it will not be built right.'

The man then asked the Gobán what it was. The Gobán said that no one would get it but [the owner's] own son. When he reached the Gobán's house, the boy's wife welcomed him and she made some tea for him. After he had partaken of a fine meal she asked him what he wanted. She then got a deep box and told him he would have to get it himself as she could not reach it. When she got him stooped taking out the article, she caught his feet and threw him into the box and put the lid on it.

When the owner saw his son so long away, he got uneasy. He sent a messenger to the house, but he got an answer, that he would not be let home until the Gobán and his son would return home.

So the Gobán Saor was let home free, where he received great welcome, and the old man's son returned home to his father's house and that put an end to the Gobán Saor and his son.

3
GHOST STORIES

'When, logic, law and every other avenue are exhausted, there's still fierce power in a curse or a good ghost story.'

SMALL WONDER THAT *Dracula* was conceived by an Irishman! We have a deep tradition of frightening the life out of each other and, fortunately, there is a remarkable treasury of ghost stories in the National Folklore Collection. The very first story in this small selection came as a right shock to me and involves the legendary Biddy Early, once described to me by folklorist Eddie Lenihan as a *bean feasa*/woman of knowledge.

The story tells of a restless soul wandering a railway line as penance for her father's sin. He was Tom Hayes, a member of the jury that wrongfully found John Twiss, a Kerryman, guilty of the murder of James Donovan in 1894. Despite a plea of innocence, a flimsy case against him and a massive public outcry, Twiss was hanged in 1895.

This story of the spirit wandering on foot of her father's deceit was gathered in 1937 and I first encountered it in November 2021. Within weeks of reading it, I was stopped in my tracks when I heard RTÉ News announce, 'President Michael D. Higgins today welcomed the descendants of John Twiss to Áras an Úachtaráin for the formal issuing of a presidential pardon. The emotional ceremony was the sixth such pardon ever issued in the state, and just the third issued posthumously.' Justice done after 126 years.

Apart from the brilliantly dramatic narrative, consider the practical value of this ghost story. Having failed to secure an innocent man's release, the powerless poor are left with only the word of a ghost to continue the case for John Twiss. The shady testimony of a restless spirit is enough to keep the good name of John Twiss alive. Folklore sustained the people where law had failed them. I have little doubt that the telling and retelling of this story fed into the torrent of support that ultimately led to his pardon.

When logic, law and every other avenue are exhausted, there's still fierce power in a curse or a good ghost story. Many of us grew up on moral tales with endings like '...and that landlord or his family never had any luck since.' You just can't argue with a declaration from 'the other side'. Whether it be a call from the Blessed Virgin to say the rosary, or Biddy Early's 'curse' on the Clare hurlers, you'd be a fool to ignore it. According to legend, Biddy Early ensured that Clare will never win an All-Ireland hurling title (even though she died in 1874, a full 10 years before the GAA was founded!). One thing is sure, however: John Twiss has finally been pardoned and the guilt-ridden ghost of Tom Hayes' daughter can now rest in peace.

A good story is always enhanced by a good storyteller. The telling has to be credible, with a few breadcrumbs dropped along the way: clues that prompt thoughts in the listener like, 'Mmm, I always found that place creepy too.'

One of the great techniques of a good salesman, magician or storyteller is understatement. By casting some doubt on their own story, they can elicit a reaction like '...but it could be true, though, couldn't it?' Many a great *seanchaí* would dismiss his or her own story at the conclusion with a shrug and a throwaway *'Sin é mo scéal ar aon nós,'* or 'Yerra, I dunno, but that's how 'twas told to me anyway.'

This is brilliantly illustrated here by an informant from Termonfeckin named Michael. He cleverly uses a throwaway line to draw you in as he begins his first-hand account of a ghostly pub crawl: 'I'll tell it as it happened. If you don't believe me you needn't.' Nor does Michael stretch the listener's credulity by overstating the veracity of his story: 'I ordered two pints and I drank one. I didn't see him drink his but I seen the tumbler leaving the counter and coming back empty.' I'm all ears at this point.

Other storytellers draw on outside sources to lend support to their tales. Eighty-year-old Dr Albert Edward Croly tells us an entirely credible tale of bodysnatching in Dublin's Rathfarnham, complete with newspaper evidence to back it up. When living in the same area, I actually heard this story myself in the Yellow House pub.

There are common threads running through the weave of Irish ghost stories: the power of holy water, spirits being trapped in the liminal space between this world and the next, shape-shifting black dogs, the power of the priest or a compassionate ear to 'settle' the restless spirit and the ghost disappearing 'in a ball of fire'.

Prepare yourself to meet a cast of characters that includes a 'half-lunatic', smoking ghosts, pint- and whiskey-drinking ghosts and a king who inserts an advertisement in a newspaper. You will be introduced to 'Petticoat Loose', an evil spirit who specialises in killing unbaptised children. Hot on her heels was *An Dúlachán*, the headless horseman, sometimes known as *Gan Cheann* (No Head), who spirits away the dead in a coach made of human skin while brandishing a whip made of a human spine.

Disclaimer: If you are reading this book on your own and it's dark outside, I'd save this chapter for the morning.

They went to Biddy Early

SCHOOL: *Birdhill, Cooleen, Co. Tipperary*
TEACHER: *Micheál Ó Meachair*
COLLECTOR: *Thomas Teefey, Coosáne, Birdhill, Co. Limerick*
INFORMANT: *parent: Michael Teefey, railway worker, Coosáne, Birdhill, Co. Limerick*

The only ghost story I ever heard of was John Mac Mahon, a railway employee, went into Killaloe one night to a tailor who was making a suit of clothes for him. When he arrived in Killaloe the clothes were not finished. He said he would wait until they would be finished. He had them done at twelve o'clock midnight. He then started to walk home and he came along the Killaloe Branch railway.

When he entered the straight road he saw a white object approaching from the direction of Birdhill. She was walking between the two rails and he was walking outside. They both passed each other and neither of them spoke. He thought she was the most beautiful woman he ever saw. She was dressed in pure white. He walked on about one hundred yards; then he looked back and she was disappeared. It was then he got frightened as he heard that the place was haunted. He struggled home as best he could and got sick after going home and was on the point of death. It was then he told his people what occurred to him coming from Killaloe.

They went to Biddy Early and when she saw them coming up the lane she told them their business and she said that there was only the one cure. That was to go back and walk that railway every night for a week and to speak to her and ask her what was troubling her. He did as he was told and she told him her name and she said she was a daughter of Tom Hayes, the well known pact juryman who brought a verdict of guilty against a man named John Twiss of Kerry. He well knew that Twiss was innocent and she said that she was doing penance for her father, who was in the fires of Hell for his false conscience. She bid him good night and told him to never walk that railway at that hour of night and so he did not.

He remained a half-lunatic until he died

SCHOOL: *Moyne, Co. Longford*
TEACHER: *Bean Uí Tháibh*
COLLECTOR: *Peggy Mc Shane, Legga, Co. Longford*
INFORMANT: *Michael Mc Shane, Legga, Co. Longford, farmer*

One time there was a man. His name was John Colum Sonnagh. A ghost travelled with him every night from sunset. Every night the ghost went with him on his CÉILÍDHE. He had three or four stiles to cross. The ghost lifted him across each stile. He went one night to a gamble. The ghost went with him. The ghost told [him] not to stay later than nine o'clock as there would be a man killed in the house before morning. The man stood on till half past nine. They raised a row. It was settled. He advised them to quit. The man came outside the house. He met the ghost. The ghost said, 'I thought I told you not to stay long or pass any remarks to them.' Colum and the ghost started for home. As they were going home a man came after them for the priest. A man was killed with a POUNDER. 'Ha, ha,' says the ghost, 'didn't I tell you there would be a man killed?' They went home.

A week later he was asked to go to a fair with a man with cattle. The man rose in the middle of the night. He had no clock. The ghost met him outside and ordered him to go back, that it wasn't near daylight yet. The man refused. He said he would go ahead. He went to his journey's end and when he was going in on the gate the ghost attacked him. He had to be carried home. He remained a half-lunatic till he died. The priest settled the ghost at a lone bush in a farmer's field. The priest told them never labour within THREE PERCH of it or if they would the ghost would break out again.

CÉILIDHE: *social visits.*
POUNDER: *either a wooden mallet for mashing or pounding potatoes, or a wooden tool used when planting potatoes.*
THREE PERCH: *approximately 75 square metres.*

The cock was crowing all night

SCHOOL: *Urhin, Co. Cork*
TEACHER: *Eimile Ní Urdail*
COLLECTOR: *Cáit Ní Shuilebháin, Caherkeem, Co. Cork*
INFORMANT: *Cáit Bean Ní Shuileabháin, Caherkeem, Co. Cork, mother*

Long ago there was a man from Cahirkeem working in Allihies mines. He was going home one Saturday night. He was very anxious for a smoke but he had no match to light his pipe. Then he saw a fire on the road before him. While he was lighting his pipe he saw a man coming to him. They walked on together until they came to Eyeries; they never spoke. He went into a public house for a drink. The ghost waited outside. He offered a drink to the ghost; he did not take it. They walked on again till they came to Ballycrovane.

Then the ghost spoke. 'Well,' he said, 'we must separate now from each other. I must be in Waterford before cockcrow and you will be going home to Cahirkeem. I will give you advice not to be out late any Saturday night from this out. Be off with you now,' said the ghost, 'for a crowd of people will be going this way soon and if they catch you out you will pay for it.' The ghost shook hands with him. Then he looked into the ghost. He knew him. He was a neighbour from the village who died six years ago. He went off and did not see him since.

The man was gone a quarter of a mile when he heard the great noise after him. He did nothing but throw himself into a thicket of brambles. He was not long there when away down came the great noise. There were horses there; they were knocking sparks out of the road. There were gentleman and ladies there. He knew some of them. They all went away and the man got out of his hiding [place] and away home with him. Just when he reached home it was cockcrow and his wife asked him did anything happen to him. She said the cock was crowing all night. He did not tell the story to her until a few days after.

Three crocks of gold

SCHOOL: *Croom, Co. Limerick*
TEACHER: *Bríd, Bean Mhic Eoin*
COLLECTOR: *Nancy Kirby, Croom, Co. Limerick*
INFORMANT: *(name not given), parent, male, 50 years*

Long ago there lived a family who bought a fine big house. But when they went to live in it they found it was haunted by a ghost. Every night the ghost appeared in the kitchen and went rattling around the place so that no one could sleep. At last the owners left the house altogether, and offered a reward to anyone who would rid the house of the ghost. Many tried to do so but all fled in terror from the apparition.

At last a soldier who happened to be passing and heard the story said he would stay in the house for one night anyhow if he got plenty of whiskey, whether he would hunt the ghost or not. They said they would, and they made up a good big fire for him and left him sitting in a fine comfortable chair beside it with his glass and bottle within reach and the curtains drawn across the windows.

Came the hour of midnight and with it the ghost – an old man with a long beard nearly down to his toes. Before he had time to talk the soldier jumped up and reached him a glass of whiskey. 'Here,' said he, 'drink this and we can talk afterwards.' The ghost drank the whiskey and sat down. 'Couldn't I cut that whisker for you and trim your beard?' said the soldier.

'Ah for many a day I have wanted some one to do that for me, but no one would wait for me to ask them,' answered the ghost.

So the soldier trimmed his beard and cut his whiskers and the ghost was truly grateful to him. When he was finished the ghost said, 'In that wall there are three crocks of gold. Give two to my son and keep the other for yourself.' With that he disappeared and was never seen again.

In the morning the owners of the house came and found the soldier gay and well. He told his story and they looked for the crocks of gold. Sure enough they were in the wall where the ghost had said. The people of the house gladly gave them to the soldier to do with them as the ghost had asked him and they were never again troubled in their house.

The palace ghost

SCHOOL: *Lankill, Co. Mayo*
TEACHER: *Seán Ó Cibhil*
COLLECTOR: *James Reid, Knappabeg, Co. Mayo*
INFORMANT: *Walter Walsh, Knappabeg, Co. Mayo*

Once upon a time there lived a King and his brother died and he left him a palace. The next night after his brother died he went into the palace and he was sitting at the fire. At twelve o'clock he heard a ghost coming down the steps and he ran out to his own home again.

Then he inserted an advertisement in the paper saying that he would give a hundred pound to anyone who would sleep in the palace for one night. A man came to him and said that he would sleep in the palace if the King would give him a hundred pounds and the King said he would. The man went into the palace and at twelve o'clock he heard a ghost coming downstairs and he ran out too.

A few nights [later] another man came to him and said that he was not afraid of any ghost and he went into the palace. At twelve o'clock he heard a noise up stairs and the ghost walked down and sat beside the man. After a while the man asked the ghost would he have a smoke and the ghost said [he] would.

The man lit the pipe for the ghost and handed it to him the pipe. After the ghost had enough smoked, he let the pipe fall and broke it in a hundred bits, and the man said nothing. After a while the man asked the ghost would he take a cup of tea and the ghost said he would. The man gave him a cup of tea. When he had enough of tea drunk, he let the cup and saucer fall and broke it in a hundred bits. The man asked him did he want [to] fight and the [ghost] said he did. The two of them started to fight. With the first RATTLE the man gave to the ghost he tumbled him in the ashes, and with the second rattle the man gave to the ghost he tumbled him head-long on the floor.

Then the ghost said that the man had him beaten. And the ghost said that he would never trouble him again. He told him to raise up a certain FLAG and that there was a crock of gold under it. The man did so and he got the crock of gold, and he also got a hundred pounds from the King and he was rich for ever. The King lived in the palace for the rest of his life.

RATTLE: *a blow.*
FLAG: *a flagstone.*

The alm of salt

SCHOOL: *Aubane, Millstreet, Co. Cork*
TEACHER: *Tadhg Ó Corcaráin*
COLLECTOR: *Eileen O'Brien*
INFORMANT: *her father (name not given)*

There was a girl in Ballyvourney long ago and a ghost used appear to her nearly every night. Any other person in the house usedn't see the ghost, only herself. The little girl was greatly frightened and her parents went to the priest. The priest didn't take any notice of it and said that it was only an imagination of the child. The ghost continued to appear.

Some wise woman told the mother of the child to give alms of salt to some poor person for the sake of the soul that was haunting the child. The mother did this and the child didn't see the ghost for more than a year, but she appeared again, attacking the child worse than ever.

They then went and told the priest that it was no imagination of the child and that the ghost was attacking her now worse than ever. The priest told them to tell the child when she would see her again to say in God's name what was troubling her. When the ghost came again the girl said, 'In God's name, what is troubling you?'

The ghost said, 'If you spoke to me when you saw me first, my purgatory would be mostly ended — and your mother, whoever advised her to give the alm of salt kept me in darkness for twelve months so that I couldn't see you.' She also said that she was living in Meath before she died and that she promised TO PAY A ROUND in Ballyvourney. She hadn't time to finish it and she got the privilege of showing herself to this girl to finish the round. The girl paid the round and as she was finishing it the ghost appeared again and vanished out of her sight into heaven.

TO PAY A ROUND: *to walk a circuit at a holy well.*

The ghost lived with John for the rest of his life

SCHOOL: *Caddellbrook, Co. Roscommon*
TEACHER: *Bean Uí Dhocraigh*

There was once a man, and his name was John Shannon, who lived with a ghost in Corlis. At night, when John would come home from rambling, the ghost would have the door bolted and all the furniture that was in the kitchen at the door, and John would burst in the door and he would go in on top of his head across all the furniture and break his shins. Then when John would be putting down the fire, the ghost would be throwing turf down on John's head and John would throw up the turf at the ghost again, and they would keep on throwing turf at one another until John would go to bed. Next morning when John would get up out of bed the ghost would have the fire down and the ghost lived with John for the rest of his life.

A figure in a white sheet

SCHOOL: *Ballina, Co. Mayo*
TEACHER: *D. P. Ó Cearbhaill*
COLLECTOR: *Charlie Doherty, Ballina, Co. Mayo*
INFORMANT: *Annie Mc Andrew, Bonniconlan, Ballina, Co. Mayo*

Once upon a time there lived two men in the same house. But you wouldn't call them friends because they were always fighting. They never had a good word for each other and one night one of them, whose name was Pat, said to the other, whose name was Mick, 'I will haunt you when I die, whether you are dead or alive.'

Not long after that Pat died and he kept his word. For he was only dead a few days when one night, as Mick was coming home from a fair, suddenly out in front of him came a figure in a white sheet. Before Mick could do any thing the figure, which was Pat's ghost, jumped on him. They rolled over and over on the ground and at last Mick got the better of the ghost. And he took the sheet off him, for he knew that the ghost couldn't do anything without it. Mick brought the sheet home and hid it.

The following night Mick was sitting at the fire when he heard tapping at the window. He went over to the window and looked out. Outside was the ghost from whom he had taken the sheet. He lifted up the window and asked the ghost what he wanted. The ghost said, 'I want my sheet.'

'Well,' said Mick, 'you won't get it.' And he went outside and hunted the ghost away.

The following night he heard the same tapping and he did the same thing. The next night Mick was listening for the tapping but he didn't hear any. Then when he was going to bed he heard rattling behind him. He looked 'round and saw the ghost taking his sheet out of the press where Mick had hid it. Mick ran over but he [was] too late, for the ghost put on the sheet, and as Mick came [forward] he said some words and Mick changed into a number of small pieces. Then the ghost put the pieces in a box and brought it away.

Soon afterwards a family came to live in the house. But they could not sleep because every night at twelve o'clock they would hear plates breaking and men fighting. But when they would go down to the kitchen they would not see anything. They put up with this for about two weeks and every night they heard the same noises. So they had to leave. Three or four [families] came to the house after them, but they all heard the plates breaking and the men fighting, and so the house had to be deserted.

When ever anybody passed by that house at night they would hear men scolding each other and the house was said to be haunted.

'Bury them dacent'

SCHOOL: *Termonfeckin, Co. Louth*
TEACHER: *Bean Uí Mhurchadha*

I met Michael one Summer evening and after we had talked on various subjects natural and supernatural I asked him – 'Did you ever see a ghost, Michael?'

'Did I ever see a ghost! Aye, I seen a ghost and talked to a ghost and walked with a ghost, a ghost that was dead more than a hundred years.'

'That was surely a ghost, Michael, dead all that time. No chance of his shamming at any rate. Tell me about him.'

'Well,' said Michael, 'I'll tell it as it happened. If you don't believe me you needn't.

'It was the time the old church spire was ataking down to build the new one. As we dug among the old foundations we came on a square space between the stones and in that space was lying the bones of a man. It was in the evening and the foreman said to me, "Michael," he said, "take them bones and bury them over at the hedge and then you can go home." I put the bones in a wheelbarrow and was spitting on my hands to wheel them over to bury them when I seen a strange man half behind me.'

'What kind of man was he, Michael?' I asked.

'He was an odd sort of a man then and fairly tall with a tall BILLYCOCK HAT on his head, and the quare part of it was, sometimes I could see him well enough and sometimes I could see the wall through him.

'He says to me, "What are you doing with them bones?"

'I says, "I'm going to bury them, Sir."

'"Well," he says, "bury them dacent, for them's my bones."'

'Were you frightened, Michael?' I asked.

'Sure,' says Michael, 'I was frightened, but what was the use, I had to go on with my work to get away out of the graveyard. I came down the walk and there he was at my shoulder all the time. When I hurried, he hurried and when I slowed, he slowed. When I came down to the road he says to me, "Come for a walk, Mister, I want to know who the people are who live round here now."

'We went down the Strand Road and every house we passed he wanted to know who lived there and everyone we met he asked their names. Every time I told him, he said something like "humph", and didn't seem pleased.

'We went up the Burrows to Baltray and he never spoke all the time, but he could slip over the rough places quite easy and never tripped. I fell a couple of times trying to keep an eye on him for I didn't know what he might do on me. Every time I fell he grunted, as much as to say, "You're a smart fella."

'When we came to Baltray I went in to get a pint for I was in a bad way, and his reverence, I mean the ghost, followed me in. I asked him would he care for a pint and he growled something. I ordered two pints and I drank one. I didn't see him drink his but I seen the tumbler leaving the counter and coming back empty.

'As we passed through Baltray the people, when they seen us coming, pulled their youngsters in and shut the doors. We went down the road to Termonfeckin. He never walked beside me but kept at my shoulder, just a little behind. Sometimes I thought he was gone but when I would SKELLY round again I could see the billcock still there. When we met people or passed houses he questioned like he did on the other road but the names didn't seem to mean anything to him.

'I went in at Termonfeckin to get another pint and when I looked round he was there at my elbow. I called for two pints but the barman said, "I'll give you a pint, Michael, but that man will get nothing here." I thought he would rear up at that but he only muttered and we both went out and up the hill. We met the priest on the hill and when I was saluting, looked to see what the ghost would do but he was gone.

'It was DUSKIE then and I thought I seen a shadow moving through the gravestones but I wouldn't be sure about that.

'I hope I'll never see the ghost again for he makes me cowld when I think of him.'

> BILLYCOCK HAT: *a bowler hat.*
> SKELLY: *to look around furtively.*
> DUSKIE: *dusk.*

A white woman

SCHOOL: *Tullogher, Ros Mhic Treoin*
LOCATION: *Tullogher, Co. Kilkenny*
TEACHER: *Mrs Winnie Murphy*
COLLECTOR: *Rísteárd Ó Dochartaigh*
INFORMANT: *James Doherty, Brownsford, Co. Kilkenny*

One day two brothers were out in the field ploughing and the draft broke, and as the nearest forge to them was three miles away they waited until evening before setting off to get the draft repaired.

In the evening one of the men set out for the forge, and he had to pass between two hills which were haunted. It was late when the smith had the draft done, and the man had his tea in the forge. The smith wanted him to stay for the night but he wouldn't because he had more ploughing to do in the morning. He set out for home and when he was passing between the hills he heard something behind him and he turned back but could see nothing. He continued on his way and a white woman came in front of him. He put the draft around the ghost. She had no power over the draft so he brought home the ghost. When he reached home his brother was sitting at the fire and he told him to put down a pot of water, but when the brother saw the ghost he fainted. So he tied the ghost to the leg of the table, and put down the water himself. Then he got the ghost and tried to [put] her down in the pot, but she roared and screamed and told him she would show him where there was a pot of gold if he take her out. So he took her out, and she showed him where the gold was, and he tied the ghost to the trunk of a tree, and dug until he found it. When he got the gold he let the spirit off and he never saw her afterwards.

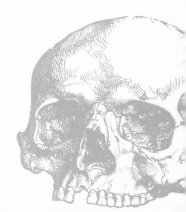

A remarkable bush

SCHOOL: *Tulla, Co. Clare*
TEACHER: *M. Ó Maonaigh*
COLLECTOR: *Patrick McGrath, Furhee, Tulla, Co. Clare*
INFORMANT: *Pat MacNamara, Tulla, Co. Clare*

It was known long ago that there was a remarkable bush in Ranna. At this bush there was a ghost seen by any persons passing by. When the ghost would see a person passing by he would leap out and kill him if he did not talk to him.

It happened one night that a man was coming riding on a horse. The horse stopped when he came to the bush. Then the man saw the ghost and he said, 'If you are coming this way I will carry you on the horse.' The ghost leaped on the horse. The horse began to stumble when the ghost got on him.

All of a sudden, the ghost said, 'Do you know who I am?'

The man said he did not know.

'Well, only for you speaking to me I would kill you,' said the ghost. 'Did you ever hear of Petticoat Loose?' said the ghost. 'When you go home tonight your horse will die.'

The man was going home and the ghost asked him to meet him in the same place tomorrow. The man agreed.

Next night he was coming, and he met the curate of the place. The two of them went together. The ghost came out in the shape of a hound and made for the priest. 'Go back! go back!' said the priest. 'Take your right form and I will talk to you.' The hound changed. The priest asked what brought him here. He got no answer. 'What is wrong with you?' he asked.

'I killed a child and I am damned,' said the ghost. Then the ghost changed into a ball of fire and was never seen again.

Petticoat Loose

SCHOOL: *Bunmahon, Co. Waterford*
TEACHER: *Íde, Bean Uí Chobhthaigh*
COLLECTOR: *Patrick O'Donovan, Ballinarrid, Co. Waterford*
INFORMANT: *John Hurley, relative, Ballinarrid, Co. Waterford*

Long ago there lived a woman whose name was Petticoat Loose. She was a farmer's wife. She used to kill children before they were baptised. When she died she was damned. Some time after her death she used to appear at a certain stone every night.

One night a boy was going home. He had to pass by the stone and so he saw the woman. He was terrified, and ran back part of the way he had come, to the priest's house. The boy told the priest the whole story. He accompanied the boy to the stone. He asked Petticoat Loose what had damned her.

She answered, 'I spat in my mother's face.'

The priest said, 'That did not damn you.'

'I used to poison the neighbour's poultry,' said Petticoat Loose.

'That did not damn you,' said the priest.

'I used to kill children before they were baptised,' said Petticoat Loose.

'That is what damned you,' said the priest. He paused and then said, 'I will banish you to the Red Sea.'

'I will sink all the ships that will pass,' said Petticoat Loose.

'You cannot,' said the priest, 'because you will be head first.' The priest had a small prayerbook with him. He scarcely had finished the word 'first' when he threw the prayerbook at Petticoat Loose. Petticoat Loose disappeared at once and she was never seen again. The priest sent the boy for the prayerbook next day. He warned him to bring it back the way he would find it. The boy did exactly what the priest told him, and brought it back safely. It is said that Petticoat Loose is out on the Red Sea ever since, making SUGANS of the sand.

SUGANS: *from súgán – rope, usually made of straw.*

A roaring bull

SCHOOL: *Roxborough, Co. Roscommon*
TEACHER: *Donncha Ó Ruairc*
COLLECTOR: *Patrick Delamere, Roxborough, Co. Roscommon*
INFORMANT: *Joseph Delamere, Roxborough, Co. Roscommon*

There lived in Barnhill long ago two men whose names were John Sgally and Thomas Sgally. One of them died and then the other man was living alone. The lone man was standing at the door one day and he seen his dead brother coming up the road in a carriage with a burning foot. The ghost went over to the man at the door and told him to meet him in a certain field that night. The man said he would. The ghost also told him he was the cause of having him damned.

Before the man went to the field he went to the priest and he gave him a bottle of holy water, and told him to sprinkle it round him when the ghost would come, so he did.

The man went to the field. At twelve o'clock the ghost came in the form of a roaring bull. The man sprinkled the holy water round him and the bull was not able to pass that spot. There did some of the holy water fall on the bull and he went away in a ball of fire.

The dead coach

SCHOOL: *Morett, Co. Laois*
TEACHER: *Elizabeth Finn*
INFORMANT: *Mr. Patrick Fitzpatrick, 50, Morett, Co. Laois*

This is the story of the dead coach. One Saturday night a long time ago, a woman was sitting at the fire alone, making a dress for herself. It had just struck twelve o'clock when the woman heard a rumbling noise coming up the road. She knew at the minute that it was the dead coach. She was so frightened that she put out the lamp and she left the sewing on the table and ran into bed. She woke her husband and he was so vexed with her that he ran out to the door and shouted after the dead coach to take his wife off with them. The woman was so frightened that she got sick and she died a week later.

A dead body was its load

SCHOOL: *Rathfarnham, Co. Dublin*
TEACHER: *P. Ó Dubhthaigh*
COLLECTOR: *Proinnsias Ó Dubhthaigh, muintéoir, Rathfarnham, Co. Dublin*
INFORMANT: *Dr. Albert Edward Croly, over 80*

The church yard at Cruagh is on the mountain side – apart from nearby houses and in a lonely and somewhat dreary spot. To the casual passerby there is nothing to be seen since a long rutty lane leads through some grazing land to it. But it is remarkable that it has what appears to be a dwarf round tower and this same tower was a pivotal point for many occurrences – violent deaths among them. The purpose of this tower was a 'watch tower' used by the relatives of the recently interred corpses to frustrate the efforts of 'body snatchers'. Many tales are told in the lonely houses of Rathfarnham to this day of the 'Death Coach' which noiseless moved about on secret errands. No one seemed to know whence it came or where it went, but all agreed that a dead body was its load and headless its horsemen and sack-muffled feet on the steeds of death.

When local people and others who had right of burial in Cruagh had deposited their relatives in the grave they took it in turns to watch the grave for at least a week of nights to fend off the body snatchers, if necessary by force of arms, and as a shelter was necessary the small 'Watch Tower' of Cruagh was built.

The real origin of the Death Coach was for the purpose of providing 'anatomical specimens' for the medical profession in and round Dublin. Since Rathfarnham mountain side gave such health to its inhabitants it was also looked on as natural by the 'medicoes' that very suitable cases for dissection would be found here. A hearse was chartered and commanded, usually by medical men themselves, to get the required 'case'. Many a scuffle and fight ending in death occurred here.

There is still in Cruagh a respected family who were ancient inhabitants two hundred years ago. As Catholic landowners of the farming class their roots went deep into the soil beloved by them – their past generations are interred at Cruagh. A fine strong healthy sturdy type of peasant farmer – eminently suited for dissection. One of them, about eighty years of age, died in 183– and in due course was interred. He was one of four brothers. Each surviving brother took his turn to watch from the Tower in secret.

On the second night a silent coach moved up to the outer gate, a very small broken-down structure. Four figures clad in black – long capes drooping from shoulders and large flopping hats down on faces. They carried spades and shovels. It was early in November and the watcher in the tower, huddled closely in his thick FRIEZE coat, must have dozed. However, a late moon shone out and showed him four figures busily engaged at uncovering his brother's grave. Had he been a young man he might have approached them and made an effort to force them off. But, being elderly and well used to the shot gun now in his hand, he fired and saw one of the figures tumble headlong into the half-opened grave. The others quickly raised the figure and staggered away with it.

Next morning showed a trail of blood to the graveyard gate. On the following day a notice appeared in the 'Dublin Evening Post' intimating the sudden death in the Meath Hospital of a very bright medical student whose people gave generations of doctors to Dublin.

FRIEZE: *a type of heavy woollen cloth.*

4
LIFE ON THE LAND

'This was a time when every animal had its own first name and a language understood by all had evolved. "Prug prug" summoned the cattle. "Tip, go on" and "Hip-off" made sense to a horse. "Cioc, cioc, cioc" would bring the hens running and "deoch, deoch, deoch" would get the attention of even the most stubborn pig. "Heck-up" was the reverse gear in Johnnie's donkey.'

Knockraha,
County Cork.
3/7/1967

Dear Mammy and Daddy

I hop you are fine. Do you know how to kill a hen? Bridgie shode me.

Get broom and put on floor. Get Hen. Thigh his legs together. Place his head under broom. Stand on broom. Grab his legs. Pull hard.

Can you bring down my footbal boots. I miss you.

Lots of love,
Mister John creedon

HAT POSTCARD FROM my former self was found amongst my father's possessions after he died. I only vaguely remember writing it, but it's clearly in my handwriting. So, guilty as charged. I spent every summer of my childhood on some farm or other, away from the dangers of the city. On this occasion, I'm staying with Johnnie and Bridgie, a childless couple, on their 14-acre mixed farm in East Cork.

Thanks to the copybooks gathered by the Irish Folklore Commission in the 1930s, I'm taken right back to my own childhood, thirty years after those copybooks were written. Apart from the steep decline in the standard of spelling, as illustrated in my postcard, little had changed. It was the same sour smell of a turf fire and a paraffin lamp as we shooed an inquisitive hen or sow out the back-kitchen door and across the vague threshold that separated our lives and theirs.

The Celts were farmers. Many of our ancestors shared a roof with their livestock for mutual warmth and safety. As farming methods evolved, animals were moved out to their own *bothán*, often a stone shed adjoining the gable-end of the house, later on to an outhouse and eventually to the industrial-style slatted units of today.

The great industrial and economic leap forward of the 1960s and '70s came right in the middle of my childhood. How inconsiderate. I had been enjoying myself up to then. But there's no stopping 'progress'. The vision of Seán Lemass and Donogh O'Malley presided over the arrival of rural electrification, international airports, Irish television and secondary education for all. Ireland's membership of the EEC (now the EU) heralded an irreversible shift in rural life. Modern farming methods were seen as more hygienic and productive and people began to live longer.

However, the Dúchas collection brings us back to a time when family and farm animals were a tight interdependent unit. The scenes described reverberate to a cacophony of children's voices.

This was a time when every animal had its own first name and a language understood by all had evolved.

'Prug prug' summoned the cattle. 'Yip go on' and 'Hip-off' made sense to a horse. 'Cioc, cioc, cioc' would bring the hens running and 'deoch, deoch, deoch' would get the attention of even the most stubborn pig. 'Heck-up' was the reverse gear in Johnnie's donkey.

I'm reminded of '*Cúl an Tí*' by Muskerry poet Seán Ó'Riordáin, who brilliantly captures the goings-on in the haggard as viewed from the back window. He describes the scene as '*Tír álainn trína chéile*', loosely translated as 'A wonderful, disorderly world at the back of the house':

> There are hens here, with a clutch of chicks,
> A humble duck, with a focused mind,
> A big black hound with a cross look
> Barking loudly like a good watch-dog,
> and a cat sun-bathing.

Family welfare was linked directly to animal welfare. Animal care was based on a mix of superstition and science. Although these two disciplines are often at odds, both agree that prevention is better than cure. So an elaborate system of spells and charms was employed to protect the family and the animals. These *piseogs* involved everything from marking eggs with soot to tying a red rag to the tail of a calving cow as protection from malevolent fairies. The children tell us of singing to the cow as she was milked and using the froth off the top of the bucket to make the sign of the cross on her when finished. Our very first report, from young Máire de Búrca of Tonacooleen, County Galway, lists the dos and don'ts of poultry care. Máire includes her grandmother's system to ensure a successful hatching: 'Little boys were far luckier than little girls, so she used to make one of my brothers count the eggs ... Thirteen and fifteen were her lucky numbers.' She'd have been a dab-hand at the Lotto.

Another popular practice was to bury animal skulls under the flagstones of a new house, both for luck and to give a nice hollow sound for the dancers above. A coin was also buried for luck. Indeed, I remember well Johnnie and Bridgie did so when building a new bungalow to replace the old cottage. As the youngest person in the household, I was proud as punch when they asked me to bury a penny in the wet cement as the foundations were laid. Mind you, I was a little miffed a few months later when they asked a priest, not me, to come back and bless the finished house.

Pisreóga about clutches

SCHOOL: *Shrule, Co. Mayo*
TEACHER: *Bríd, Bean Uí Éanacháin*
COLLECTOR: *Máire de Búrca, Tonacooleen, Co. Galway*
INFORMANT: *Mrs. Burke, mother, 40, Tonacooleen, Co. Galway*

Long ago the old people had very funny ideas or PISREÓGA about clutches. They would never set a clutch but when the sun was setting in the sky in the evening and when all of the birds of the air were silent. They said that it was the best time the hen would lie the eggs. When my grandmother would get the box ready for the clutch, she would shake and shake the straw to make it soft and cosy for the eggs. She always said little boys were far luckier than little girls, so she used to make one of my brothers count the eggs and lay them down carefully. Thirteen or fifteen were her lucky numbers. Then she used to take three wisps of straw, and light them over the hen, and the clutch, and three shakes of holy water. You would want to be a real friend of hers, before she would part with A CLOCKING HEN. She said it was most unlucky to give away a clocking hen. Some people do so, providing they get her back again, when the chickens are reared, or in her place a young pullet. They say round eggs are the best for pullets, and the long eggs are for cocks.

When the clutch is eleven days hatching, they get a candle, and light it, and take the eggs one by one in turn and put them between the candle light. The egg there is a bird in would be empty over-head and very dark at the other end. If there were many empty ones the cock was often scolded. Some old people used not to like to exchange eggs for a clutch for fear they would have any ill luck at all. My grandmother often told me she put down a big egg to hatch one time. This was for curiosity. She never dreamt of any harm. I suppose there were two yolks in the egg, and it happened there were two birds in that egg, and they were joined together. They died in the egg. They were too weak to scallop the egg. That very year she buried a fine man of her family, and nothing would convince her but it was the big egg that brought the death on him.

It is right to eat the first egg a hen lays, and you would have the luck of good horses. It is not right to cut hens' tails, but to burn them. It is not right also to put a white hen hatching eggs, or to keep a white cock. If a black hen is put hatching eggs, all pullets will be in that clutch. It is not right to give away a hen after the sun has set. Before giving a hen to anyone it is right to pull out some of her feathers. If you were putting down two clutches of eggs, it is right to put two hens of the same colour hatching them. It is right to put a mark of soot on every egg before it is hatched for fear the fairies would bring the chickens when they come out. It is right to take three wisps out of the nest, where a hen is to be put hatching, and to hang them on a rafter of the hen house, until all the chickens are out. It is not right to throw away shells which chickens came out of, and it is right to put three grains of ashes into the shell that the first chicken came out of in the clutch.

Before a hen is put hatching eggs a few of her feathers should be pulled out and left on top of the eggs. When eggs are hatched for about a week, it is right to turn the thin top of them up.

PISREÓGA: *piseóga, superstitions, charms.*
A CLOCKING HEN: *a clucking hen, a broody hen.*

Very useful animals

SCHOOL: *Cloncarneel, Co. Meath*
TEACHER: *Máire, Bean Uí Bhreacáin*
COLLECTOR: *James Garry, Barnisle, Kildalkey*

Sheep are very useful animals and are kept on a lot of Irish farms. The sheep's coat is soft white wool. In the Summer they are washed and shorn. Then the wool is taken to the wool market and sold. Then it is spun and clothes are made out of it. There are different kinds of sheep such as: Mountanies, Suffolks, Galways, Cheviots, Shrops, and Oxford-Downs.

In the winter when there is snow on the ground the farmer has to put in the sheep and he gives them hay and turnips.

In Spring they have lambs and the people are very busy minding them because a fox night might kill them. When there are lambs the sheep are given pulped turnips and cracked oats. In May and June the lambs are taken from the sheep and sold at the fairs and markets nearby.

Fanny and Nancy

SCHOOL: *Termonfeckin, Co. Louth*
TEACHER: *T. Ó Corcoráin*
COLLECTOR: *Laurence Mullen, Blackhall, Co. Louth*

We have two horses on our farm at home. These horses' names are Fanny and Nancy. When you are driving the horses you should say, 'Yip go on.' When you want the horse to stop you should say, 'Wey.' When you want him to turn the right hand side you say, 'Hip back,' and when you want him to turn left you say, 'Hip off.' When you want to catch the horse you give him a little oats on a dish and then you catch him by the mane.

There is a long manger in the horse-stable and there are two divisions in the manger. There is a halter attached to each manger for the two horses. The horses are tied by the neck with these two halters. There is a window on this horse-stable. The horses eat hay and oats and mangolds and turnips and grass and they drink water. The horses are shod about every three months by the blacksmith who is in the district. The horses are clipped with a horse clippers in the winter.

A sheep-dog

SCHOOL: *Foynes, Co. Limerick*
TEACHER: *Eithne Ní Mhaidín*
COLLECTOR: *Caitlín Nic Uilleagóid*
INFORMANT: *Mr. T. Mc Elligott, age 73, Foynes, Co. Limerick*

There was a sheep-dog in the district of Glin. He used to go out every morning and evening and bring in the cows. This morning he went out for the cows and he was a long time away. After a while he came and there was one cow missing. He began to bark and bark, and when they had one cow milked they put the milk into a tub in the yard. He went over and put his tail into the tub and ran off. The cow had calved and he put his tail into the calf's mouth, so the calf sucked the milk off his tail and the dog brought him along.

Prug, prug, prug

SCHOOL: *Mullen, Co. Roscommon*
TEACHER: *B. Mac Siúrtáin*
COLLECTOR: *Kathleen Breslin, Leitrim, Co. Roscommon*

We have two cows, four calves, and an ass at home. We call one cow 'the grey cow' and the other 'the MAOL COW'.

When we want to bring in the cows we generally say 'prug, prug, prug', and the cows come. We tie the cows in the cowhouse. They are tied with a chain around the neck, which is fastened to a stick, that goes from one sidewall to the other. We put the hay inside this stick for the cows. The calves are put in a stable, and the hay is put in a rack for them. The donkey is tied in the same way as the cows.

About five o'clock in the evening the cows are given hay, and at half past eight they are milked. At ten o'clock they are given straw, and in the morning they are given hay.

In the olden times the cows were not tied in the same way as nowadays. There were ropes made of straw which were called 'sugans'. The sugans were tied to the cows' horns, and fastened to stakes, which were put in the floor.

When a cow was calving some people tied a red rag on her tail. This was done so that nothing would happen the calf.

When a beast died, the crúbeens or horns were cut off, and placed behind the COUPLES in the house. After a cow is milked, the sign of the cross is made, with milk on the cow's hip.

We have about thirty hens. When we are feeding them we call 'cioc, cioc, cioc', and all the hens come running to the feeding.

We have four pigs. When we want to put in the pig in the sty we say, hurrais, hurrais, hurrais, or deoch, deoch, deoch, and the pigs come and walk into the sty.

MAOL COW: *a cow with no horns, literally 'a bald cow'.*
COUPLES: *rafters or roof beams.*

Fan an socair

SCHOOL: *Ballindine, Co. Mayo*
TEACHER: *Séamus P. Ó Gríobhtha*
COLLECTOR: *Patrick Grogan, Newtown, Co. Mayo*
INFORMANT: *Thomas Gilmore, 71, Ballindine, Co. Mayo*

Long ago the people used to call the cow 'Bet'. They had no stables at that time. They used keep the cow in their own houses. They used tie the cow with a straw rope which they called a 'sugán'.

They had strainers at that time. They used to strain the milk with a cloth which they called a nopigan. When they would be milking they used sing. When she would be milked they used put a cross on the cow with froth. When they would be driving the cow they used say 'hurch'. They used have a horse shoe hanging inside on the back door for luck. When a person would be milking and if the cow did not stay quiet he would say, 'FAN AN SOCAIR.'

When they would be bringing the cow in the evening they would stand at the gate and say 'hurch, hurch', and cow would come to them. When a cow would be after calfing they used boil milk and it used to get hard; this used to be called BEASTINGS MILK. They used boil bread in the milk which was called sops. This custom is still observed in neighbourhood. When a cow would be after calfing they used tie a red rag to the calf's tail. This custom is still observed in my locality for the past thirty years.

They had no lanterns at that time. They used put a lighting candle in a can to show them light. They used tie a [saucepan] to the calf's mouth for fear he would eat hay or grass and choke. This custom is still observed in my neighbourhood.

FAN AN SOCAIR: *stay quiet.*
BEASTINGS MILK: *colostrum, the first milk produced by a cow after giving birth.*

Black-leg in a beast

SCHOOL: *Clooncullaan, Co. Roscommon*
TEACHER: *Liam Mac Leastair*
INFORMANT: *Michael Brady, 76, Curcreigh, Co. Roscommon*

1. As a preventative of Black-leg in a beast, it was customary for the old people of this district to give to the young calf on the day of his birth, and before he would get any milk, three small bits of an old baked cow-dung mixed with peat ashes and which was used to hold the twelve rush candles on the previous Twelfth Night. This old dried mixture of cow-dung and ashes was carefully kept from the previous Twelfth Night — usually stowed away in the roof behind the rafters so as to have it in readiness to give to the calf after birth.

2. Another preventative of Black-leg was put a split in the calf's right ear on the first Friday after its birth.

3. Still another preventative for Black-leg was to insert a bit of copper wire in the dew-lap of the beast. It was inserted just under the skin to protrude again, to be knotted in a ring and left permanently there.

4. Quite a common custom among the old people was to tie a red string on the cow's tail as a preventative to her being over-lucked by evil-minded people.

Filling the firkin

SCHOOL: *Caherlustraun, Co. Galway*
TEACHER: *Pádhraic de Chlár*
INFORMANT: *Mrs. P. Clair, Kilcornan, Co. Clare*

Before the advent of creameries and fresh butter markets — farmers used to lend butter to each other to help to fill a firkin. The wives of the neighbouring

farmers would form a kind of a co-op society for that purpose. Each woman had her appointed day for filling the firkin. The kitchen and all vessels were thoroughly washed and spotlessly clean. The aim was to get all the butter into a firkin while it was fresh and sweet.

Each woman would bring her own quota of butter from 14 to 28 lbs or more according to time of the year. The quantity — in wooden basins or cans or tubs.

The women had a pleasant time chatting and laughing, mixing the butter, washing it and putting PICKLE in it. The butter was thoroughly washed two or three times or more, maybe, in cold spring water. Then they coloured salt (6 lbs per 4 or 4 1/2 stone of butter) with saffron juices which was drawn like tea. This was thrown on the salt in basin, mixed up evenly in basin or dish. This was worked into the butter with butter cups and lukewarm pickle to temper the butter. If the butter were very hard the women used warm their hands before fire and use their hands to work the butter. Sleeves were rolled up to shoulder almost and of course thoroughly washed in hot water before any work was done. The pickle was made by dissolving a fistful or two of salt in a pint or quart of water and allowed to become lukewarm. The colouring was called saffron — a threadlike substance bought in shop. It gave the butter a rich yellow colour. The pickle was added to the butter while being mixed to give it a proper texture.

When the butter was ready it was put in a firkin a small barrel made by a cooper. The firkin was lined with paper. Wt [weight] of firkin and butter was 6 stone. Wt of firkin was 14 lbs. The quality of butter was first class. White aprons were worn by women. Firkin butter is still done by some farmers. The butter cups were wooden like plates. A hearty meal was eaten after filling firkin. If weather were very cold or very hot, they couldn't make butter of cream and used the cream for making bread.

PICKLE: *brine.*

The farmer had no more trouble with his butter or milk

SCHOOL: *Shannagh, Co. Donegal*
TEACHER: *J. Hutchman*
COLLECTOR: *Mary McGroary, 11 years old*
INFORMANT: *Mr. James McGroary, 60, father, Shannagh, Co. Donegal*

Once upon a time there was a man who had five cows. He milked them every night and used to churn their milk but no butter came on it. He then went to a woman he knew and told what had happened and she promised to put a stop to the trouble.

The next night when they churned the milk, to their surprise butter came on it. When they had it nearly churned, a woman came to the door and asked if any butter was coming on the milk and they told her there was. A couple of minutes later they heard a noise outside. The man ran for his gun, went outside and, walking over to the byre door, saw a woman standing at the door. He shot at her and thought he had killed her, but when he ran to the spot what did he see but a hare picking the shot out of its leg.

It appeared that the woman was a witch who could change herself into a hare when she wished. From that day out, however, the farmer had no more trouble with his butter or milk.

Since flax was grown in Oranmore

SCHOOL: *Oranmore, Co. Galway*
TEACHER: *Micheál Ó agus Máire Bean Uí Shuilleabháin*

Flax was a common crop in the parish of Oranmore some years ago. Many of the older inhabitants remember its being grown quite well.

When it was grown it was pulled and 'drowned' in a hole of water. It was left there for about two weeks. Then it was taken out of the water and dried. It was then beaten against a rock. Afterwards it was put into a weaver and woven. Then it was taken home and boiled in order to be made white.

It is some fifty years ago since flax was grown in Oranmore. It was used locally to make shirts, sheets and bags.

The principal crop

SCHOOL: *Kilmackowen, Co. Cork*
TEACHER: *Domhnall Ó Hurdail*
COLLECTOR: *Jack Harrington, Milleens, Co. Kerry*
INFORMANT: *Jeremiah Harrington, 48, Milleens, Co. Kerry*

The principal crop grown in this part of the country is potatoes. First the field is ploughed or turned. Then the dung or manure is spread. If the field is ploughed the 'SCULLAIDHES' are taken.

Long ago the farmers used never bring the horse through the ridges, from once they were turned until the potatoes were dug. They used bring the dung in the car and leave it inside the gap of the potato garden. The women used draw it from there with a 'CISEÁN'. When the farmers were short of farmyard manure they got seaweed. I heard my father saying that his mother used cut seaweed. She used go out to the rocks on the side of a horse swimming. The seaweed was cut from the rocks and was brought to the strand on a horse or in a boat. It is left there for a few days and then it is drawn home.

The potatoes are dug in the Autumn and the farmers place them in pits. Long ago the farmers used leave the potatoes in the pits all the year round.

SCULLAIDHES: *possibly related to sciolán, seed potatoes cut up for planting.*
CISEÁN: *a basket.*

The old rules still hold good here

SCHOOL: *Burren, Co. Cork*
TEACHER: *Eibhlín Ní Bhriain*
INFORMANT: *William Ó Driscoll, 67, farmer, Burren, Co. Cork*

Up to 50 years ago potatoes used to be set here in ridges. The farmer spread manure on a BÁN FIELD. He ploughed it in ridges – 6 sods to each ridge. He hacked the ridges with a GRIOFÁN to break the sod.

The SCIOLÁNS were cut at least a fortnight before sowing. Then when the ridges were hacked men and women got their 'pouches', tied them across under one arm and over the opposite shoulder. They filled them with scioláns, got their spades and 'stuck' them. When the youngsters were able to handle a FAIRICHÍN they were made close the 'holes'.

They used set the potatoes about St. Patrick's Day. When the stalks appeared above the ground they dug the furrow with a plough (furrow plough) having no board, drawn by two horses. This earth was thrown up on the ridge. The horse drew the plough when digging the furrow for second earthing.

The people here near the sea spread no manure before making the ridge, but when the stalks appeared 7 men used to get a boat and go out to the Barrel Rock and even to the Old Head of Kinsale for seaweed. They had poles ten feet long with hooks at the end of them. Out at the Rock one man guided the boat while the six used cut the seaweed with the long pole and hook off the sea-bottom. They used drag it into the boat and when the boat was full they rowed home again. They had about a load of seaweed per man when it was divided. That load manured quarter of an acre of garden. They spread it on top of the ridge before earthing it. This produced grand potatoes. They called that seaweed DÚLAMÁN.

They still put it on the land before ploughing it up for drills for potatoes, but it is seldom it comes in and when it comes in there is a great rush for it. The old rules still hold good here. If a man sees the dulamán coming in with the tide he watches the chance until the tide has just turned to go out. He goes along with his pike and just draws it on the dulamán so that he makes little heaps of it. Once he has it heaped it is his. If another neighbour comes on he works away at another part of the strand 'marking' the dulamán in the same way until he meets the first man. Each draws his own as soon as ever he can and while he is drawing the dulamán from the strand to his farm he can claim all the weed that comes with each tide to the spot he has 'marked' with the pike. Sometimes, even still, the farmers go out as early as four or five o'clock in the morning with a lantern 'marking' dulamán.

No one here goes out in a boat for it now. Several people cut the small weed off the little rocks near the coast when the tide is out still and they place this weed under the ordinary manure between the drills.

BÁN FIELD: *a grassy field or pasture.*
GRIOFÁN: *a heavy-duty hoe.*
SCIOLÁNS: *seed potatoes cut up for planting.*
FAIRICHÍN: *a small mallet for covering up the newly sown potatoes.*
DÚLAMÁN: *seaweed often used as fertilizer.*

Mickey the mower

SCHOOL: *Scoil an Churnánaigh, Newcastle, Co. Limerick*
TEACHER: *Pr. Ó Fionnmhacháin*
COLLECTOR: *John Joseph Harnett, Barnagh, Co. Limerick*
INFORMANT: *Thomas O'Grady, 86, Meenyline South, Co. Limerick*

Long ago there lived a great mower whose name was Michael Enright. He was more commonly known as Mickey the Mower. Mickey's main work in life was cutting hay with a scythe. At this time there were no mowing machines and the hay had to be cut with scythes. There were many great mowers in the locality and sometimes they used to challenge one another to find who was the best and fastest mower. Mickey was in every challenge and was always the winner. One evening a farmer went to him and asked him would he cut two acres of hay for him. 'I will,' said Mickey, 'but I have to go to Limerick after for a new scythe.'

'But,' said the farmer, 'you will not have the hay cut in time to go to Limerick.' Mickey had neither a clock or a watch so he got up very early the next morning and went and started cutting the hay. When the farmer got up, Mickey had one acre cut, and he had the second acre finished before his dinner. After eating his dinner he went off walking to Limerick. On his way he saw three men inside in a meadow mowing hay. One of them was lagging behind and was not able to keep up. Mickey saluted them and asked the last man what was wrong to say he was not able to keep up.

'I have a bad scythe,' said the man, 'and I cannot keep any bit of edge on it.'

Mickey stepped inside the ditch and took the scythe from the man, gave it two rubs of the scythe board and handed it again to the man. The man started mowing and passed out the two more men and mowed twice as much.

Mickey went away on his journey and bought the scythe. When he was returning home he asked the man what way was the scythe since.

'Ah,' said the man, 'I never edged it since you left and it is mowing great.' Mickey went inside the ditch and took the scythe, gave it two more rubs and took the edge off of it. When Mickey went away the man took up the scythe and it was worse than before.

Mickey often mowed two and three acres of hay in a day and the people believed that he had a charm for mowing.

There was also another great mower in my district and his name was Martin Stevens. He used go around from place to place on his hire. There was a farmer in the district that had a lot of hay to cut and he let the cutting of it to Martin. The whole lot amounted to about twelve acres and the farmer wanted to have it all cut in a week. Martin went off one night with his scythe on his shoulders to start mowing the hay. He went into the biggest meadow in which there were about four acres. He edged his scythe and looked at his watch and it was just midnight. He was drawing the first stroke with his scythe when a small man hopped behind his back and told him to cut a swath full round the meadow by the ditches and not to attempt to look back. Martin did as he was commanded and when he had arrived at where he started, the whole meadow was cut down for him by the fairies.

The turf are cut in the last days of April

SCHOOL: *Drung, Co. Donegal*
TEACHER: *Seán P. Mac Gabhann*
COLLECTOR: *Edward Toye, Quigley's Point, Co. Donegal*

Around this district the turf are cut in the last days of April, or the first of May. Some of the people in this district cut their turf with a broad spade as they are easier dried than the ones cut with a turf spade. Anyone, before going to the hill to cut turf, PARES THE BANKS, as you could not cut turf without the banks being pared. The banks in these hills are five turf broad and three deep. In this district it is turf that is used as fuel, and very little coal is used.

The way they cut turf is: one man who has a turf spade cuts the turf out of the moss, and another man who takes the turf away as he cuts them is called the 'holer'. The reason for calling him so, is because he takes the turf out of the hole. The 'holer' throws the turf in 'couples' at a time to the capper, who catches them and spreads them evenly on the 'spreading field'. In about a week after the turf are cut — if it is good weather — the turf are turned over.

The reason for this is to let them dry on both sides. In about a week's time after they are turned, they are 'stood up' on their ends in sixes to dry, and this is called 'footing'.

They are left in the 'footings' for three weeks, and then they are taken to the road by horse and SLIPE, there they are built in a stack to keep the rain out.

Any one cutting turf on his own land carries them home in a CREEL as he needs them.

When the farmers get their turf to the road, they draw them home, and build them in a stack beside the house.

PARES THE BANKS: *to remove the top layer of soil from a bog.*
SLIPE: *a small wooden sledge.*
CREEL: *a wicker basket.*

This tedious work

SCHOOL: *Cartronavally, Co. Roscommon*
TEACHER: *Cáit, Bean Uí Cheallaigh*
COLLECTOR: *Rose A. Guihen, Cartron Beg, Co. Roscommon*
INFORMANT: *Charles Flynn, 59, Cartron Beg, Co. Roscommon*

During the Autumn months farmers are very busy gathering all their harvest and making provisions for the cold Winter.

When the people of this district have their oats saved they bring it into the HAGGARD and make stacks.

Afterwards it is prepared for the threshing process. This work is done by means of a threshing machine or a flail. When a machine is used five or six men are employed, one of whom is working the machine, another unbinding the sheaves and the rest putting the sheaves into the machine.

In this district corn is generally threshed with a flail, as the people are too poor to buy a threshing machine. The flail is made of strong hazel or ash. When it is used, two or three sheaves are left on a barrel or box and given a few strokes of the flail.

After this tedious work the grain has to be separated from the chaff by means of a RIDDLE. This being done, the grain is taken to a mill and ground into oatmeal. This meal is used in making porridge and oat-cake.

HAGGARD: *a yard for storing stacks of hay or grain.*
RIDDLE: *a large sieve.*

Implements used in preparing the land

SCHOOL: *Shannagh, Co. Donegal*
TEACHER: *J. Hutchman*
COLLECTOR: *Jim McGroary, 13, Shannagh, Co. Donegal*

The implements used in preparing the land for potatoes are ploughs, harrows, rollers, grubbers, spades, shovels, GRAIPS, and barrows. A plough is used for ploughing up the land and a harrow is then required to break the lumps of soil, and sometimes a roller is used for this purpose also.

When the potatoes are ready for shovelling the SHOUGHS are grubbed with a grubber drawn by a horse. This implement is made of iron with three 'toes', two behind and one in the front, and it is these that dig up the soil. Then this soil is shovelled up on the ridges with a shovel. The shovel is composed of a long wooden handle, and at the bottom is a flat piece of metal wide at the top and narrowing towards the bottom.

A barrow is used for wheeling out the manure on the ridges. It is made of wood with two legs and two handles and has one wheel which is also made of wood but has an iron hoop on the outside of the rim. A graip has a short handle with four iron toes each about a foot long. This implement is used for spreading manure and also for filling it into the cart. It is also used in cleaning out byres, stables, etc.

GRAIP: *a large digging fork.*
SHOUGH: *a furrow.*

5

THE OLD TRADES

'The monotony of rural isolation was broken when people gathered at a workshop or at someone's home for collective work. The meitheal when saving the hay or harvesting any crop was an opportunity to mix and make merry.'

**HESE ARE STORIES** of self-sufficiency, before self-sufficiency had been invented. Farming households took responsibility for their own food, fashion and fertilizer. A piece of twine was never discarded, and recycling saw pigs fattened on leftovers and hens pecking away happily at their own discarded egg shells. *Rotha mór an tsaoil*: the big wheel of life.

Some of these stories rekindle memories of my own urban boyhood, when many neighbours kept a pig or a few hens and the neighbourhood dads worked as dockers, coopers, butchers and bakers. All of those tradesmen have since died. So too have many of their trades. Others, in a greening economy, have seen a renaissance in, for example, thatching and kelp gathering; these days kelp is prized for its therapeutic benefits. The next time your hotel leaves complimentary little soaps with flecks of dried kelp, to revitalise and moisturise your skin, you might spare a thought for our leather-bound ancestors who dragged freezing, wet seaweed from the rocky shoreline with only a wicker basket, a donkey and grim determination. 'Tis fine for you!

A vital trade in those days, and one still important in my youth, was that of the blacksmith. Fourteen-year-old Thomas Hayes paints a picture of Joseph Mulhare's forge at Cree, County Offaly, that brings me straight back to the sounds and smells of Ned Ring's forge on John Street in my native Cork City. Ned made his living in the shadow of Murphy's Brewery and its enormous dray horses, who would literally darken the sunlit entrance to the already smoke-filled forge.

One of these compliant beasts, weighing over half a ton and taller than Ned, would wait stoically as Ned reddened and readied the new shoe, before stooping beside the horse's knee and, tapping her with the back of his free hand, say, 'C'mon now, hup!' The gentle giant would obediently raise a huge shaggy fetlock and rest it on Ned's knee. With a hiss of steam the shoe was fitted and tacked to the mare's hoof. I was unaware of the health benefits of the steam until I read young Thomas Hayes' account.

John Street was known locally as 'Little Baghdad' on account of the huge number of small industries that huddled together in sheds, yards, houses and lean-tos. Within a hundred yards of Shandon steeple the air was thick with the sound of men at work. 'Haul away, Paudie!' 'Back her up there … aisey now, aisey.' There were Lenihan's penny sweet factory (a two-man operation), tinsmiths, scrap-iron dealers, the flock where old rags were recycled, Franciscan Well Lemonade bottling, Paddy Daly's Yard (a cabinet maker), and more, all dominated by the jewel in the crown, Murphy's Brewery, and across the road a large house with a particularly large door. I mean particularly LARGE. I often wondered what that door was for.

No one, other than his family, was really sure what Ned Ring looked like beneath those layers of soot and smoke, stuck with sweat. He was a hospitable man, who welcomed small children and huge horses in equal measure. There was a rhythm to Ned's work. It went something like this: 'CHING! ... Ching ... ching ... ching ... ching ... ching.' The hammer's ding-dong was the song of the forge as Ned, wearing a full-length leather apron, raised his powerful forearm over the anvil, like some heroic Russian worker in a Communist poster. He then brought the hammer down like the KGB.

Sometimes he'd let us have a go. Holding the iron tongs in his left hand, he'd reach into the fire for the white-hot metal and place it on the anvil. Then he'd add his right hand to the two little hands struggling to raise the heavy hammer. 'Now let the weight of the hammer do the work,' he'd say. The paltry 'Chang ... krang' sound was met with 'Good man, you're getting into the swing of it. Step out of the way now and I'll finish it off. Good man.'

The much-welcomed social aspect of visiting the forge or the mill is a common thread amongst these first-hand accounts. The monotony of rural isolation was broken when people gathered at a workshop or at someone's home for collective work. The *meitheal* when saving the hay or harvesting any crop was an opportunity to mix and make merry. The same was true for people who gathered at the tradesman's door.

From Tipperary we hear of rope-making, where people would twist a súgán rope. The rhythm of the work gave us the beautiful Irish song '*Casadh an tSúgáin*'. Similarly, we have some fine songs written to the rhythm of butter-making and the waves when fishing. These vivid accounts of disappearing trades, and particularly the detail of the various processes involved, are invaluable additions to the national database. This information is gold, not only for social historians, but for craft workers and artists in search of authenticity.

I took a walk along John Street yesterday and met Danny Cronin, an old neighbour and contemporary. We were recalling days of catapults, runaway knock and Ned's forge.

'And y'know the house across the road with the huge front door? I always wondered what that was all about?' I asked him.

'That's a good one,' sez Danny. 'The cooper who supplied the barrels to the brewery lived in there. He worked out in his own back yard, but had to get the barrels out the front door when he had them ready. That's why he widened the doorway. My grandad used to call him "Roll out the barrel".'

It's always good to ask.

Kelp-making

SCHOOL: *Leaffony, Co. Sligo*
TEACHER: *Bean Mhic Fhionnlaoich*
COLLECTOR: *Mary Finnerty, Rathlee, Co. Sligo*

Kelp-making was an old industry carried on in this district. In the month of May the people went down to the sea with their donkeys and CREELS and put up the seaweed on top of the shore and spread it out to dry. When the seaweed was dry it was COCKED and after a while it was put into one big cock. When summer came the people took out the dry seaweed and put it in a heap and built a fire round it. When the seaweed was burned and cool it was put into sacks and sold to the nearest kelp merchant and was afterwards sold to the chemist for the produce of iodine.

SLAP-MARROWS make the best kelp but it is hard to get them. Kelp making has died out in this district as the Government is not buying it at present as there is a glut of iodine in the market.

CREELS: *wicker baskets.*
COCKED: *stacked like hay-cocks.*
SLAP-MARROWS: *probably the species known as 'slack marrow' or 'slata mara',* Laminaria hyperborea.

The tan-yard

SCHOOL: *Tagoat, Co. Wexford*
TEACHER: *Pádraig Coilféir*
COLLECTOR: *Peggy Doyle, Drimma, Rosslare, Co. Wexford*
INFORMANT: *Peter Ellard, Ballycowan, Tagoat, Co. Wexford*

The local industries of long ago were spinning, weaving, starch making, candle-making and tanning. The tanning industry was carried on about fifty years ago in the townland of Cottage, about AN IRISH MILE from this school, where Mr. Doyle now resides. The yard in front of the kitchen door there is still known as the tan yard. It was owned by people named Sinnott.

The hides were obtained from the local farmers when animals were killed. At that time farmers used to kill their own cattle for meat. In preparing them for the making of leather two deep holes were dug in the ground in the yard, which is now opposite the kitchen door. In one of these holes water was put and the hides were steeped in it for some months. Lime was put in the other one, into which the hides were put after taking them out of the water. As each one was put in lime was put on it. They were then put through other processes to make them into leather. Twenty and thirty men were employed there and their wages were sixpence a day.

When the leather was manufactured it was sold to the local shoemaker, and it was also sold for making harness. Different kinds of leather were sold for making harness and making boots.

AN IRISH MILE: *2240 yards, about 1.27 imperial miles.*

The right stuff to make a sugán

SCHOOL: *Kilmurry, Ballyneill, Co. Tipperary*
TEACHER: *Joseph Manning*

The art of making a 'sugán' is a very old one and it came into being through necessity. Long ago there was little known as to how to make the ropes and cords that we use nowadays. Hence the necessity for some thing to supply our wants. It is surprising the strength and durability of the 'sugán' when properly made. The right stuff to make a sugán was bog hay or hay grown in a bog.

It was used for many purposes. A single plait was used to tie down the hay-cocks and when doubled it was used to take the place of our modern reins. There was no better article to hold on the thatch on the homes and when kept dry held its own for more than a century. One thing I've heard is that after forty years in use, it defeated the strength of two men to pull it asunder. They used it to make 'bosses'. A boss was a very comfortable fire-side seat and was made of rings of straw fastened together by a 'sugán'. It was also used to make a neat floor mat and also for clothes lines.

It was quite possible for two men to make a hundred yards of 'súgan' in a half-hour. One man spun the hay and the other turned the 'PHILIBÍN'.

PHILIBÍN: *a hooked piece of wood used to twist the súgán.*

A famous basket-maker

SCHOOL: *Oldcastle, Co. Meath*
TEACHER: *Máire D. Ní Nualláin*
INFORMANT: *Mr. Carolan, Fennor Upper, Co. Meath*

Over forty years ago there lived a man whose name was Michael Lynch. This man was a native of Ross. He was a famous basket-maker in that district for many years, and was noted for that occupation all through the country. His father was a basket maker before him. He would make shopping baskets, basket chairs, potato baskets and turf creels. First he would go out to the hills and get a large amount of SALLIES. Then he would put on a big fire and put a pot of water on to boil, and put some rods in it and peel the skin off with boiling water. This man died at the age of eighty five years, and was sadly missed.

SALLIES: *willow rods.*

They used to make the baskets

SCHOOL: *Ballindine, Co. Mayo*
TEACHER: *Séamus P. Ó Gríobhtha*
COLLECTOR: *Sean McHugh, Branraduff, Co. Mayo*
INFORMANT: *John McHugh, 49, Branraduff, Co. Mayo*

The people used to make baskets long ago. They used to go to the bog and cut a SCRAW the size of the basket. They used to make the baskets in the house or in the barn. They used to get four strong sally sticks and stick one at each corner of the scraw. They used to stick the sticks at each corner because the sticks could not stand on the ground. They used to stick two more sticks at each corner and other sticks around the scraw also. Then they would get the thinner parts of the sally and weave them around the sticks.

They would keep weaving the thin parts of the sally around the sticks till the basket was made. The baskets were used for putting out the turf in the bog. The baskets were put on an ass's back attached to a STRADDLE. The bottom of the basket is called the cliathog.

The SCIBS were made with sally sticks. They would get some sally and turn the tops of them up and weave the bottom with sally sticks. They would weave the sides of them the same way. The scibs were used for bringing in turf, and for turning the potatoes after being boiled into it to cool.

The clothes baskets were made the same way as the scibs. The thin sally sticks were peeled and boiled. There was a handle on the clothes baskets. There was a great basket maker named John Martin Branraduff who is still living.

SCRAW: *a rectangular piece of sod.*
STRADDLE: *a small saddle used for carrying baskets
or attaching a cart.*
SCIB: *a type of basket.*

Our useful little mill

SCHOOL: *Killea, Co. Leitrim*
TEACHER: *Séamus Mac Coilín*
COLLECTOR: *Francis Gordon, Derragoon, Kiltyclogher, Co. Leitrim*
INFORMANT: *John Gordon, Derragoon, Kiltyclogher, Co. Leitrim*

It is not more than sixty years since our useful little mill ceased to grind the grain which the industrious and hard working farmers of ancient times produced. This mill was situated in a very cosy spot on the southeastern side of a high hill which prevented north western winds from destroying anything at the mill. It was built by a man of the name of Pat Gallagher who was locally known as Pat the Miller. There was a kiln built at the same time for the purpose of drying the oats before it was ground, as oats was the chief grain which was ground there. When a man brought oats to the mill he had to bring turf also, to light a fire in the kiln for the purpose of drying and loosening the hulls on the oats before grinding it. The person who brought the oats had to dry it but the miller and his ground it.

There is a river about one hundred yards from the ruins of the mill and it was the power of its waters that turned the grindstones in the mill. There was a 'mill race' from the mill to the river and it was in it that the water was conveyed to the mill wheel and allowed to go into a small stream, which was running by the mill and which eventually ran into the big river again. That mill would probably be in use yet only for a severe illness which Pat got about a year before his death and from which he never recovered. His sons were working in America when his death occurred and they did not return till the roof of the mill was rotten. Its walls are as sound as the day when it was built long ago.

How thatching is done

SCHOOL: *The Rower, Inistioge, Co. Kilkenny*
TEACHER: *Labhaoise Nic Liam*
COLLECTOR: *Máire Ní Galváin, Cullentragh, Co. Kilkenny*
INFORMANT: *her grandmother, over 70, The Rower, Co. Kilkenny*

Years ago practically all the houses in Ireland were thatched. In other parts of Ireland there are still many thatched houses but in this district there are very few. In the course of a few years the thatched houses will have disappeared in this locality and with it the art of thatching. I shall now describe how thatching is done.

I shall first tell how a newly built house is thatched. When the walls are built to the required height the house is roofed with rough timber. Straw is spread over it and sewed to the roof by means of a straw rope called a sugán. When the roof is covered in this manner another layer of straw is put over it. This second layer of straw is put on in bundles. It is pushed into the first layer by means of a pointed stick. Each bundle of straw is then secured by a forked sally rod called a scallop. The loose straw is the best straw for thatching. It was then cut off with a sharp knife and the roof made level. The roof is covered in this manner by the straw. After four or five years this coat of straw will have decayed and then a fresh coat is put on the roof.

The commonest classes of straw used for thatching houses are wheaten, oaten, and rye. Wheaten straw is the best straw for thatching, and rye is better than oaten for thatching, but rye is not grown in this district. Before the straw is used for thatching it is pulled by the hand and tied in bundles. It is then wet to make it tie better on the roof.

It is a pity that the thatched houses are disappearing in Ireland. There are very few things as picturesque as a neatly kept white-washed well thatched cottage.

The burning of lime

SCHOOL: *Raharney, Co. Westmeath*
TEACHER: *S. Ó Conmhidhe*
INFORMANT: *James Dargan, 84, Ballinahe, Raharney, Co. Westmeath*

The burning of lime is a very old industry in this country. Long ago nearly all large farmers had their own lime kilns as they put the lime on their land as a fertilizer. The kiln was built in a dry field; some were built of stone, others were built of fire bricks. To make lime you would want large lime stone rocks from a quarry. In the olden days the owner of the lime kiln would burn lime with turf. He covered the floor of the kiln with turf and then put a layer of stones broken in small pieces on top of the turf. Then he started the turf on fire and repeated this every day until he would have the kiln of lime burned. Then he sold it by the barrel to any one that would need it, such as butchers and builders for plastering and stone work and farmers for white-washing and putting on the land as a fertilizer.

'So they were saying at the forge.'

SCHOOL: *Cree, Co. Offaly*
TEACHER: *Mrs. Dennison*
COLLECTOR: *Thomas Hayes, 14, Lisduff, Co. Offaly*
INFORMANT: *Joseph Mulhare, 45*

There is one forge in this district. The smith's name is Joe Mulhare. His father and grandfather and his great-grandfather were smiths. The forge is situated near a crossroads and a river.

The forge is a large square room with no windows. There are a lot of horseshoes and old irons around the doorway. There is a square doorway with a huge horseshoe nailed to it. There is one fireplace in the forge. The bellows is a large oval leather thing with a pipe out of it into the fire. The bellows are fastened in a stand and is blown by pulling a bar up and down. The bellows are made in a bellows factory. The smith uses a hammer, a tongs, and a punch to bore square holes when he is working.

The smith shoes horses and asses. Cattle are not shod in this district.

The smiths do not make ploughs nowadays. The implements are repaired in the forge. When the smith is shoeing a horse he has to try the shoe on to see if it will fit. A green smoke rises as the smith LEAVES the shoe on the horse's hoof. This smoke is supposed to contain a cure for consumption.

Long ago people used to gather every evening at the forge. When a person told a story, if another person asked him where he heard it he would say, 'So they were saying at the forge.' This saying is still current in Ireland.

We have a story in our books about Conor Mac Nessa visiting Culann the smith. In olden times the smiths were very important. A smith was next to the king in olden days because the smith used to make armour and arms for the soldiers and king to fight with.

LEAVES: *places.*

The blacksmith did many a good deed

SCHOOL: *Bundorragha, Co. Mayo*
TEACHER: *Siúbhán Bean Uí Bhúrca*
COLLECTOR: *Máire Ní Niaidh, Leenane, Co. Galway*
INFORMANT: *Mairtín Ó Niaidh, 38, Co. Galway*

We have no blacksmith or forge in this place, but there is a forge in Leenane and another in Killeen, and it's to those places the people of this place go when they require a blacksmith to do any work for them. It is not thatch that is on the forge which belongs to this place. The door of the forge is a very wide door, being much larger than the door of a house. The blacksmith has all sorts of tools such as the hammer, the anvil, the water trough, the bellows, and iron of every description. He keeps water in the trough at all times for cooling the iron when he is finished with it. The blacksmith can make all sorts of iron. He makes iron gates, horse shoes for horses and many other iron articles. It is inside the forge he works. The bellows is a big thing with a handle which he uses for blowing the fire when he has iron in it.

It was a custom in olden times in this place to give special gifts to every blacksmith such as a 'pig's head' or the head of a cow. In olden times people gave every blacksmith a special present because the blacksmith did many a good deed for the people. The blacksmith was supposed to have great power to hunt rats and mice out of any house. The blacksmiths are very brave and strong men and in olden times they made war implements.

The making of bricks

SCHOOL: *Leitrim, Co. Monaghan*
TEACHER: *E. Ó Maitiú*
COLLECTOR: *Dan Mc Grory, 14, Leitrim, Co. Monaghan*
INFORMANT: *Francis Mc Grory, 82, grandfather, Leitrim, Co. Monaghan*

Bricks were made in several places in this school area in olden times. They were made from blue clay which is plentiful in this district. Around the school there is an abundance of blue clay. It is found about a foot below the surface of the ground. In the meadows near the school there are a large number of deep rectangular holes now filled with water. These holes were made by men removing blue clay for brick-making about forty or fifty years ago. The bricks were made in the townlands of Leitrim, Tamlet, Carrowkeel and Lappan. They were used by the people of the parish for housebuilding and also in the towns of Monaghan, Castleblaney and Ballybay as well as in the country districts in north Monaghan. Many small farmers like the McGrorys of Leitrim, the Hughes of Lappan and Carrowkeel made a living at this work. The making of bricks has stopped about thirty years ago. The McGrory family made some in 1933 but no more was made since. The bricks in Tyholland Creamery are Tyholland-made bricks. Francis McGrory and his sons made them forty years ago.

When the clay is removed from the hole it is allowed to remain for a few days. It is then made wet and is made into shapes of bricks in wooden moulds. These are left out in rows to dry by the heat of the sun. When they are hard enough to be handled they are collected and built in the shape of a square around a coal fire ready for lighting. An opening in the bottom of each side is left to admit air and the bricks built to about the height of a man. This structure is called the 'kil'. The outside is plastered with mud and the fire is lit. It is kept lit for about a fortnight and it is said that it requires two tons of coal to burn the bricks before they are fit for use. About 30,000 bricks are usually burnt in one kil.

In olden times crowds used to collect around the brick kil when the fires were lit and spend the evening dancing and singing.

The landlord of the townland of Tamlet once stopped the making of bricks. His name was Mr H. J. Johnston. On the farm now owned by Frank Gray are many brick holes for the previous owner. Patrick Finnegan made bricks. One day clay was being removed for brick making in a field near the road, when work was stopped by the order of the landlord and no bricks were ever made since. The clay remains where it was piled up beside the hole from which it was raised and may be seen yet, for it was never removed.

In every town there used to be a cooper

SCHOOL: *Ballindine, Co. Mayo*
TEACHER: *Séamus P. Ó Gríobhtha*
COLLECTOR: *John Kivneen, Logalisheen South, Co. Mayo*
INFORMANT: *Patrick Kivneen, 46, Logalisheen South, Co. Mayo*

There was a cooper living in this locality. There were many trades in olden times which are all dead and done away with now. In every town there used to be a cooper, who used to make churns, barrels, and other wooden vessels.

There is still one living in Crossboyne about two miles from here. His name is James Cleary. There was another in Ballindine and his name was Thomas Kelly. He used to bring barrels, tubs, and churns to every fair round the place and sell them.

When he used to be working he used to sit on a long stool. He used to sit on one end and leave his work on the other end. First he used to plane the wood with a hard piece of oak timber with a good edge on it. He used to rub it hard on the long piece, and in that way he used to clean and plane the wood.

Then he used to make the bottom of the churn. He used to put six wooden hoops on every churn. They were all made of oak timber. The hoops were made of ash because oak would be too hard. He used to make the barrels out of oak and sometimes out of ash. He used to put wooden hoops on the barrels also.

Only one weaving loom in Beare Island

SCHOOL: *Cobh Labhráis, Rerrin, Co. Cork*
TEACHER: *Áine, Bean Uí Shúilleabháin*
COLLECTOR: *Kathleen Meade*
INFORMANT: *Mrs. Meynell, 56, farmer, Cloughland, Bere Island, Co. Cork*

There was only one weaving loom in Beare Island long ago, which was owned by Mr P Mc Carthy, who lived near our house. First of all the wool was spun and carded into thread before it went into the weaving loom. Then it was wound into a big BEAM and the spools were filled at the spinning wheel and they were spun in the shuttle. As the weaver weaves it comes through two or three reels to make it into cloth. He has to move both hands when working at the reels to make the cloth. The feet are also used when working the loom. When the cloth is woven the weaver measures it with a rule called a BANDLE. For six bandles he used to get 4S 0D. The cloth when woven was called flannel and frieze and also sheets. The shuttle which was used when spinning the wool was shaped like this. As there was only one weaving-loom in Beare Island long ago, every person used to come with the thread to get flannels and other things made and also people used come from the Allihies to get things spun.

BEAM: *a circular piece of wood where the warp thread was wound.*
BANDLE: *this would have measured two feet in length.*
4S 0D: *four shillings and no pence.*

He makes baskets. He thatches houses also.

SCHOOL: *Cappataggle, Co. Galway*
TEACHER: *Antoine Ó Monacháin*
COLLECTOR: *Deirdre Mullarkey, Gortnahoon, Cappataggle, Co. Galway*
INFORMANT: *Mr. Thomas Maloney, Cappataggle, Co. Galway*

In olden times people used to make candles with tallow. On twelfth night they used to light rush candles steeped in tallow. There is an old man named Patrick Dolan living in townland of Donaree in the parish of Cappatagle, and he makes baskets. He thatches houses also.

Long ago thread was made out of the wool of sheep. After it being taken off the sheep, it is teased and mixed with a little oil, and carded into little rolls, and spun into thread. Then it is taken to the weaver to get it woven into cloth.

It had to be warped on four warping bars. They are put up on a square. There are twelve pegs on each of the two side bars and two pegs on the top one. Two balls of thread called warp, weighing about twelve pounds, are warped on those warping bars. When all the thread is up it must be counted; on the top bar at the two pegs should have at least five and a half hundreds of thread. It is then taken down and twisted into one ball and drew into a loom. It is rolled up on a large beam, with some holes in one side, to twist it up with a piece of a stick. Then it is drew into an affair called gears, which is made up of twines. The thread has to be put up between these gears in order to keep it separated. Then it has to be drew into a reed of cane slits and then start to work.

Mr. Thomas Maloney lives in the townland of Donaree in the parish of Cappatagle, aged eighty-six years, used weave and make frieze, flannels, blankets, linen sheeting and linen towels by hand looms. Those looms were worked by the feet and by the hands with shuttle and [treadles]. The treadles were worked by the feet to keep the thread open for to run the shuttle across through the thread with the hand.

There are two kinds of thread used in the manufacture of flannels, friezes etc, namely; 'warp' and 'woof'. The warp is used on the length and the woof on the breadth. The woof is wound on small quills made of pieces of timber, with holes in the middles of them to twist on a spindle, in order to twist the thread on them.

Long ago people used to dye frieze and thread for socks. Frieze was dyed with elder branches and bog mud boilded [boiled] down. Thread for socks was dyed with moss pulled off the rocks and boiled down.

The weaver wove

SCHOOL: *Rashinagh Co. Offaly*
TEACHER: *S. Ó Cinnéide*
INFORMANT: *Mrs. Maria Kennedy, Bloomhill, Ballinahown, Athlone, Co. Offaly*

There was a weaver named Mullen, who lived in the townland of Castlerea, in the parish of Millane and Ballinahown, and in the County of Offaly. At that time the people of this district used to grow flax. The people used to take off the bark of the flax and spin the fibre into thread and bring the fibre spun into thread to the weaver. Then the weaver wove the thread into linen sheets, tablecloths or towels.

There was a weaver named Patrick Fox in the townland of Ballyduff, parish of Milane and Ballinahown, Co. Offaly. He made coarse linen sheets and towels, and material for shirting. When well bleached they looked well and lasted for a lifetime. Material that he made sixty or seventy years ago is still kept by careful mothers and has passed from one generation to another.

Wool was carded and spun in a good many families but never woven. The thread was used for knitting stockings, socks, jumpers, jerseys, etc.

6

THE FOOD WE ATE

*'The Inuit are reputed to have 50 words for snow.
The Irish had 50 recipes for spuds. A pinch of salt,
a spoon of sugar, a splash of milk or a fist of flour
would transform the humble spud into boxty,
pandy, griddle cake, farls and a huge range
of recipes that are new to me.'*

 WAS ELECTED BY the plain people of Ireland,' declared Jackie Healy-Rae on foot of his surprise election to the Dáil as TD for Kerry South in 1997. When quizzed by TV journalist Brian Farrell as to who exactly 'the plain people of Ireland' might be, Healy-Rae thundered, 'The plain people of Ireland are the people who have their dinner in the middle of the day.'

Healy-Rae's statement carried a lot of truth even when reconstructed to read, 'The people of Ireland had a plain dinner in the middle of the day.' I expect the best of them still do.

The testimonies gathered for the Schools' Collection suggest that as late as 1939, poorer farming households depended primarily on three staples: milk, potatoes and flour. Not unlike the diet of today's global poor, many of whom survive on a basic diet of rice, the mainstays of the Irish menu were also white and bland. When the opportunity arose, a little pork or salted fish was a welcome bonus. A head of cabbage or a turnip was another pleasing addition and in some areas oats or Indian meal were staples. Either way, dinner was in the middle of the day and it was plain.

The Inuit are reputed to have 50 words for snow. The Irish had 50 recipes for spuds. A pinch of salt, a spoon of sugar, a splash of milk or a fist of flour would transform the humble spud into boxty, pandy, griddle cake, farls, and a huge range of recipes that are new to me. Young Eddie Carroll of Derrynahinch, County Roscommon, notes the sweet and sugary flour-based 'flummery' and the savoury 'scailtín'.

The plain people of Ireland were equally creative with milk. My father, whose family ran the Inchigeelagh Dairy Butter & Egg Company, spoke of thick milk, sweet milk, sour milk, buttermilk, cream and Grade A butter. He truly was a connoisseur and had no difficulty swigging and rating sour milk. When yoghurt came on the scene in the 1970s, he thought it was hilarious that such a thing would be viewed and packaged as 'fashionable'.

A glass of cold fresh milk to wash down the last of a stew or a bacon dish was usually marked with '*Ahh ... bainne an bó breac*' ('Ahh, the milk of the speckled cow'), regarded as the sweetest, creamiest milk of the herd. I didn't realise at the time that his blessing on the cow was actually a play on the Irish word for the cowslip, *bainne bó bleachtáin*. Either way, my father's Grace After Meals was a fine addition to the already extensive list of Irish toasts and blessings. I still salute a cold, refreshing glass of milk with his words. I, too, love a glass of sweet milk and firmly believe there is no place for red wine on a table serving boiled potatoes. Red wine with pasta or beef, of course. But with boiled potatoes? A pint of plain (milk), people, is yer only man!

Given Ireland's well documented love affair with tea, it might come as a surprise to be reminded here that it only became widespread after the Famine. It first arrived from India to Ireland in the early 1800s, but was regarded as a luxury product and the preserve of the wealthy, whose tea parties were highly fashionable social events. One informant from Castletown, County Donegal, reports that tea only became popular in that area as late as the 1890s.

We have a fascinating and detailed account from Newtown, County Tipperary, of the waste-not methods of keeping and slaughtering a pig. Every single part of the pig was put to good use. I'm reminded of the story of a Victorian visitor to Cork's English Market who, on viewing the array of pigs' heads, trotters, tails and puddings on display, was moved to remark, 'It appears the only part of the pig not eaten by the Irish is the oink!'

Gratitude for a full belly is a recurring theme amongst the informants. Given the hand-to-mouth existence of tenant farmers, nothing was taken for granted, and a prayerful Grace before and after meals was recited in many of the kitchens of my own childhood. My sense of gratitude has deepened with age. So at mealtimes I have taken to simply acknowledging how fortunate I am to have such quality and variety of nutrition before me. It truly is a blessing.

Enjoy the awaiting feast, but remember, you might need to bring your own seasoning.

Thick milk, butter milk and sweet milk

SCHOOL: *Calhame, Co. Donegal*
TEACHER: *Seán Mac Cuinneagáin*
INFORMANT: *P. Mc Closkey, Castletown, Co. Donegal*

People in olden times took four meals a day. These were breakfast, dinner, tea and supper. The breakfast was taken at eight o'clock, dinner at one o'clock in the afternoon, tea at six and supper at ten. Milking of the cows and cleaning of the byres was done before breakfast time. The breakfast consisted of oat bread and milk, dinner consisted of potatoes, turnips, milk and salt, tea of oat bread and milk and supper of potatoes and milk. Potatoes was the most common food and milk was drunk.

All sorts of milk were used, thick milk, butter milk and sweet milk. The table was usually placed convenient to the wall and was hung up against the wall when not in use.

The bread was usually made of potatoes or oat meal. Potato bread was made in the following way: First they boil some potatoes and take the skins off them. Then they mix them with milk and some flour until they have a kind of dough. Afterwards they pound it into a circular shape and cut it into parts with a knife. Then they put it on to fry on the pan. Oat bread was made in much the same manner: The woman of the house used to mix the oatmeal with a little hot water or milk, until it became a dough. Then it was flattened out with a roller and cut into shapes. Then it was put on an iron in front of the fire until it became quite hard. It was now ready for use. Meat wasn't eaten often, but what was eaten was usually salted. Mutton was the meat mostly used. Fish was plentifully used especially round about the coast. People did not know very much about vegetables.

Long ago people used to eat 'SOWINS', a dish partly made from the fresh ground oat-meal. It wasn't usual for people to eat late at night.

Different kinds of food were used to suit the different seasons. For instance, they used fish during Lent and all Fridays of the year. On Halloween they used to make Boxty bread. This bread was made from potatoes and flour. First they used to take the skins off the potatoes, then they used to grate them on a tin, covered with holes. This tin was called a grater. Afterwards they used to stew the water out of them with a cloth, and mix together with some flour. Then the mixture was flattened out in a circular shape and put on to fry on a pan.

In olden times Christmas was a great time of feasting. They used to kill and eat geese, turkeys, hares, rabbits and sometimes goats. Tea was used for the first time about forty years ago. Bowls and PANDIES were used most commonly before cups came into vogue.

> SOWINS: *a dish made from oats which were soaked and left to ferment for some days before cooking.*
> PANDIES: *tin mugs.*

A basin of porridge and a can of milk

SCHOOL: *Droichead na Ceathramhna, Derrycashel, Co. Roscommon*
TEACHER: *S. Pléimeann*
COLLECTOR: *Eddie Carroll, Derrynahinch, Co. Roscommon*
INFORMANT: *John Gildea, 57, Derrynine, Ballyfarnon, Co. Roscommon*

Long ago the people used to take three meals a day — breakfast, dinner and supper. Before the breakfast the people would do two hours' work; then they would take a basin of porridge and a can of milk and eat it with wooden spoons. Then they would take potatoes and buttermilk and sometimes they would take 'scailtín', which consisted of flour, onions, pepper and salt all boiled on milk and water. They used to take porridge for the supper or sometimes Indian-meal-bread or oatmeal cake. The oatmeal cake used be made with oatmeal and wet with water and then baked on a tongs. The young children used to take 'flummery', which was flour boiled on milk and sweetened with sugar.

Before they set sail for America

SCHOOL: *Clochar na Trócaire, Navan, Co. Meath*
TEACHER: *An tSr. Concepta le Muire*
COLLECTOR: *Eileen Watters, Flower Hill, Navan, Co. Meath*
INFORMANT: *Mrs. Watters, 45, Flower Hill, Navan, Co. Meath*

Long ago the people had no tea. They used to take porridge for their breakfast and supper, potatoes, bacon and cabbage for their dinner and often potatoes for supper. Very seldom meat was used only on special occasions, at Christmas, Easter and on big feasts. Long ago they used to have cakes made of wheaten meal. The people used to make oaten bread before they set sail for America and take it with them. The table was usually placed in the centre of the floor. The people used to go to work before breakfast in the mornings and come home for breakfast.

A good stomach

SCHOOL: *Gabhal tSulchóide, Newtown, Co. Tipperary*
TEACHER: *Donnchadh Mac Thomáis*

In olden times people used only three meals a day, these were breakfast dinner and supper. A couple of hours' work was done each morning before breakfast, especially by farmers, who always milked the cows, fed calves and pigs before breakfast. Dinner was the principal meal and was eaten about 1 o'clock. Supper was taken when the work in the fields was finished at about seven o'clock.

The breakfast in olden times consisted of porridge and skim milk. Stirabout was used by the poorer people. Porridge was made from oat-meal and new-milk, while stirabout was made from oat-meal, water and salt. The dinner consisted of potatoes and salted new milk. Those who could afford it used a little butter with the potatoes. Meat was used only on Sundays and Feast Days. The table was placed in the centre of the floor when the family was big and after each meal it was placed beside the wall. The table was never hung up against the wall when not in use.

Whole meal bread was eaten or brown bread as it was called. It was made with skim-milk, salt and soda and was baked in an oven over the fire; burnt sticks called SPREECE were placed on top of the lid to help to bake the top of the cake.

A pig was usually killed in the winter time to give meat. The killing always took place before Xmas so that there was great feasting of puddings about the Xmas. The meat was salted after being cut up. The salt was rubbed into each piece of meat with the hand, and all holes, where bones were, were filled with salt. Pickle was then made and put into a barrel and the pieces of meat were put into that and left there for about two-weeks. The meat was then taken out of the pickle and hung up on hooks on the outside of the chimney, where it was made brown and sweet by the smoke. The smoke from SALLY-RODS was considered the best smoke for meat. The head of the pig and the feet or 'crubeens', as they were called, were put in pickle by themselves and were the first to be eaten. This was done because it was considered very hard to cure them owing to the numerous bones. Brawn was sometimes made from the head and feet, but this was very seldom.

Each pig that was killed was at least two hundredweight, and that pig was let roam about while young so as to grow. When being fattened he was fed chiefly on boiled potatoes and POLLARD, hence the meat afterwards was very firm.

Puddings were made from the blood. The intestines of the pig were used in making the puddings. They were washed and turned several times in a running stream. Oat-meal and salt were mixed with the blood for filling the puddings. When filled they were boiled for a little while to make them hard. They were then hung up inside the chimney where they were well smoked and dried. Before being used they were fried and were very sweet.

The fat of the pig was taken out and rendered in an oven over the fire. The dripping or lard was stored in jars and used during the years to dress potatoes when the meat was out.

Fish were not eaten very often except trout or eel which were caught in the rivers on Sundays. During Lent herrings were bought and these were also hung up in the chimney inside. But apart from this season fish were very seldom used.

Cabbage was always eaten with meat in Spring and Summer. In winter when cabbage was scarce turnips or carrots were used. In May nettles were eaten and were supposed to be very wholesome and to keep away all sickness. Rhubarb was also used. Jam was made from crabs (wild apples) in Autumn for use in Winter and Spring.

People never ate late at night. The last meal was about seven o'clock and this nearly always consisted of porridge or stirabout. A cup of water was always taken before going to bed and this was considered a very healthy practice.

A number of eggs were always eaten on Easter Sunday. There was always a competition on between members of a family to see which of them could eat the most eggs. Even amongst the neighbours the number of eggs eaten was always the subject of conversation on Easter Sunday, and the young man who could not eat at least a dozen eggs on that morning was considered a weakling. The person who could eat about two dozen eggs on that morning was supposed to be healthy and to have 'a good stomach'.

On November Eve all kinds of fruit were eaten and games were played.

On Shrove Tuesday pancakes were eaten.

Tea was not used until sometime after the Famine, and even then it was only the well-to-do who could afford to use it.

Little tin saucepans were used before cups. These were very often made by tinkers, who travelled about from place to place.

SPREECE: *from Irish sprios, hot embers of wood or turf.*
SALLY-RODS: *willow rods.*
POLLARD: *spoiled grain fed to pigs.*

Potato cake, boxty and oaten meal

SCHOOL: *Carrowbeg, Co. Donegal*
TEACHER: *Rachel Nic an Ridire*
COLLECTORS: *Constance Norris, Tremone, Moville, Co. Donegal and Emma*
Hutchinson, Carrowmenagh, Moville, Co. Donegal
INFORMANTS: *John Norris, 64, Tremone, Moville, Co. Donegal; James Elkin,*
72, Tremone, Moville, Co. Donegal; Robert Campbell, 82, Ballymagaraghy,
Moville, Co. Donegal

Bread was made from barley, wheat and corn in olden times. The people grew their own barley and corn from which they ground the meal. No one that I know is quite sure whether the flour was made locally or not. The people bought only a very little flour at a time because it was very scarce and dear and very often they had to do without any. They had grindstones or querns, as they were sometimes called, with which they ground their own oats. No one that I know remembers the querns being used but there are still a few disused ones in the district. It is up to two hundred years since the querns went out of use. Knocking stones were in use before the querns but it is rare to see one of them nowadays.

In olden times the people made three kinds of bread called potato cake, boxty, and oaten meal. When making potato bread, the potatoes were boiled and then skinned and bruised with the bottom of a tin pan when cold. The bruised potatoes were mixed with a little flour if the person had it. No milk, water or soda was used but a little pinch of salt was added. The potatoes and flour were kneaded together and rolled out and cut into farls. The farls were hardened on a griddle hung over a bright fire. They were a brownish colour when baked and were fairly hard and tough.

In making oaten bread, oaten meal was put into a dish with a little salt and mixed with a little lukewarm water and then put on the bake board and rolled out with a rolling pin. It was rolled out to a large cake about half an inch thick. It was let stand for a quarter of an hour and then put on a grid iron to HARN on front of the fire. It was usually eaten when cold.

Boxty bread was made with raw potatoes. The potatoes were washed, skinned and grated. Then the grated potatoes were kneaded together with a very little flour and some salt was added. When rolled out and cut in farls, the boxty was baked on a griddle over a bright fire. It had not much of a taste.

In olden times people were thankful when they got enough bread baked to keep the hunger away. No one that I have enquired from has ever heard tell of any marks being cut on the top of the bread. The vessel on which the bread was baked in olden times was called a griddle or frying pan. It was often baked in front of the fire standing against a support which was called a grid-iron. This thing was made from iron and called a brander. These grid-irons or branders, as they are sometimes called, are still common in the district. There was a little griddle bread made in olden times. No one that I can find out from has ever heard of any special bread being made on any occasion. The following is an old rhyme about the making of the boxty bread:—

> The Boxty Mill began to shill
> To remind you of a fiddle,
> She gave it a squeeze betwixt her knees
> And clapped it on the griddle.

HARN: *fully bake.*

By means of querns

SCHOOL: *Cappagh, Co. Kerry*
TEACHER: *T.F. Sheehan*

The people in olden times crushed their oats and wheat by means of querns or large flat circular stones with roughened surfaces. The grain was made into flour when crushed between these stones. When making into bread the flour was wet with milk, kneaded and baked on a flag on the hearth. In many cases this stone flag was never removed but acted for baking purposes. When required it was only necessary to brush the fire aside and place the cake on it. Besides oaten meal and wheaten bread, cakes were also made from potatoes – one kind from boiled potatoes called potato cake, and the other potatoes which were grated raw and peeled of their skins. The grated potatoes were dried by being wrapped in a cloth and squeezed. It was then mixed with a little flour and baked in the ordinary way being wet with milk. This was stampy or boxty bread. It was the custom to make a number of cakes when potato digging was finished, usually at Michaelmas.

Give the churn a few turns

SCHOOL: *Clochar na Trócaire, Cappamore, Co. Limerick*
Teacher: An tSr. Benin
COLLECTOR: *Cáit Ní Nuanáin, Dromsallagh, Cappamore, Co. Limerick*
INFORMANT: *Nóra Ní Chonghaile, Cappamore, Co. Limerick*

Every family, or almost every family, had a churn in the old days in this area. However, each family did not make their own butter each week. One person churned for all the neighbours, all bringing their cream to one house. Each person took a hand at the churn, and if any stranger came in, they too were requested to give the churn a few turns. That was before a creamery was established in Cappamore. The people used to go to Limerick and Tipperary to sell the butter at the butter market.

There was an old custom which was faithfully observed. The woman in whose house the churn was being made always made a hot cake. It was made thin like scones, but not cut up until it was baked. It was baked in an oven without a lid. Then when the work was finished, all the women sat down to tea, and had the hot cake and freshly churned butter. So the workers had their own reward; the women would not think the butter making properly finished if the day's work was not celebrated with hot cake, tea and fresh butter.

7

HOME CRAFTS

'The accounts gathered here bring us back to a time when the necessities of life were coaxed from the earth. Expertise was paid for only when necessary.'

Mellow the moonlight to shine is beginning
Close by the window young Eileen is spinning
Bent o'er the fire her grand grandmother sitting
Is crooning and moaning and drowsily knitting.
Merrily, cheerily, noisily whirring
Swings the wheel, spins the wheel, while the foot's stirring
Sprightly and lightly and merrily ringing
Sounds the sweet voice of the young maiden singing.

THESE LINES, beloved of my mother's generation, paint a scene of domestic contentment, where work and leisure harmonise in the cosy homes of rural Ireland. A romantic vista, perhaps, but one similar to the picture painted here by the testimonies of our informants.

Yes, money was scarce, but the man who made time made plenty of it. Everything on the table was homemade and everything from work to courtin' took place in the kitchen. Home was where the heart was.

In recent decades Ireland has become a 'wage economy'. The formula is simple and repetitive. You give your labour, you get your cash, you buy your stuff, you go home. Repeat weekly. We now have more money and less time. These days 'homemade' is something you're more likely to encounter on a supermarket label.

The accounts gathered here, however, bring us back to a time when the necessities of life were coaxed from the earth. Expertise was paid for only when necessary. Food, fabric, dye, soap, even bulrush candles, were harvested from the land and made fit for purpose by the family. Sheep produced the wool that was spun and knitted into socks and sweaters on-site. Similarly, flax was sown, harvested, soaked and woven in the home. The travelling tailor was only sent for to finish off the garment, in the same way as the butcher was only sent for to finish off the pig.

Young Bridie Collins from North Cork tells us that the women spun their own woollen thread from which they made stockings and jerseys. Provided they brought 10 pounds of their wool to Shaughnessy's mill 'they got a good heavy blanket, only to give 4 shillings for the weaving.' So, where possible, do it yourself.

Kitty Mac Hale of Lahardaun, County Mayo, documents the dyeing techniques of 'our fore-mothers'. Elsewhere, from an unnamed informant in Cappamore, County Limerick, we have a heart-warming account of a small child witnessing her own 'little coat and cap' being homemade. She recalls her grandmother at the spinning wheel, which 'hasn't been used for over twelve years now'. A picture that tells its own story. But the warmth of the memory, as much as the little coat and cap, lives on. Would that all of us might be blessed with such hands-on nurture, at least once in our lives.

In fact, this account of 'the hand that gives' had me thinking of my recently departed friend Jim Heffernan. Jim was born in Templeglantine, County Limerick, in 1936, just as this collection of folklore was getting underway. Although six feet tall, Jim saw himself as a 'small farmer'. A non-smoking teetotaller, Jim's tastes were simple – he liked the occasional toffee and a few lively tunes. He loved to dance polkas. Jim was a tidy worker: there was a place for everything and everything was in its place. He kept a clean farmyard and wasted little. The cattle and the house were sheltered by sturdy pine trees, planted by his uncle Paddy when Jim was just a boy.

However, to every thing there is a season, and so Jim and his trees aged together. Eventually, in February 2014 Storm Darwin got the better of the mighty pines.

It's an ill wind, they say, and this windfall was harvested with the precision of a surgeon, limbs removed, trunks split into blocks and stacked to dry, before being placed, block by block, into recycled animal feed bags. Any time I visited Jim, he'd always say, 'Will you take a few bags of blocks back to Cork with you?'

And I'd always say, 'I will, Jim, if you can spare them.'

I've always loved an open fire. Each one has its own personality. Jim's fires, like himself, were neat and lively. His blocks come in a nice variety of shapes, but all are a tidy fit for a fireplace. The wood is bone dry, no sparking, just perfect.

In 2018 Jim went off to where, I hope, the toffee is free and the polkas go on forever.

At his funeral mass, the priest declared, 'Fruit of the vine and the work of human hands.' I thought of all the farmers who had dutifully provided for family and friends.

I still miss Jim. Particularly in the winter when I light the fire. I have never once added a block to the pyre without thinking of his kindness and the fact that I am now handling the very same home-grown timber that he handled as it went into the bag. For as long as we're allowed, I'll keep the open fire going. I only have a few bags of Jim's homemade timber left anyway, so the last block isn't that far away.

When the day comes, I expect a stray wisp of wood-smoke might well sting my eye.

A spinning wheel to be found in almost every house

SCHOOL: *Knockeenbwee Lower, Dromdaleague, Co. Cork*
TEACHER: *Dd. Ó Ceallaigh*
COLLECTOR: *Maigreadh Ní Muirthille, Lahanaght, Co. Cork*
INFORMANT: *Tadhg Ó Muirthille, Lahanaght, Co. Cork*

The clothes that were worn in former times were much better than the clothes that are wearing at present. They were made from homemade frieze and manufactured at home. There was a spinning wheel to be found in almost every house. The people kept a large number of sheep. The wool was carded and spun by the women folk.

When the thread was made into large balls it had to be taken to a weaver and afterwards to a TUCKING MILL, then it was fit for use. There are no spinning-wheels in use at present as the wool is taken to a mill where it is manufactured. The original colour of the cloth was usually a mixture of black and white. If it was wanted a different colour it was sent away to be dyed as required.

Tailors were more numerous at that time than they are now-days, the country tailors especially. The tailors' instruments were sewing machine, scissors, thimble, needle, and chalk. The people generally brought the tailor to their houses to get their clothes made; they found that way cheaper than to send them out. The tailors usen't work at their homes, only they travel from house to house.

> **TUCKING MILL:** *a small factory that cleaned and processed cloth, also known as a fulling mill.*

They buy it in the shops

SCHOOL: *Rockchapel, Co. Cork*
TEACHER: *Donncha Ó Géibheannaigh*
COLLECTOR: *Bridie Collins, Lyraneag, Co. Cork*
INFORMANT: *John Collins, Lyraneag, Co. Cork*

There is no tailor in this district for the past few years. The last tailor who was here was Patsy Murphy. He lived in a thatched house in Glounakeel. Three years ago he left this district and is since living in Meelin village. Forty-five years ago, there were two tailors living and working in this district. One was John McCarthy, who lived in a mud cabin on the side of the road in Tooreenagrena, near John Buckley's gate; he was a lame man but a very good tailor. The second tailor was John Fitzgerald, who lived in Stagmount.

A travelling tailor comes to the district every November. Tadhgh Doody is his name. He is about sixty years of age and travels in a donkey car from place to place. He spends the winter in this district, a week or few weeks, in the farmers' houses. Whilst in the house, he makes any clothes that is required for the family. The people buy the cloth in the shop. He is very cranky.

Mrs Nolan of Glounakeel is the only woman who makes some woollen clothes at home, in this district at present. She cards and spins the sheep's wool and with the thread makes jerseys, cardigans, pull-overs and stockings. Mrs Nolan has a spinning wheel and uses it. Mrs Ellen Mulcahy of Mileen also has a spinning wheel, but no use was made of it for years.

When my mother was a young girl, they made all their own clothes at home. From the wool of the sheep, they made woollen thread, with which they made their own stockings and jerseys. From the woollen thread, Edward Scanlon, the weaver, made flannel and tweed. The women made flannel waist-coats and under-pants for the men, skirts and under-skirts for themselves out of the flannel. The tweed was taken to the tailor for making the men's clothes.

The flannel was also made into blankets and quilts. Nano John Connell was a quilter in this district. When the women wanted blankets, they took wool to Shaughnessy's mill at Feale's Bridge, or to Shaughnessy's mill at Coolbawn, near Freemount, and for ten pounds of wool, they got a good heavy blanket, only to give four shillings for the weaving.

From the flax, the women made linen thread. The thread was sent to the weaver, who made it into bandle-cloth sheeting. The bandle-cloth was made into shirts, and the sheets for the house were made from the sheeting.

In every house in this district the women knit their own stockings and socks for the men. The thread is not spun in the homes now, they buy it in the shops.

The implements used by the tailor are — A lapboard, on which he creases and presses the clothes. An iron of about 7 ½lbs for pressing. A scissors, needle, thimble, a measuring tape, and a sewing machine.

> There was an old tailor in Macroom,
> And all he wanted was elbow room.

Spinning and knitting with the light of the fire

SCHOOL: *Gortaveha, Co. Clare*
TEACHER: *P. Wiley*
COLLECTOR: *Cáit Ní Chorra*
INFORMANT: *Thomas Corry, 60, Derryfadda, Caherfeakle, Co. Clare*

They used to get the wool off the sheep. Then they used card it with hand cards and make it in to rolls and then spin it. The old women used sit all night in the corner, spinning and knitting with the light of the fire, and weave BONEENS. Then they used to sow flax and pull it with their hands. Then they steeped it for three weeks in a bog hole covered up with sods. After that they would spread it out in the fields to dry and bleach and then pound it. Then they combed it with a combing tongs, and made it into bundles.

There was a little stick with three prongs on the spinning wheel to hold the bundles. They worked the spinning wheel [with] their feet and kept drawing down the flax round the wheel and make it in to rolls. Then they drove pegs in to the wall and passed the thread in and out of them. Then they wound it in to hanks and send it off to be weaved.

There was a man over in Faha named Madden who used to weave. There was another below in Feakle near Joe Canny's named Hugh Madden. There was another further down named Culloo.

They used to weave the flax into big sheets and then make shirts and sheets and blankets and towels and dresses. And used colour some of them.

BONEENS: *bawneens, woollen jackets or waistcoats.*

I can plainly remember the spinning wheel

SCHOOL: *Clochar na Trócaire, Cappamore, Co. Limerick*
TEACHER: *An tSr. Benin*

There is still a spinning wheel in our home, but it hasn't been used for over twelve years. When I was a very small child I had a little knitted coat and cap which was home-made. The wool was sheared in the district and my grand-mother spun it. I can plainly remember the spinning wheel. It used to fascinate me seeing the wool going to the wheel in a tangle and winding at the other side on the spindle as thread. The coat and cap were also knitted and dyed in the locality.

A pleasant day scutching

SCHOOL: *Cornadowagh, Newtowncashel, Co. Longford*
Teacher: P. Eustace
COLLECTOR: *Séan Ó Fearghail, 11, Newtowncashel, Co. Longford*
INFORMANT: *parent (name not given), male, Newtowncashel, Co. Longford*

In olden times flax was grown in this district. Almost all the farmers sowed flax. The seed was sown in Spring time, the same as oats, and pulled in the harvest time and tied in sheaves and brought to a bog hole and left there for some time. After a week it was taken from there and spread out to dry and tied again into sheaves. Then it was brought into the house and broken up with BEETLES until it was [well] softened. Then a party of girls came with a SCUTCHING STOCK AND HANDLE and spent a pleasant day SCUTCHING.

Then the young people collected, and had a dance that night. After that the flax was carded and spun with a spinning wheel. It was then brought to the weaver and woven into linen which was used for sheets and shirts, and other articles. Almost all the women at that time knew how to spin and had their own spinning wheels, and the weavers at that time were Tomas Clarke, Loughown, and Berney Smith, Derryshawn, who are now dead. This story was told to me by my father, who saw this work done.

BEETLES: *mallets.*
SCUTCHING STOCK AND HANDLE: *the stock was a board on which the flax was placed and then beaten with the handle, a long, narrow board.*
SCUTCHING: *beating the flax stalks to separate the linen fibres from the straw.*

Our fore-mothers

SCHOOL: *Lahardaun, Co. Mayo*
TEACHER: *Mairtín Ó Ceallaigh*
COLLECTOR: *Kitty Mac Hale, Caffoley, Ballina, Co. Mayo*

Long ago the people used to dye the wool that they used for making their clothes with moss. The moss that is used for dyeing grows on rocks, and has to be scraped off with a knife. It is then put into a pot of hot water and given a very long boil. Then it is taken up and strained and the wool is put into it, and boiled again, for about an hour. Then the wool is taken up and put out to dry. If the wool be dyed well it becomes a nice saffron colour. This method of dyeing wool and cloth was used very much by our fore-mothers. And some people use it yet for dyeing wool for socks.

Weeds, dock leaf, nettles and coarse hay

SCHOOL: *Annaduff, Co. Leitrim*
TEACHER: *Thomas Morahan*
INFORMANT: *Hugh McGuinness, Fearnaught, Dromod, Co. Leitrim*

Soap was made in the townland of Fearnaught by the O'Rourke family.

They made it out of weeds, dock leaf, nettles and coarse hay. First they cut and dried these and then burned it into ashes. They then wet the ashes that remained with water until they got it into a thick paste. They made small sections of the paste and left these to dry until they got hard and firm. These blocks were used in washing linen so as to make it white. The linen was put into a pot and a section of this soap was boiled with it. After this the linen was spread on the grass and suds thrown on it to make it still whiter.

Lights they used to have long ago

ACHOOL: *Cloonfad, Co. Roscommon*
TEACHER: *Mrs. Flood*
COLLECTOR: *Mary Teresa Noone, Gurteen, Cloonfad, Ballyhaunis, Co. Roscommon*
INFORMANT: *Mrs. Maria Fleming, 75, Gurteen, Cloonfad, Co. Roscommon*

About sixty years ago rush candles were made in my district. The people would first get about twenty rushes and peel the green skin off. Then they used to make gravy out of lard and dip the rushes into it and leave them to dry. Sometimes they would give them a second coat. They used to be good light from them.

They had no candle-sticks. They used to get a rod about eight or nine inches long and split it down about two inches and stick the other end into a soft sod of turf and put the candle into the top of it. One candle would last about one hour.

Some people used to light 'BOG-DEAL' instead of candles. They used to go to the bog and get a block of bog-deal and bring it home and saw it into little blocks. They would put a block into the fire and it would show as good a light as a candle. That is the kind of lights they used to have long ago.

BOG-DEAL: *wood found preserved in bogs.*

8

FROM HEDGE SCHOOLS
TO NATIONAL SCHOOLS

*'A concerted effort was made to stamp out any ember
of learning that dared to glow in the ashes of Gaelic
Ireland. The destruction would have been complete,
had the last of the bards not managed to take to the
roads and pass the torch of learning to
raggedy children.'*

**RELAND'S INTERNATIONAL REPUTATION** as a place of great learning is probably underestimated by those of us who still live here. My home town of Cork was founded in 606 AD as a monastic school by St Finbarr. Today it's home to several universities and third-level institutions, and Irish graduates are considered amongst the finest in the world. I expect Finbarr would be pleased.

But just why are the Irish so keen on 'the books'? It's a long story that precedes even Finbarr and begins with the pre-Christian bardic tradition. This sophisticated system of learning saw a hierarchy of poets, from bard to *fileadh*, memorise vast amounts of information, usually in verse form. These people were the repositories of history, law, medicine, genealogy and everything else to do with 'the story of us'. The bards were walking reference books.

Actual books didn't arrive here until the fourth century. From that point, monastic schools busied themselves transcribing not just sacred text but, with the assistance of the bards, secular material too. This sourcing, recording and teaching went on unaffected by the fall of Rome. So, as Europe entered the Dark Ages, the flame of knowledge burned brightly on this little island. Teachers from the Land of Saints and Scholars were in high demand across Europe.

However, England's grip on Ireland became a stranglehold in the 1600s with the establishment of the Penal Laws and the outlawing of 'non-conformist' religions. A concerted effort was made to stamp out any ember of learning that dared to glow in the ashes of Gaelic Ireland. The destruction would have been complete, had the last of the bards not managed to take to the roads and pass the torch of learning to raggedy children.

The Catholic clergy were outlawed, so Mass was hurriedly said at secret sites. In some cases, all that now remains are a few stone markers and place names like '*Carraig an Aifrinn*' (the Mass Rock). Similarly, teachers set up 'schools' with only brambles for shelter from the weather and as camouflage from the eyes of the law. Placenames like *Páirc na Scoile* (the school field) and Schull (*Scoil*/School) in West Cork are often the only trace left behind.

Wandering bards, some carrying ancient manuscripts, formed a living link between hungry children and an Irish literary tradition that stretched all the way back to the great Gaelic chieftains and kings. In Poulacapple, County Tipperary, we encounter a penniless hedge schoolmaster who once counted the Earls of Ormond amongst his muses.

Life at a hedge school could be difficult and even violent. Pat Forkan of Broher, County Roscommon, paints a bleak picture with his matter-of-fact list of what they didn't have — no windows, no heat, no pens, no ink, no desks, no blackboard, no light. Writing was taught at the entrance to the hovel because they had no other daylight. In this environment the children learned the classical languages of Greece and Rome. From Currans, County Kerry, we get a horrific scene of corporal punishment, meted out from a distance by a schoolteacher brandishing a long whip.

It's important to remember that hedge schools were not a system as such, but a series of underground cells without any set standards, exams or resources. Some taught through English, others Irish. Because of the demands of seasonal farmwork, attendance was often casual. Stephen Duffy of Kilcurly writes, 'It was a common sight to see boys with long trousers and moustaches attending school, not to mention big courting girls.'

The Catholic Emancipation Act of 1829 finally paved the way for the National Schools system. By the late 1880s most of the hedge schools had faded from the landscape, but not from folk memory. Indeed, many of the elderly contributors to this collection witnessed first-hand these humble hovels.

I come away from this collection of memories with a better understanding of my parents' generation and their fixation with 'the books'. They scrimped and saved and turned a blind eye to corporal punishment to ensure an education for their children. 'Education is your ticket to freedom!' roared our second-class teacher. I was only seven years old at the time and didn't really understand, but I get it now. This is the same motivation, I expect, that led most of Ireland's political prisoners straight to the prison library. Education is the key that eventually unlocks liberty.

Generations of scholars have been motivated not only by a pride in the pinnacles of our bardic, monastic and National School systems, but also by the fear of ever again falling into the dark valley of penal times. A valley that would have been an abyss, if not for the stopgap provided by the hedge schools.

A little centre of learning

SCHOOL: *Ridge, Leighlin, Co. Carlow*
TEACHER: *Bean Uí Airtnéid*
COLLECTOR: *Kathleen Darcy*
INFORMANT: *Patrick Darcy, Coone, Co. Kilkenny*

In 1831, the National system of Education came into operation in Ireland. Previous to this there were no schools and no Catholic could get any education because no children could be sent to foreign countries to be educated. The only means of education that the people had were the hedge schools which were held in barns and out houses. These schools were conducted by a young teacher who was self-educated. From twelve to twenty pupils, both boys and girls, attended the schools. The only remuneration the teachers had was a weekly contribution of a penny or threepence from the lower classes and sixpence from the higher classes. The teacher also got contributions from the farmers such as bacon, vegetables, and fuel. By these contributions he was able to live. The subjects taught were English, spelling book, writing letters and composition, arithmetic and calculations. The progress was astonishing. On account of the pupils having few subjects their knowledge of those subjects was sound and thorough. The pupils took great advantage of the schools.

There was one school in Revanagh. The teacher who taught there was named Mr. Nolan. My father heard his parents talk of a hedge school in Coone East at the top of the Pike Road where now lives a family named Hennessy. He has no recollection of the teacher who taught there. This school was a little centre of learning in its own humble way.

In this school the ragged pupils were taught

SCHOOL: *Ring, Dalahasey, Co. Dublin*
TEACHER: *M. Ní Reachtaire*
COLLECTOR: *Kevin Whyte, 13, Dermotstown, Co. Dublin*
INFORMANT: *father, Dermotstown, Co. Dublin*

The 18th century was the darkest period in our Irish history. During the troubled times the terrible Penal Laws were in force, and the Irish suffered much from land troubles especially the landlordism. Owing to the hard laws made against Catholics no Catholic children were allowed to attend school. The Protestants burned down the Catholic schools. As a result simple structures were erected in fields and remote places and schoolmasters taught the ragged children in those schools, which were called Hedge-Schools, and the teachers were called Hedgeschoolmasters. All over the country there are remains of those old schools. Now I will tell of local remains in my District.

At Walshestown, Lusk, Co. Dublin, about one mile south of our school, there are the remains of an old school in which children were taught in those dark days. It is situated beside a farmhouse surrounded by trees about fifty yards from the road. It is a wooden structure apart from the bottom, which is built with brick and clay a foot from the ground and is round-shapen. The roof, which is round, is wooden also and has two round holes cut in the wood as windows and is still in a perfect state of preservation.

A small village two and a half miles south of our school is Hedgestown. This village, which got its name from the hedge schools, has no remains except in a remote glen far from the road there are the butts of clay walls now green with grass – in this school the ragged pupils were taught – it is said to have been found by the Protestant [soldiers] and wrecked despite their hidden efforts.

The hedge schools lasted in Ireland until the Penal Laws were over and Emancipation act was passed in 1829. Then they fell to ruins as they were of no use any more, there were plenty of Catholic schools now with teachers. Although the hedge schools are gone their ruins remind us of the dark Penal Days.

A man of quiet disposition

SCHOOL: *Poulacapple, Mullinahone, Co. Tipperary*
TEACHER: *Séan Ó h-Icidhe*
INFORMANT: *Mrs. Patrick Vaughan, Garryricken, Co. Kilkenny*

About the year 1800 Mr John Dunne was born in Poulacapple. In those days schoolmasters were very few, and school children on account of that had to travel a long distance to school. As well as being a schoolmaster he was a poet and an orator. He wrote many poems in connection with the Ormond family, also on local marriages and [wren boys].

He was a fluent Irish speaker and wrote many of his poems in Irish. He was a man of quiet disposition. He was keenly interested in improving the Irish people in education, which was sorely needed at the time. He taught school up to a very advanced age. He wore a swallow-tail coat, a tall hat, and a KNICKERS. He died in the year 1895 and was buried in Killamory grave-yard.

KNICKERS: *knickerbockers.*

A famous, though fugitive, hedge-school master

SCHOOL: *Kilbonane, Lios an Phúca (Beaufort), Co. Kerry*
TEACHER: *Dll. Ó Clúmháin*
COLLECTOR: *Tadg Ó Concubhair, Coolroe, Co. Kerry*
INFORMANT: *Charles Connor, 54, Coolroe, Co. Kerry*

In the parish of Listry there existed what was known as a hedge school. The name of this particular school is unknown, since in those times it was forbidden by law to conduct any kind of institution for teaching. It is well known, however, that there once travelled through the parish a famous, though fugitive, hedge-schoolmaster who was known by the name of Dan O'Hanlon. It is well known that the old hedge school was conducted by this famous school teacher on what was once known as the old road, Coolroe. The school was an old cabin from which the occupants had been evicted years before. Within the crumbling walls of this deserted cabin Dan O'Hanlon secretly taught his fifteen boys the classical languages of Greece and Rome. Here sitting on the mud floor and arranged in groups of three the teacher imparted his knowledge to his pupils, who, without books or script of any kind, maintained his work within their memories. Dan O'Hanlon thus taught the boys of the parish the foundations of their future knowledge standing with his back to the wall.

Ink was got from black berries while quills served them as pens

SCHOOL: *Castlemaine, Co. Kerry*
TEACHER: *Máire, Bean an Chaomhánaigh*
COLLECTOR: *Kitty Horgan, Rusheen, Co. Kerry*
INFORMANT: *Timothy Mc Carthy, 42, Ardmelode, Co. Kerry*

One of the fields near my home is known as PÁIRC NA SCOILE. Between 70 and 90 years ago a so-called hedge school was built in this field. It was built up against a ditch and covered with rushes, a part of it being the home of the schoolmaster. To this school went a lot of young men from the locality. The master's name was one Micheal O'Connell. It was said that he was a descendant of Daniel O'Connell.

Each scholar had to pay the master for his education. Irish was the principal language spoken. The school was not equipped with seats, ink or pens as plenty as they have them now. Ink was got from black berries while quills served them as pens. The remains of this hedge school can be seen yet and some of the scholars who attended it still live and are fairly educated.

PÁIRC NA SCOILE: *the school field.*

He would rise black stripes on them with a long whip

SCHOOL: *Currans, Co. Kerry*
TEACHER: *Cormac Ó Muircheartaigh*
COLLECTOR: *Mr. John Fitzgerald, Tulligrabbeen, Castleisland, Co. Kerry*
INFORMANT: *Mrs. Ellen Roche, 77, Curranes, Castleisland, Co. Kerry*

Two hedge schools existed in this neighbourhood, until Currans National school was built. One existed in upper Dulague and the other was situated in Portdubh. The school in Dulague was held in the house of Mr. Garret Fleming, and the other was held in an out-house on the farm of Mr. John Cahill. The latter school was taught by Master Murphy, a cripple. His school consisted of one room, a fire place, a large table around which were placed logs of timber hewn into something like rough benches for the pupils to sit on. The other school was taught by Master Rollins, who had his school in Mr. Fleming's granary. The teachers were lodged in the houses of their pupils, and were [paid] by contribution of the parents.

Master Murphy, the cripple, could not get up to slap his scholars if they were not minding their lesson, but he would rise black stripes on them with a long whip which would reach to every corner of the room, so that their only chance of escape was to keep near the door. But the master at Flemings who had the use of his limbs would blacken the dunces' hands if they had not their task. Another method of punishment was hoisting; which was done by a big boy standing in the middle of the room, and the dunce was put up on his back, and then the master started FLAKING him with an ash plant, but sometimes if the master were a bad shot he would hit the big boy instead.

The subjects taught in the hedge-schools were Reading, Spelling, Writing, and Voster (An arithmetic published by Mr. Vere Foster Dublin). The great difficulty was that neither master nor pupils could write a decent English letter. Every letter should begin with 'I take this pen in hand to [write] you these few lines hoping to find you in as good state of health, as the mailing of this letter finds me at present, thanks be to God for his mercies to us all' etc. etc. Some people today look down with scorn on the hedge-schools, but it was really their labours that kept education alive in Ireland during the Penal Times.

FLAKING: *beating.*

'I know what is in my master's mind'

SCHOOL: *Kiltormer, Co. Galway*
TEACHER: *Pádhraic Ó Muineacháin*
COLLECTOR: *Augustine Lyons, Ardranny Beg, Ballinasloe, Co. Galway*

Once there were two little boys named Jack and Billy. They were twins and they were so much alike that you would not know one from the other. They had only one suit of clothes so they could go to school only every second day.

One day Billy went to school without Jack and the master asked him where was Jack that he was not at school. Billy answered that they had but one suit of clothes and they could go to school only every second day. The master said that he would get him a suit of clothes if he answered the following three questions. – 'What was the weight of the moon?' 'What was the depth of the sea?' and 'What was in your master's mind?'

He went home and he told the story to Jack but he himself could not answer the questions. Then Jack said he knew the answer and that he would go to school the next day. When he entered the school next morning the master asked him the questions. He asked him what was the weight of the moon, and Jack said four quarters, one CWT. He asked him what was the depth of the sea, and Jack said the throw of a stone, because when a stone is thrown in, it goes to the bottom, and that is the depth of it. He asked him what was in his master's mind, and Jack replied, 'Oh! It's well I know what is in my master's mind. You think it is Billy you have here but it is Jack.'

So they got the suit of clothes and they went to school every day from that day forth.

CWT: *a hundredweight, 112 pounds.*

Big enough to beat the master

SCHOOL: *Kilcurly, Co. Louth*
TEACHER: *T. Ó Cuinn*
INFORMANT: *Stephen Duffy, pensioner, plasterer, Kilcurly*

The present school is a new building erected in the year 1927 by the late Rev. Bernard Canon Donnellan P.P. at a cost of £2,100, one third of which was raised locally. This school replaced an older building, which was situated between the church and Tankardsrock road, just to the rear of the residence of Thomas Mulholland. It was a one-story slated building, barn-shaped, and divided into two compartments by a wooden partition. It was erected in the year 1830. The boys and girls were kept in separate rooms. The following are the names of the teachers: Mr and Mrs Nugent, Mr Mulholland, Mr Lavelle, Mr Boyle, Miss D'arcy, Miss Mathews. Mr and Mrs Nugent used to live in a house where Jem McGeough lived but the house is in ruins now. It was situated in the townland of Kilkerley. Mr Mulholland used to live where the Mulholland family in Plaster now live. It is common property round Kilkerley, that the house he lived in was then the teacher's residence. He stayed on in the house after retiring from teaching and was allowed to keep it as his own private property. This house adjoined the old school and is a two-story thatched building — the only one of its kind left standing in the district.

The children were taught all the usual subjects: — Arithmetic, English, Reading, Writing, Spellings and Grammar, History in English. Geography, Algebra and Drawing. The children used to play in the chapel yard and Lavelle's Field. No lavatory accommodation was provided in the old school up to the time it was demolished. The children hung their coats on nails on the wooden partition. There was a fire place in each room and during the winter months the children used take sods of turf for the fire. On Monday certain children would be told to take sods on the following day and so in turn each child would be asked to bring sods. Every morning one of the bigger boys would be put standing at the door with a slate, on which he would write down the names of the children who took sods and the number of sods taken. Those who failed to take any sods were punished and those who took extra sods were allowed to sit nearer to the fire. This old custom died out about the beginning of the present century.

The children in those days usen't to come to school till they were anything between six and ten years of age. Very few of them wore boots, even in the Winter. Most of the younger boys wore petticoats or skirts when they went to school first. They seldom took lunch with them and when they did it consisted of a few scallops (slices cut very thickly) of dry homemade bread. (Dry bread means bread without butter or jam.) The boys remained at school for four or five years and few of them were regular attenders except during the Winter months, when there wasn't much work to be done on the land. Some of them continued on at school until they were big enough to beat the master. It was a common sight to see boys with long trousers and moustaches attending school not to mention big courting girls.

An ounce of tobacco to pay the master

SCHOOL: *Baile Nua, Ballymacarbry, Clonanav, Co. Waterford*
TEACHER: *Pádraig Ó Cearbhaill*
INFORMANT: *Michael Treahy, Knockalisheen, Co. Waterford*

In olden times there were no schools in this parish except the ruins of an old house which stood in a field near Castlequarter; it was owned by a farmer named Patrick Mulcahy. Grown-up men and girls used come there, sometimes to day-school and sometimes to evening-school. Some scholars used bring a few pence and others an ounce of tobacco to pay the master. It was the custom at that time for the scholars to bring a few raw potatoes, light a fire in the field and roast the potatoes for their lunch. One very severe winter the roof of the old house fell in. The scholars had to leave and there was no school for the rest of the winter and the teacher, Patrick O'Keeffe, was without his pennies and tobacco.

As the weather got finer the people gathered under the hedges in the roadside in front of a farmer's barn in Newtown. This barn was owned by a farmer called Michael McGrath. As the winter came on again people could stay no longer under the hedge, so they asked Mr. McGrath to let them into the barn and he kindly consented. They managed to have a day-school there and the Parish Priest, Father Finn, asked the people to subscribe and buy the barn and they did so. They raised enough money to buy the barn, convert it into a schoolhouse and also erect a teacher's residence.

Nothing to write on but slates

SCHOOL: *Rathgormuck, Carrick-on-Suir, Co. Waterford*
TEACHER: *Mícheál Mac Créigh*
COLLECTOR: *Seán Ó Dálaigh, Park, Co. Waterford*
INFORMANT: *Pádraig Ó Dálaigh, Park, Co. Waterford, 50, father of collector*

About a hundred years ago there was a school in the townland of Glenpatrick and nothing is to be seen there now but the foundation and two trees, up against which the school was built. This building had a slate roof and walls built of clay and stones. A man named Mr. Power, who was a stranger, is supposed to have taught there. All Irish was taught in this school and the scholars had nothing to write on but slates. A man named John Quinlan, when going to this school, had one of the oldest books concerning Columcille.

Some years before that there was a hedge-school in Croonyhill and the man who taught there was afterwards a beggar going the road. His name is not known. This man had also a hedge-school in Park and at the place where he had his little school a house now stands. Irish was the subject taught in these schools too.

Men of great ability and of poetic fame

SCHOOL: *Butlerstown (Kilburne), Co. Waterford*
TEACHER: *Seán Ó Flannagáin*
COLLECTOR: *Jackie Power*

Long ago Ireland was called the 'Island of Saints and Scholars'. It was called so because of its numerous schools and colleges. The nearest school that was famous in ancient history was in Lismore. This school sent out men of great ability and of poetic fame. The only ruins of old schools in this parish are those of the schools that preceded the present ones. The site of the girls' school is now joined with the church yard. The boys' school is still there and is now occupied by a family. In olden times the schools were not as comfortable and they had no books.

Those schools were made of the brambles of the tree

SCHOOL: *Tonroe, Co. Mayo*
TEACHER: *Máirtín Ó Giobaláin*
COLLECTOR: *Eibhlín Ní Gabhláin, Tonnagh, Co. Mayo*
INFORMANT: *Pat Forkan, 80, farmer, Broher, Co. Roscommon*

Long ago the schools in our district were not so plentiful as they are now. The schools made then were much smaller than the schools nowadays.

Long ago the schools that existed in our district were called hedge schools. Those schools were made of the brambles of the trees. The brambles of the trees were woven in and out. The inside was lined with bags. The roof was also made of brambles. On top of the brambles SCRAWS out of the bog were put in order to keep out the rain. Those schools were built in the middle of the district in a shady place.

The best learned man in the district always came and taught in these schools. Sometimes strange teachers came through the district and taught for their living. Every child paid those teachers a penny or twopence each every Monday morning. The names of those teachers were Garret Burke, Michael Veasey and Martin Casey. Those people travelled from district to district teaching. Those teachers lodged in the village in which the hedge school was built. Those teachers taught also in farm barns. There was a barn in our district belonging to Peggy Owens. Michael Veasey taught in this barn about a hundred years ago. It was in this barn that my grandmother's mother was taught.

In these hedge schools the only subjects taught were writing and reading. There were no pencils or pens at that time, but a piece of chalk and a slate were used. When the master was teaching a child how to write he brought the child out to the door and taught him how to form the letters. Masters had to do this because there were no windows in their barns or old schools where they taught. Irish was spoken by master and pupils, because they knew no English.

There was only one book used and that was a twopenny primer. There were no desks or chairs at that time. The desks then were big blocks of wood. What they sat on were small blocks. They sat also on a few sods of turf on the top of one another. There was no blackboard, but a big slate left on top of a block of wood was used for instruction.

SCRAWS: *sods.*

No such thing as Irish

SCHOOL: *Davidstown, Dunlavin, Co. Wicklow*
TEACHER: *Róisín Bhreathnach*
COLLECTOR: *Larry Nolan, Donard, Co. Wicklow*
INFORMANT: *Murtagh Nolan, father, circa 60*

When my father was going to school he went to Davidstown. Miss Mac Hugh was the teacher. At that time, they used to learn English. Of course there was no such thing as Irish.

The way they spent the day was — from the time they went in, at about ten o'clock, until twelve they were at sums, writing and reading. Then at twelve they said their prayers and then they were at their Catechism until half-twelve. They got out until one o'clock for their lunch, and the teacher had a little bell and she would ring it at one o'clock to call them in. From one until three o'clock they did writing and were at the map.

When three o'clock came they were let home, and the teacher used be along with some of them, as she lived in Fanagh where Nolans are now. Every morning she would have to walk with a big shawl around her, which was the fashion at that time, and of course there were no bicycles at that time.

When my Grandfather was going to school, he was taught in a hedge-school. There were no schools at that time. Some nights they would gather together and go to a neighbour's house and be taught there, and another night to another neighbour's house and that was the way they were taught.

Sods of turf to sit on

SCHOOL: *Listowel, Co. Kerry*
TEACHER: *Brian Mac Mathúna*
COLLECTOR: *W. Keane, Listowel, Co. Kerry*
INFORMANT: *Mrs. Purtill, 76, Ballydonohoe, Co. Kerry*

There was a hedge school at my grandmother's house in Ballydonohue and it was taught by Bathail Stack. Every evening after school he fell asleep in a hide in the school. They used to call his wife Peggy the WINDGALL. This woman wore no shoes sometimes. They had sods of turf to sit on, and each boy had to bring a sod of turf for the fire. They used write on a big flag in the middle of the hearth. Their chalk was a lump of lime. The boys had bogdeal tapers on bits of newspapers. They often wrote with feathers and the ink was bog wood which was a dye in that time. They put it into water. He slapped the boys with a twig.

WINDGALL: *a sore, blister or cyst.*

The children could come and go any time they liked

SCHOOL: *Cornadowagh, Newtowncashel, Co. Longford*
TEACHER: *P. Eustace*
COLLECTOR: *Séamus Mac Suibhne, 14, Derrygowna, Newtowncashel,
Co. Longford*

In this district about ninety or one hundred years ago, there were several old schools. There was school held in my townland, in a cow-house owned by Patrick Shanley. When the cows were let out, the children used to come and attend school. In other places it was held at the backs of ditches and in all kinds of old houses. At that time any good scholar could be a teacher. A man named Bob Connelly, from Lanesboro, used to teach in this school. He used to lodge in the children's houses. Each of the children used to bring him to their houses on their turns. Each child used to bring one penny each to the teacher every Monday, this is the way he was paid. If the children did not bring the money they would have to leave the school. At that time there was no roll book, the children could come and go any time they liked. They used to have a fire in the school also, and each child used to bring two sods of turf under his arm. Sometimes they used to steal the turf from houses on the way to school. If they happened to forget the turf, they would be put beside the door for the whole day. The subjects taught were: – Reading, Writing and Arithmetic, there was no Irish taught. They used to write on slates with sharp stones. All the books the teacher used to have would be divided round on the scholars to read. The children used to have to sit on their heel. There was no blackboard in the school. The teacher used to remain a certain time in the school, then he would pack up and go to some other school.

9

GAMES AND PASTIMES

'1930s gaming required just a few friends, a big imagination and the God-given right to roam. Even the poorest children enjoyed "the freedom of the city", and their country cousins also rambled till hunger drove them home.'

AMING, MY GRANDCHILDREN ASSURE ME, is a solitary pursuit, usually played online in a youngster's bedroom with remote friends. It's a low-energy, high-buzz pastime, and 'Batteries Not Included' can lead to off-grid Christmas morning meltdowns. The children of the Schools' Collection, however, lived in an era when batteries were neither included nor required.

1930s gaming required just a few friends, a big imagination and the God-given right to roam. Even the poorest children enjoyed 'the freedom of the city', and their country cousins also rambled till hunger drove them home.

Much of the year was spent outdoors trapping birds, fishing, picking flowers, gathering nuts and acting out nursery rhymes and verses. Apart from favourites like tig, there were many local variations of games, some with names that could grace a Grand National starting line-up: 'Skipping Lad, Lord Luke, Limping Tom … and they're off!'

As the days grew shorter, the craic moved indoors. Like everything else in 1930s Ireland, pastimes were seasonal, so the old box of draughts or snakes and ladders would be taken down. Seasoned chestnuts were run through with a string to play conkers, or chessies, as we called them. With the instincts of gamblers, children could create a game of chance from anything. Every child in the household would throw a nut on the fire and whoever's nut was first to crack and be spat from the flames would be the first to marry. Similarly, homemade bulrush candles would be lit by each member of the household, and whoever's candle burnt out first would be next to die. Great craic. Perhaps *Resident Evil 2* isn't so scary after all.

I had forgotten how much time small children spend at role-play. My own four little girls spent hours in a game they created themselves where they were all called Mary. Much confusion and merriment ensued. I expect today's 'smallies' would knock the same sport as their ancestors did from the nursery rhymes and re-enactments in this collection, like Jack the Bread is Burning, Little Silly Saucer, Ghost in the Garden, Frog in the Well and Thread the Needle Dan.

Pretending was popular amongst adults too. Elsewhere in the Schools' Collection I have read accounts of role-playing at wakes and funerals. The assembled adults would act out an improvised courtroom scene with hilarious results. When you are poor and powerless, it must be nice to be a judge or a priest or a lawyer for an hour. Patrick Niland of Newbrook, County Mayo, informs us here that hand-slapping was also popular at wakes. Two men would take turns to slap each other's palm until one of them gave up, often with the blood 'streaming out of the tips of their fingers'. Clearly, not every man leaving the house of the deceased in floods of tears was keening!

It comes as a surprise to many to learn that in the late 1800s cricket was the most popular field sport in Ireland. However, the Gaelic revival saw the re-emergence of native games. By the 1930s, Gaelic games had been re-established as the sport of the masses. This was a source of some pride and relief to Sr Fionbharra, of the Mercy Convent in Roscommon, who oversaw the following essay from one of her students: 'There are many games played in Ireland to-day which are not Irish games such as cricket and rugby but still the majority are Irish and Ireland should be thankful she is not connected with England in graver matters. The two most famous of our Irish games are football for boys and camogie for girls.'

Like children's games, field games also had regional variations. Until the GAA was founded in 1884 and rules were standardised across the land, it was a case of 'house rules apply'. One informant, Denis Foley of Glounecomane Lower in County Cork, remembers hurling when local rules most definitely applied. If 'rules' isn't too big a word for it.

Denis tells us that men from Freemount used go up to Tullylease after Sunday Mass. Up to this point, it's the same as it ever was. However, the modern game and traditional ways meet a sharp fork on the road directly after Mass. Teams were typically 50-a-side. There was no referee, no sidelines or goalposts. Any stick with a twist at the bottom could be used as a hurley and a goal was scored by driving the horsehair-stuffed leather 'sliotar' over the opposing team's ditch. Denis also tells us that games could be six hours long and about twenty goals per side would be typical. There was no final whistle. However, he says, 'It was usual to have a good fight between the rival players for a finish.' We're back on track with the modern game here, as this tradition is still upheld from time to time!

In fairness to modern gaming, I've never heard of someone grazing a knee while on a console, but I am glad I took my chances at tig and the rough and tumble of the schoolyard.

The children of 1930s Ireland are waiting to tell us more.

'I'll race you to the gate ... ready ... steady ... go!'

Our special games

SCHOOL: *Loughros, Co. Leitrim*
TEACHER: *Stiofán Ó Braonáin*
COLLECTOR: *Rita McGuire, Kiltyclogher, Co. Leitrim, 16 years old*
INFORMANT: *mother, Kiltyclogher, Co. Leitrim*

Games are our special pastimes and for every season we have our different suitable games. During the Winter we have to remain indoors so that all we can play are house games. In Spring, Summer, and Autumn we play outside so our games are much more pleasant than those of the Winter. During these three seasons our games are much the same, and we play them in the open air. In the fields and woods and on the hillside.

Our special games during the year are card playing, blind man's buff, hide-and-go-seek, skipping lad, times, colours, tig, broken bridges, JUSTY-BLUE BELLS (there the same a gipsy riding), the ghost in the garden, Lord Luke, Lord John. We play cards and other games in the house, during the long Winter nights, or sit around the fire, listening to stories told by some old man of the neighbourhood.

During the Summer, we go around the ditches, gathering strawberries, and looking for birds' nests, and later on, in the Autumn, we go around the hedges, picking blackberries and pulling apples, currants and gooseberries. In the end of Autumn we go to the wood to pull nuts, and often when we would return home, we would spend the evening cracking them and throwing some in the fire, to see which nut would let the best shot. Then when the frost comes we go to pull sloes. And that ends our fruit for the year.

JUSTY-BLUE BELLS: *probably the playground song
and dance commonly known as Dusty Bluebells
or Dusting Bluebells.*

Games smarten up boys

SCHOOL: *Dean Kelly Memorial, Athlone, Co. Westmeath*
TEACHER: *D. Cahalene*

The games I play are mostly outdoor games. I prefer those games because when you play them you exercise yourself and that keeps you very healthy. When you play indoor games you do not exercise your muscles and you become delicate. The outdoor games I play are football, hurling, and handball. Games like those bring out the good qualities in a boy. I play those games on THE BATTERIES every evening with other boys.

There is no handball alley in Athlone and it is a shame to have boys playing handball on the streets and at the gable ends of houses.

When the winter comes the boys cannot play outdoor games so they play indoor. I play those myself. I play ludo, cards, draughts and some others. Games such as cards and draughts sharpen up the player's mind. I play very often and I like it very much. There are many games in cards, such as twenty five, fifteen, rummy, banker, and a lot of others.

Games smarten up boys and bring them more onto contact with one another and in this way introduce a good spirit amongst them.

> **THE BATTERIES:** *an open area on the outskirts of Athlone, which was once the site of gun emplacements and was later used as a public park.*

Girls have their own games

SCHOOL: *Easky, Co. Sligo*
TEACHER: *Seán Ó Tioralla*
COLLECTOR: *Betty Gillespie, Easky, Co. Sligo*

Boys and girls play different games at certain times of the year. Boys have their own amusements, such as football, hurling and tennis. In Autumn boys and girls go out picking blackberries, and in the Summer they go bathing. Girls have their own games also, such as hopscotch, skipping, hide and seek, my man Jack, Jackie show light and round the mulberry bush. In the Winter they sit around the fire and tell stories, they also play cards and crack nuts in the fire, and if the nuts jump out, you will be the first married in the house. I will tell you a story about a girl that was dying to get married, she put two nuts into the fire, and the nuts shot down through the house, and she got married soon after.

At wakes they play games too. I will tell you one, one fellow acts as a priest and he would marry another boy and girl, and they would have great fun at the sermon.

'All work and no joy'

SCHOOL: *An Clochar, Kilbarron, Co. Donegal*
TEACHER: *Mother Philomena*
COLLECTOR: *Sheila Mc Cauley, Lissahully, Ballyshannon, Co. Donegal*

When children get an interval at school they like to pass the time playing games. These games take their minds off their lessons, as the old proverb goes: 'All work and no joy makes Jack a dull boy.'

There are many different games which we play at recreation such as 'Ring of Roses', 'Fair Rose', 'The Grand old Duke of York', 'Old Rodgers' and 'The Farmer'.

There are certain times when special games are played. Now as the Springtime is with us, we enjoy ourselves skipping, playing handball, or playing tig.

In Summer time we play 'Fair Rose', 'The Farmer' and such like games that do not require much exertion.

In Autumn and Winter the games are rather alike. Boys and girls play marbles in these seasons. Boys play different games to girls. Some play top-spinning, others play marbles, while others play handball, conqueror, or chesnuts.

In the Winter season, when the wind is howling outside, we like to remain indoors. Some children play 'hide-and-seek', 'blind-man's-buff', while others pass the time around the fireside playing draughts, ludo, cards, snakes-and-ladders, dominoes, and hiking.

Boys pass the dreary Winter days making birds cages called 'claveens'. They set these to catch birds, which they release when they see them.

The game which I like best is 'The Grand Old Duke of York'. It is played as follows – a number of children gather together. Each takes a partner and they turn round half-face. On turn every pair acts as 'The Grand Old Duke of York'. The children all sing the old poem.

> The Grand old Duke of York,
> He had so many men,
> He marched them up to the top of the hill.
> And he marched them down again
> When they were up they were up,
> And when they were down they were down,
> And when they were only half-ways up,
> They were neither up nor down.

The children on each side then march in opposite directions, led by the first pair. Each pair in turn acts as 'The Grand old Duke of York' until the game is finished.

Making bird traps and rolling snow

SCHOOL: *Kilbrannish South, Bunclody, Co. Carlow*
TEACHER: *Cáit Nic an Ultaigh*
COLLECTOR: *Tom Foley, Craan, Co. Carlow*

The games that I play are football and picking blackberries. I play cards at night. The games that I like best are football and picking blackberries.

The games that are the hardest to be played are football, handball and playing cards. I crack chesnuts in the fire at night. I like playing games. The games I play on a snowy day in winter are putting a box standing up in the snow, and tie a cord to it, and put oats or crumbs of bread under it. When I see the bird eating the crumbs I pull the cord, and the box will fall on her and catch her.

The other games I play in Winter are making snow-men and rolling big rollers of snow. I play games mostly in Summer. I fish in Winter, and hunt rabbits. The games that are played mostly in Winter are making bird traps and rolling snow.

We all join together

SCHOOL: *Knockbeha, Feakle, Co. Clare*
TEACHER: *Pádraig Ó Maolruanaidh*
COLLECTOR: *Nancy Hoey*

There are many games played in this vicinity by the young folk at certain times of the year.

We play High Gates in Summer when the weather is fine; we all join together and then one of us run and another follows her around the school yard until she catches her.

We play Púca in Winter when the weather is cold. All of us join together in the porch then one of us put a PÚICÍN on her face. Then she tries to catch one of us.

Five people can only play Corners, four have corners and one in the middle called the fool. Then they change and the fool stands in the middle watching her chance. If she gets the corner the one put out is the fool.

We play Limping Tom in the Summer. We all join together then one of us go into the middle and another go around the ring. The one in the middle says, 'Who goes round my stony wall?' and the one outside says, 'No one but poor limping Tom.' 'Will you take any of my chicks?' 'No, only this little one.' Then we all run and one follows us, another saves us.

We also play Little Silly Saucer in Summer. We all join together and we sing a verse.

> Little silly saucer
> Sitting on the water,
> Turn to the east, turn to the west
> Turn to the girl you love best.

PÚICÍN: *a blindfold.*

'What drops on the floor comes in the door'

SCHOOL: *Ennis, Co. Clare*
TEACHER: *Proinnsias Ó Fionnmhacháin*
COLLECTOR: *Brendan Ryan, Clonroadmore, Ennis, Co. Clare*

There are many different kinds of games we play, both indoor and outdoor games. The outdoor games we play are marbles, conkers, hide and seek, tig, time, rounders, handball, catching birds in bird baskets, picking blackberries and nuts, and four corners, throwing stones, cricket. The indoor games we play are draughts, ludo, cards, finding the a in a book, racing games, and table tennis, and snap-apple.

When the players are playing cards, if one of the cards drops on the floor, the players say, 'What drops on the floor comes in the door.' The games we play at school are tig, handball, and gangs. When the chestnuts are ripe in Autumn, we go out the country and pick supplies of them. We then put them up until they are well seasoned. When then they are seasoned we put a hole in them with a nail. Then we put a piece of cord with a knot in the end of it through the hole. We have great sport trying to break the chestnut. One boy holds the chestnut while the other boy tries to break it. They got every second chance to hit it.

Rounders

Rounders can be played during any part of the year. It is played with an even number. Boys go out playing rounders every day after school. A number of boys gather in a field and they have an even number on each side. They then place four stones around in a circle. One of the boys stands in the centre of the circle. He fires the ball to the man in the goal, he strikes the ball to with the palm of his hand, after that he makes a run and if the boy fielding out catch the ball and strikes one of the stones, he is out. This game is very popular around the town of Ennis.

Hide and Seek

Two or more boys can play this game. Some boys go off hiding and other boys follow them. If the boys who follow are not back to den, and the other boys catch them, it counts five for every boy they catch.

Nuts

The time for picking nuts is August and we go picking them. The nuts are green and unripe when we pick them. We leave them out in the sun every day for about a month. Then they are seasoned. We eat many of them on NOVEMBER'S NIGHT. Hazel trees are very plentiful around Ennis.

Blackberries

When the blackberries are ripe we go out the country and we bring a tin-can with us and we fill it up with blackberries.

The House that Jack Built

This is played around the fire. You get a stick and you pass it around the fire. If they are not quick enough to answer your question they will be slapped.

NOVEMBER'S NIGHT: *Halloween.*

The games I play

SCHOOL: *Kilcullen, Co. Kildare*
TEACHER: *Na Siúracha*
COLLECTOR: *M. Byrne (female), Mary Walshe, Mona Christie*

Ghost in the Garden

A child is chosen to be the ghost and hides somewhere. Then the mother tells one of the children to go to the garden for something such as cabbage. The ghost intercepts them on their way. The child returns and says, 'There is a ghost in the garden.' The mother informs her that there is no such thing as a ghost, and sends another child. Each time the ghost comes out of her hiding place. At last the mother goes herself and sees the ghost. A conversation is held, the last words being 'Why do you want to sharpen your knife?' The ghost answers, 'To eat you up,' and gives chase, as the others run away.

Blind Man's Buff

One child is blindfolded and then swung around by some other girl. All who are playing go and hide and the blind man goes and looks for them. When passing by a hiding place, her frock would be pulled — the blind-man would then search that place in vain. Whenever she would catch anyone she would be made cry like a lamb, thus she would be able to discern her name, but if she would not she must remain blindfolded until she discovers one child's identity.

Match Man

A group of children stand in a circle. They are named Monday, Tuesday, etc. A girl called the mother, and another called the maid, stand before the children. The mother going out tells the maid to take care of the children.

A man comes in and asks for a match. The maid tells him to get it in the kitchen. He says, 'No, the dog is barking.' The maid goes down herself and while she is gone the man takes one of the children. When the mother comes back she finds one missing. The maid makes some silly excuses, as 'I was making a cake and Monday fell into it.' The game continues like this till all the children are gone. Then the mother looks for them, finds them and brings them back.

People's hands were harder than they are now

SCHOOL: *Sruth Nua, Ardnacally, Co. Mayo*
TEACHER: *Tomás de Brún*
COLLECTOR: *Bernard Niland, Newbrook, Ballyglass, Co. Mayo*
INFORMANT: *Patrick Niland, 64, Newbrook, Co. Mayo*

Long, long ago there was a game played at wakes called Slapping. A man would get up [and] put his hand behind his back with his palm outwards. Then he would challenge any man in the house for slapping. Then a man would get up and give him three slaps on the hand as hard as he could draw them.

Then they would change places and keep on like that every second time till one could give in. Sometimes before they would give in the blood would be streaming out of the tips of their fingers. That time people's hands were harder than they are now.

We spend hours cracking nuts

SCHOOL: *Clochar na Trócaire, Kinvarra, Co. Galway*
TEACHER: *Siúracha na Trócaire*
COLLECTOR: *Kathleen Fallon, Kinvarra, Co. Galway*

Games are played throughout every district in Ireland. There are numerous games which I play. I play different games for the different times of the year.

In Spring I play skipping, hide and seek and many other games. The games we play in Spring keep our feet very warm. In Summer the most common of our games is swimming, because it keeps us cool. We also play tennis in the evening, because the evening is the coolest time for tennis and because it is a very warm game. On Sundays we hardly ever play games; we either go for a long walk or if the Sunday happens to be calm we go for a cycle.

Autumn is the time that children play the most games. The games we like best in Autumn are nut-picking, berry-picking and apple-picking. We spend hours cracking nuts and eating them. The part we like best about apple-picking is climbing up the trees to get the apples and when we come down we see which of us has gathered the most apples.

Another game we play most time of the year is the 'hop scotch'. When we are playing that game we first draw a square. Then we draw smaller squares inside the big square and then we mark off the square in consecutive numbers starting from the number one. Then one of us gets a stone and throws it into one of the squares. Then one hops into the square on one foot. If her foot touches one of the lines in the square she is out of the game.

In Winter we play hardly any games as the weather is too cold and wet to go out. We sit round the fire and tell stories. We sometimes play ludo and cards, draughts and snakes and ladders. When the snow falls we make snow-men. That is one of the games we like best in Winter. We also like sliding and skating.

The noisier the game the merrier it is

SCHOOL: *Clochar na Trócaire, Roscommon, Co. Roscommon*
TEACHER: *An tSr. M. Fionnbharra*

There are many games played in Ireland to-day which are not Irish games such as cricket and rugby but still the majority are Irish and Ireland should be thankful she is not connected with England in graver matters. The two most famous of our Irish games are football for boys and camogie for girls.

Children's games, of which there are many, are most enjoyable. The famous outdoor games of the children are Highgates, Dan Dan tread the needle, Tig, Colours, Corners and skipping. The famous indoor games are draughts, snakes and ladders, Ludo, Musical chairs, Musical oranges, Jackstones and Hide the Button. Musical Chairs and Hide the button are a bit noisy but the children think the noisier the game the merrier it is.

There are some games which some people would call customs which are played at Christmas and on Hallow E'en. The day after Christmas Day the little boys all dress up as wren boys and go around the roads with a money box, gathering money. They look upon it as the game of the year. On Hallow E'en the children duck for apples and consider it great fun. They also tie an apple to the ceiling and try to bite it and it swinging round the room.

All children love games and certainly agree with the old proverb 'All work and no play makes Jack a dull boy.'

The stronger side wins

SCHOOL: *Carrowcrin, Co. Roscommon*

TEACHER: *Mrs. Devine*

We play different games at home and at school. The games we play at school are Ring a Ring of Roses, my Lord Luke and my Lord John, Sally Sally Walker, Bull in the Ring and Cat and mouse. The games we play at home are Tick, Hide and Seek, Frog in the well, Frog leap and Fox and Geese. The games we play inside are Púcóg, Button, and Horth.

We play certain games at school as we could not play them at home because we want a lot of children to play them. This is how we play my Lord Luke and my Lord John. All children catch hands and two children go away and get the names of two different things and then they hold up their hands, and all the other children pass under their hands, and the last child is asked which thing would she like, and she stands behind the child who had chosen that thing. Then when they are [divided] up into two companions they catch hands and pull and the stronger side wins.

This is how we play Bull in the Ring. All children join up in a ring and one goes in to the middle of it and if she gets out all the others run after her. Whoever catches her will be the bull the next time.

This is how we play Frog in the well. There is one child who is called the frog, and the other is called the old mother. All the children go to the mother and show her their hands, and she tells them to go to the well and wash their hands. They go to the well and when they reach the well, the child that is called the frog jumps out at them. Then all the children come back to the old mother and tell her there is a frog in the well. Then she goes to the well and asks the frog what she wants and she tells her what she wants. Then the old frog runs after the children and catches them.

This is how we play Sally, Sally, Walker. All the children join up in a ring and one child goes into the ring, and all the other children say these words.

Sally, Sally, Walker, land and sea,
rise up Sally and choose to thee,
choose to the east, and choose to the west,
and choose to the very one you love best.

Then the child that is in the middle of the ring takes in whoever she likes best. Then all the children say other words and skip around them and then the first child goes back to her place in the ring, and the other child in and the game is played all over again.

We play different games inside to what we play outside. It is Púcóg. One child gets a cloth and puts it over her eyes in order that she will not see and tries to catch the other children and who-ever she catches three times will be the Púcóg the next time.

In the Springtime we go looking for birds' nests and in the Autumn we go nut-cracking and black-berry picking. In the Winter we amuse ourselves while sitting around the fire telling old stories and giving out riddles and the others trying to answer them.

Boys play different games to girls. In the Winter boys make bird-traps with sticks, for catching birds, and they catch a lot of birds during the frost and snow.

A great number of rhymes

SCHOOL: *Dennbane, Co. Cavan*
TEACHER: *T. Ó Cionnaigh*
COLLECTOR: *Veronica Galligan, Denbawn, Carrickaboy, Co. Cavan*

I am a schoolgirl and I play a great number of games every day.

We say a great number of rhymes while we are playing these games. When we are playing 'Around the green gravel the grass grows green', all the children join hands and go round in a ring. While they are doing so they say

> Around the green gravel the grass grows green,
> many a lady was fit to be seen,
> washed with milk and dried with silk.

The last pops down, and whoever is last popping down has to go into the middle.

Maeve of the golden hair
This is the way we play Maeve of the golden hair. A crowd of children sit in a row and one child gives them colours. Another child comes and raps at another one's back and the both talk in this way. 'Who is there?' 'Maeve of the golden hair.' 'What do you want?' 'Colours.' 'What colour?' 'Black', and whatever child has black has to become Maeve of the golden hair.

Heaven and hell
This is the way we play Heaven and hell. All the children stand in a row and take names of birds. Then two of them stand opposite each other, one the Angel and the other the devil. The Angel then calls out some bird and the Angel and devil follow it and if the Angel catches it, it is in heaven, and if the devil catches it, is in hell, and if it is not caught it is in Purgatory. The children who are in Heaven go round the Angel saying, 'Here is the good Angel that brought us to Heaven.'

See this pretty little girl of mine
The way we play 'See this pretty little girl of mine' is as follows. A group of

children catch hands and go round in a circle with one in the middle and say the following rhyme:

> See this pretty little girl of mine,
> she brought me many's the bottle of wine,
> a bottle of wine she brought me too
> and see what my little girl can do.
> Down on the carpet she must [kneel]
> where the grass grows green upon your feet
> so stand up right upon your feet
> and point to the very one you like best.

Then the person in the middle takes in the one he likes best. Then the rest of them say,

> Now there is a couple and many to enjoy,
> first to a girl and second to a boy,
> seven years after and seven years ago,
> kiss one class and kiss no more.

Broken Bridges

The way broken bridges is played is as follows. Two girls catch hands and hold them up. Then the rest go under their hands saying,

> Here is the robbers passing by, passing by, passing by.
> Here is the robbers passing by, Y.O.U.
> What did the robbers do to you, do to you, do to you.
> What did the robbers do to you, Y.O.U.
> They stole my golden watch and chain, watch and chain,
>   watch and chain.
> They stole my golden watch and chain, Y.O.U.
> Chip, Chop, Cherry, last man's head cut off.

This rhyme is continued until every head is cut off. Then the game is ended with tug-o-war.

Dirty Coat, Clean Coat.

The way to play this game is as follows. A crowd of children stand in a row and one goes round from person to person, saying, 'Dirty coat, clean coat.' When she has finished she throws the grass at some other girl and that girl has to follow her.

My love Juke and my love John

The way to play this game is as follows. A group of girls catch [each] other by the waist one after the other and they say while doing so, 'My love Juke and my love John, let them all pass by but the very last one.' Then the other two girls plan and choose, one an apple and the other an orange. Then the other children pass out under their hands. Then the two girls ask the last one which is it an apple or an orange she would prefer. If she prefers an apple she goes behind one girl and if she prefers an orange she goes behind the other girl's back. This game is finished with tug-o-war.

The men were so strong they did not notice the hard knocks

SCHOOL: *Knocktemple, Freemount, Co. Cork*
TEACHER: *Bean an Bhreathnaigh*
COLLECTOR: *Hannah Ó Donoghue, Ballybahallow, Co. Cork*
INFORMANT: *Denis Foley, Glounecomane Lower, Co. Cork*

In former times, 'SCUAIBÍN' was played, and twenty-one men were on each side. The hurlies they used long ago were every kind of a stick with a turn in it.

The balls were made of thread and sewn with horse hair. Hurling was played between two parishes in olden times. The ball was thrown up centreways and whichever side would hurl the ball into their own parish would win the day. Hurling and football matches were played locally between two districts.

The big games were played between parishes. The winner of the games were whoever kept the ball in their own parish. The ball was put in the bounds ditch between two parishes. The ball was made of horse's hair by the people themselves.

Handball was also played. There was an alley in which the handball was played in Freemount. There was also jumping, weight-throwing, and lifting weights carried on in the district.

Hurling matches used to be played in Tullylease long ago. The men of Freemount used go up to Tullylease on some Sundays after mass. They used have about fifty men. When they arrived a big field was usually selected. There used be about fifty of the Tullylease men also. Two men were first selected from each side as leaders. They then tossed for first call and the man who won the toss called the best man in his side and the other man called the best in his side and so on until all the men were called. The ball was then [thrown] up in the middle of the field between the men. The ball was about sixteen inches in circumference. There used to be no referee or no goal-posts or no side-line, but when the ball went out over one of the fences on either side of the field it was counted as a goal. They kept playing until it was time to go home. They used be about six hours playing and there used be a score of about twenty goals at each side. This method was very rough and it was a terrible struggle to get the ball across a fence. The men were so strong they did not notice hard knocks and it was usual to have a good fight between the rival players for a finish.

SCUAIBÍN: *literally 'little brush', also an early form of hurling.*

10

FOLK MEDICINE

'When we're stuck, most of us are glad to reach for science, superstition or faith, and to this day healthcare is still a blend of conventional medicine and alternative or complementary medicines. The Schools' Collection provides further evidence that wellness in Ireland has long been a heady potion of miraculous medals, doctors, healers, folk cures, holy wells, pilgrimages and, if all else fails, a rub of the relic and a flat 7Up.'

MAN WITH A TWINKLE in his eye once gave me a cure for influenza. He said, 'Drink one glass of whiskey, followed by one glass of water. Turn your backside to the fire and when the water boils inside you, you'll be cured.' It hasn't worked yet.

When we're stuck, most of us are glad to reach for science, superstition or faith, and to this day healthcare is still a blend of conventional medicine and alternative or complementary medicines. The Schools' Collection provides further evidence that wellness in Ireland has long been a heady potion of miraculous medals, doctors, healers, folk cures, holy wells, pilgrimages and, if all else fails, a rub of the relic and a flat 7Up.

Traditionally, each healer had a specific area of expertise and the cast of characters included bone-setters, blood-letters, 'the man with the medal' and 'an bean feasa', meaning 'woman of knowledge', who was variously credited with powers of prophecy, second-sight and healing.

A healing 'gift' was closely guarded and would only be revealed to the healer's understudy, usually a family member of the opposite gender. So quite often the healing power would pass from mother to son and then to his daughter and so on. Out of modesty and respect for their special power, many healers would display a reluctance to offer a cure at first asking. Payment was rarely sought, but a hansel, meaning a gift, of tea, potatoes, porter or whiskey was generally welcomed.

I grew up in a time when manufacturers were not obliged to put the contents on the label, so many folk medicines involved a degree of 'faith healing'. My father swore by 'The Fermoy Bottle' for relief from his duodenal ulcer. 'Arthur Mayne's Preparations' and 'Mrs. Cullen's Powders' were also very highly regarded in our house. Indeed, to this day, most dispensing chemists disappear backstage to prepare your prescription. It sometimes reminds me of the Great Oz slipping behind the curtain to work his magic.

I had an ongoing stomach complaint for years. I tried mainstream medicine, went for tests, tried a herbalist and an acupuncturist, all without relief. Eventually I tried 'a woman with the gift' in south County Dublin. She cured me. I know, many cynics will snigger, but while laughter is often described as 'the best medicine', I'm not sure sniggering is good for anything.

James Meaney, Creevagh More, County Clare, relates some great tales about the best known bean feasa of them all, Biddy Early. For example, a man who named his two racehorses after Biddy and her husband, Tom Flannery, certainly got his comeuppance and, as you'll discover, Biddy had the last laugh. It's also said that one of Biddy's husbands became an alcoholic on account of all the free gargle left at the house by grateful clients.

The struggle between Christian and pre-Christian ways took centuries to settle. Ultimately a compromise evolved, but it was an uneasy peace betimes. From Naas, County Kildare, we hear of a tense stand-off between the legendary *bean feasa* Moll Anthony and the new parish priest. Once Moll's prowess was well and truly established a truce was called and the two streams of faith co-existed, free to practise without hindrance to one another. It's not unlike the improving relationship between conventional and complementary medicine.

In County Monaghan we encounter a popular cure for sprains that includes a charm, or incantation. It was believed the cure originated when Jesus Christ dismounted from his injured donkey and reset the animal's bone while uttering this charm. The same cure is also found, written in High Old German, in a ninth-century book at the church in Merseburg. In this case, the cure is associated with the Norse deities Wodan and Freya.

Holy wells were a great source of cures. As a small lad, I witnessed throngs 'doing the rounds' at Saint Gobnait's Well in Baile Bhúirne/Ballyvourney on the saint's feast day, 11 February. The amount of prayer ribbons, discarded crutches, walking sticks and reading glasses suggested that Gobnait had the gift. Rather than revealing the whole thing as an elaborate hoax, modern research actually suggests there's more than a grain of truth to these claims.

Luke O'Neill, Professor of Biochemistry at Trinity College Dublin, accompanied me on a recent expedition to test the theory for my television series *Creedon's Atlas of Ireland*. We headed for Ballinspittle, near Kinsale in County Cork. Apart from numerous reported sightings of the Blessed Virgin at the Marian shrine there, the area has a centuries-old reputation for natural healing. The clue is in the place name, *Béal Átha an Spidéil*, meaning 'mouth of the river of the hospital'. The hospital referred to was most likely a simple place of isolation, the only safeguard against infectious diseases before the discovery of penicillin.

So, what of any curative properties in the holy wells that dot the area? Well, Professor Luke took samples from the wells and, sure enough, one of them showed a high incidence of copper, thought to boost the immune system. The other, a chalybeate well, meaning it has naturally occurring iron salts, is a likely aid against anaemia and fatigue. Similarly, taking the waters where the sulphur content is high has long been considered beneficial for those with skin or respiratory problems.

But how did our ancestors know there was a cure in the water? They simply used their powers of observation. You don't have to wear a white coat to notice, over time, that your cattle thrive on one water source over another. Similarly, Luke pointed out that the water from one well might be seen to improve skin ailments more than another. Elementary, if you pardon the pun.

Science has also validated many old herbal cures. Plants like dock leaves, carrageen moss, kelp, garlic, sage are all now tried and tested aids to good health.

Other cures in the Collection are a little more unusual. Mrs Susan Rynn of County Leitrim testifies that she herself was cured of a fever by having her head examined by a certain Miss Brigid Darcy. I used think my uncle was only messing every time he said, 'You should have your head examined.' I didn't realise that there were healers who would actually measure the dimensions of your noggin until I read Mrs Rynn's testimony.

Schoolboys' cures for warts? I knew 'em all, but there's one here that I had almost forgotten. It involves finding a black snail or slug and rubbing it vigorously against the wart. Then you impale the snail on a large thorn. There's no evidence that it works, but you are guaranteed to feel better than the snail.

There are numerous old remedies in this collection where the cure seems worse than the complaint. For example, a poultice of ashes and cow dung was often applied to a sore. From Tipperary, we have a cure for the common cold. You simply boil a mouse in milk and drink the milk. In Cork, for measles, you boil sheep's droppings in milk and drink it. There are other cures here to rid you of invasive parasites, including earwigs and worms. For a particularly stubborn lizard in the stomach, the patient is held, mouth agape, over a frying pan full of food in an attempt to have the hungry lizard exit through the mouth.

Read on, but please ... do not try this at home!

From father to son

SCHOOL: *Faha West, Co. Kerry*
TEACHER: *Seán Ó Muircheartaigh*
INFORMANT: *Eugene Moriarty, died 1927 aged 67*

Sixty or seventy years ago 'quack' doctors for special diseases were very common in Co. Kerry. The people believed that each 'doctor' had a charm for his own special disease, and what strengthened this belief was the fact that the ingredients used in the cure were kept an absolute secret by the curers. The cure was supposed to be kept in the family and was transferred from father to son. When there was no male issue the cure died out.

These curers were not confined to human beings: cattle and horses were also cured by animal 'doctors' but these were much more common than the others.

People often travelled 15 or 20 miles to get cured of 'running' sores, skin diseases, eczema etc. etc.

A man named Crowley lived in the parish of Tuogh on the left bank of the Laune, almost opposite Ballymalis Castle, and he was a bone setter. He was an ordinary farmer with little or no education. His father, grandfather and great-grandfather were bone setters. He died about 15 years ago and left only two daughters — and so people believe his 'power' died with him.

No one for miles and miles' radius would dream of going to a qualified doctor with a broken limb while he was alive, and he had often to break and reset a limb fixed up by a qualified doctor. He never failed to set a broken bone properly.

He never took money — that was considered unlucky — but he would not object to half pint of whiskey or a small present — not money.

The power of curing

SCHOOL: *Donabate, Co. Dublin*
TEACHER: *Bean Mhic Alasdair*

The most famous 'curers' in the district were the Barnes family and one person in each generation held the gift. It was passed on from parent to child. The present holder, Mr James Barnes, does not make use of his gift and has to be coaxed to perform a cure. Yet many cures are attributed to him, especially diseases of the skin. Herbs he uses but never tells what they are.

His mother, though, was famous. People came from far and near to have their ailments cured and 'tis said she never failed. She, too, used herbs from which she made ointment given to the sufferer. If one person had a complaint, a loan of 'Mrs Barnes' ointment' from another was a sure cure, or a drink from a bottle mixed by her.

The present holder has no descendants (children of his own) and we often wonder who will be the lucky one after him.

It is firmly believed in this district that a woman marrying a man with the same name gets the power of curing. Consequently Mrs O'Callaghan, who lives in Portrane Demesne and was formerly Miss O'Callaghan, is credited with the gift. At any rate she is famous as a curer of whooping cough. The treatment consists of a mixture of jam and sugar administered by her and is thought to be infallible. I never heard that she cured anything but whooping cough. Many people, however, put more faith in 'CHINK WELL WATER'.

CHINK WELL WATER: *water from a holy well believed to cure whooping cough, which was also known as chin-cough or chink-cough, from Low German kinkhoost.*

If they believed in it they would be cured

SCHOOL: *Clash, Co. Tipperary*
TEACHER: *Cristíona Ní Chearbhalláin*

There was a well near Cloughjordan. It was a saint's well. The saint's name was St Catherine. It was said that if anyone who had sore eyes would go to the well three mornings and washed their eyes with the water, they would be cured. Anyone who had ringworm would be cured if they went three times to the well and drank the water. Anyone who had sore legs would be cured if they fasted for three days and went to the well the third day and drank some water. It is in Mr. Kennedy's field.

There is a well in Woodville; it is in Mr. Mackey's grove. It was called St Veronica's Well. Anyone who had the flu were cured if they went to the well three mornings and drank the water.

There is a holy well in Latteragh. The name of the well in Latteragh is St Odran's Well. People go there to be cured of sore eyes. There is a bush near the well in Latteragh.

There is a holy well in Latteragh in Reidy's field in the parish of Templederry. It was belonging to a saint. People go there on the 15th of August in honour of the saint. If there was anything wrong with them and if they believed in it they would be cured. They would leave a medal or a holy picture or a cross or something belonging to them in thanksgiving for being cured.

At Lisineska Cross there is a holy well and it was flowing from the trunk of a tree. It used to cure sore eyes. People used not eat any meat for a while before they would go and they would pray and rub the water to their eyes and used to be cured. They used to go there 29th of June.

It is counted unlucky to use the water out of holy wells for household work. People only drink it when they want to be cured. The holy well that is in Hodgins' of Barnagrotty in the parish of Toomevara, there is a tree over it. There are ribbons on the tree and whatever they would be leaving at the well they would leave it on the tree.

A wise woman who lived at the Red Hills

SCHOOL: *Derrinturn, Carbury, Co. Kildare*
TEACHER: *Bean Uí Mhistéil*

Many people from this district used to go to Moll Anthony, a wise woman who lived at the Red Hills — beside the Hill of Allen — for cures for persons and animals. Moll Anthony's full name was Moll Dunne. Her father's name was Anthony Dunne and to distinguish her from other Dunnes she was called Moll Anthony.

Moll Anthony died during the last century but she gave the cures to her sons, and some of these cures are in the family still, and the power to use them are given to a man and woman every second time. Mr Kennedy has the cures at present.

Moll Anthony was looked upon by most people as a kind of witch. Sometimes to cure cattle she made up two bottles of medicine and one of these had to be broken and the other given to the sick animals.

People came from all parts of Ireland to her and the name 'Moll Anthony' is well known in all parts of Leinster.

Herbs had the best cure of all the remedies

SCHOOL: *Port Laoise, Co. Laois*
TEACHER: *Sr. Treasa*
COLLECTOR: *Bridie Byrne, Clonkeen, Port Laoise, Co. Laois*
INFORMANT: *Mrs. Byrne, Clonkeen, Port Laoise, Co. Laois*

The old people believed in their own remedies for diseases, but they said that herbs had the best cure of all the remedies that could be found. Moll Anthony, who lived in the Red Hills in Cullenagh, was supposed to have great healing powers. The old folks believed in her healing of cattle; thousands went to her for remedies. To some she gave a bottle of medicine made by herself from herbs, and she ordered the person not to speak a word to anyone on the way home, and that while the medicine was being given to the animal if a drop was spilt the cure would be useless.

The cure for rheumatism was this: to get a nettle and sting yourself all over with it. This was supposed to kill the pain. To get a dandelion and boil it and then eat it was supposed to be a good cure for consumption.

The strange occurrences

SCHOOL: *Mercy Convent, Naas, Co. Kildare*
TEACHER: *Na Siúracha*
COLLECTOR: *Kathleen Coffey, Naas, Co. Kildare*
INFORMANT: *Mr. Robert Seargent, Kilcullen Road, Naas, Co. Kildare*

Moll Anthony was a witch doctor who lived in Allen about 30 years ago. She used various herbs to effect cures, but it is said that she was also in communication with the devil. She often cast charms and spells over those whom she considered her enemies, or over those who injured her in any way, either by word or deed.

Once a new Parish Priest came to Allen and soon after his arrival he denounced Moll from the pulpit, on a certain Sunday during Mass. When he returned to his home he found his beautiful horse on the point of death. Needless to say he was startled, as the horse had been in the best of health less than an hour before. The neighbours of course gathered round, and were able to explain the strange occurrences. Knowing that the priest was abusing Moll, they advised him to go to her and make friends with her. He tried every available cure, he sent for a vet surgeon, but he could not [diagnose] the disease. One thing was certain, however: that the horse was dying.

At length the parishioners succeeded in getting him to go to Moll. She received him rather coldly at first, but in the end she said, 'Your horse is cured. Go home, and in future let me alone, and I will leave you in peace.'

The priest returned to his home to find his valuable animal galloping backwards and forward through the field quite normal and fully restored to health.

The power of the devil

SCHOOL: *Dangan, Quin, Co. Clare*
TEACHER: *Stiófan Mac Clúin, Treasa Ní Chonmara*
COLLECTOR: *Mary O'Loughlin*
INFORMANT: *James Meaney, Creevagh, Quin, Co. Clare*

Biddy Early was a witch who lived in Feakle long ago. She had a magic bottle, which she looked into before she gave a cure to anyone who went to her. It is said that she got this bottle from her son, who appeared to her after his death. He told her to look into the bottle before she gave a cure to anyone.

The priests were against her because her cures were worked by the power of the devil. Any person who got a cure from her had great trouble in bringing it home. The devil always tried to make them break the bottle. When the cure was given to the sick person or animal, the bottle in which it was used to be broken and buried. The priest threw Biddy Early's bottle into a lake which was near the place where she lived. She died a Catholic.

She was married to a man named Tom Flannery. A certain man had two racehorses and he called one of them Biddy Early and the other Tom Flannery. Biddy told the man if he didn't call the horses two other names they would never win a race.

A man of the parish of Quin went to Biddy Early for a cure for his cattle. She told him to be very careful of the bottle which she gave him on a certain part of the road. When he came to that place the horse fell and the bottle got broken.

A woman named Mrs Lyons was going out the back-door of her house one morning and she slipped and broke her leg. Her husband went to Biddy Early and she told him not to open that door anymore because the fairies used to go in and out there.

Bone to bone and sinew to sinew in God's own name

SCHOOL: *Carrickatee, Co. Monaghan*
TEACHER: *Éamonn Ó Dubhthaigh*
COLLECTOR: *Mollie McMahon, Gragernagh, Co. Monaghan*
INFORMANT: *Mrs. Mohan, Tullynamaloe, Co. Monaghan*

When a person got any joint sprained he went for the cure to a person who had the cure of the sprain. This person made the sign of the Cross on the sprained part. He then said these words: 'As Our Saviour was crossing Calvary Hill His ass's foot he sprained. He alighted and He SINDED it and mended it in God's own name. Bone to bone and sinew to sinew in God's own name.' He rubbed the affected part while saying these words. He repeated this three times on the one occasion and on three successive days. When this was done the cure was complete.

SINDED: *washed.*

A very good quack doctor

SCHOOL: *Tibohine, Co. Roscommon*
TEACHER: *Úna Ní Thiomáin*
COLLECTOR: *Bernadette Mahon, Ratra, Frenchpark, Co. Roscommon*
INFORMANT: *Thomas Mahon, father, 63, farmer, Ratra, Frenchpark, Co. Roscommon*

There was once a man named Walter Sherlock. He lived at Cloonmagunane in the parish of Breedogue and he was a healthy hard-working farmer aged about 45 years. He had a fair good appetite but some how his health began to decline. He took little notice of it at first for a month or two, but this day when he came into his dinner he felt a little the worse. He was keeping the matter back from his wife Molly, not liking to discourage the poor woman, for she was not too good herself. He knew it would be the last news poor Molly would like to hear. But at long last he up and told her he was feeling bad, that after his meals he always felt worse and felt something stirring about in his stomach.

'Walter A STÓIR, I was thinking of late there was something wrong with you,' said she. 'You should dress yourself up tomorrow and go and see Doctor Dillion. Séamus over there will be going to Ballagh for meat for the BONHAMS and you can be with him on the cart.'

'I might as well,' said Walter, 'and see the matter out.'

Walter got up early in the morning, joined James and jogged along. Lucky enough the dispensary was opened and Walter was one of the first Dr. Dillion attended. He was known to be the best medical doctor in the West of Ireland. He examined Walter but was a kind of puzzled. He found his heart and lungs quite sound and he gave him some medicine and told him take a spoonful 3 times a day and to eat plenty of stirabout. After a few days poor Walter got worse. Neither the porridge nor the medicine agreed with him.

He tried another doctor and found no relief coming to him and he was growing weaker from day to day. However, this night himself and Molly were sitting around the fire lamenting that he would never be able to dig the potatoes. Molly, to give him courage, said, 'I'll speak to the lads of the village. They will be coming home from England soon and they will root them out for you a while of a day just for sport,' when suddenly they heard a step at the door. Molly got up and pushed back the bolt. Martin Brennen, their neighbour, walked in.

'Welcome, Martin,' said Walter.

'What's up with you, old man?' said Martin. 'Séamus over there was telling me you were in town to-day with the doctor.'

'Well, Martin,' said Walter, 'I can't tell, though I don't feel well for the past two months. Looking back, I think I never was the same man since the night of Nancy Giblin's wake, R.I.P.'

'Would you guess who came home for the shooting season? Who but Count Mac Dermot, and they say he is a very good quack doctor, and if I were in your shoes I'd go and tell him how I feel. He dines with expert doctors over in London, notwithstanding he is only a quack himself.'

'That's true,' said Molly, 'see how he cured old Jim Rogers of the rheumatic by putting two hot pitch plasters to the soles of his feet.'

So he prevailed on Walter to pay the Count a visit.

Lucky for him Mac Dermot was just at dinner when Walter arrived. He questioned him about how he felt and how long he was ailing. Walter explained as well as he could and told him he used to feel as though there was something stirring about in his stomach and he always felt as though he would like to vomit.

The Count asked him if he ever slept out in a swampy place and if he had any intoxicating drink at the time. So Walter remembered Nancy's wake and told him he fell asleep down near a bog hole the day after the wake, and that he had a couple glasses of poteen taken. He was scattering turf and sat down to smoke and never felt until he was fast asleep.

'I have you now,' said the Count. 'It's a frog that crept into your mouth while you were sleeping and it was the smell of the poteen that attracted him. Go,' said the Count, 'to the cook, and tell her go to the larder and cut about two pounds of that corned beef and throw it on the griddle.'

When it was partly done the cook put it on a plate, got a knife and fork, and the Count pressed Walter to eat every bit of it. It took him a long time. After he had eaten he was obliged to sit still for about 2 hours. Then the Count asked him was he getting thirsty and Walter told him he was fairly burned with thirst.

The Count asked him down to the lake for a walk and that he could drink plenty. After about half an hour, when they got to the lake, Walter was made lie down on his stomach and let his head hang down in over the water so close that his tongue could touch it. The Count told him to keep his mouth open as wide as ever he could and to lie very still. After a while Walter thought he felt something creeping up his throat, and what should it be but the frog, and nine young ones followed her and jumped into the lake. Poor Walter was very grateful and the Count cautioned if ever he drank poteen again not to fall asleep near a bog hole.

A STÓIR: *darling, love.*
BONHAMS: *piglets.*

An overdose of stout

SCHOOL: *Ballycar, Quin, Co. Clare*
TEACHER: *Liam Mac Clúin*
INFORMANT: *Miss Eliza Carrigg, 30, Kilrush, Co. Clare*

Tom O'Dea was an indifferent character. He was an ex-soldier, and religiously spent his pension on drink. He was a hard drinker, and Tom on more than one occasion slept by the roadside, being too drunk to continue home. Tom always slept with his mouth open, as some passages in his nostrils were stopped.

On one occasion, after sleeping on the roadside, he felt himself oppressed by a great longing for food. Tom had a voracious appetite and although he ate sufficient he did not seem to satisfy the longing. An hour or so after eating, the overwhelming hunger seized him again although he ate sufficient he was not fully satisfied. Thus Tom lived, eating voraciously whenever he could, but still not able to drive away the hunger pang. He became thoroughly alarmed, and consulted doctors, but their cures seemed only to increase the overpowering hunger.

At last Tom began to despair, and began to seek relief in excessive drinking. On one occasion he took an overdose of stout, and became extremely ill. He commenced to vomit, and continued to vomit periodically, until he vomited a very large lizard. Although he remained ill for a long time afterwards, he is now hale and hearty, and is as fond of the drink as ever, for, says he, ''Twas the drink that fooled me, and 'twas the drink that cured me.'

Dock dock, cure me

SCHOOL: *The Glen, Co. Sligo*
TEACHER: *Proinnsias Ó Ciaráin*
COLLECTOR: *Enda Horan, male, Drumacool, Boyle, Co. Sligo*
INFORMANT: *Mrs. Mc Keon, 70, Drumacool, Boyle, Co. Sligo*

The BUACHALÁN is a yellow weed which grows about one and a half feet high and spreads rapidly over good pasture land. This weed prevents cattle from grazing comfortably on land over which it spreads. The Thistle is a very plentiful weed which grows on pasture and meadow land. It grows about the same height as the Buachalán, is very thorny, and makes it uncomfortable for cattle to lie on land over which it spreads. The dock is a leafy green-coloured weed which does not grow high but spreads and has a terrible root which makes land hard tilled. When young boys and girls get a nettle burn, the old people send them for the leaf of a dock, which when got is put on the burnt spot, saying, 'Dock dock, cure me, nettle nettle burnt me,' and that cools the sting of the burn.

The SLÁNLESS is a weed which was used by the old people as a cure for dangerous cuts. My Grandmother told me that she often saw her mother, when anybody in the house got a nasty cut, run out and get some of the Slánless, which she washed in soft water, chomped it up with a hatchet, mixed it up with butter and clapped it on the sore like a poultice to draw the badness out of it.

Other weeds are the GÁRAWÓG, which grows in potato gardens, the FÚRÁN grows in cabbage gardens, the Chicken weed and the FORABAWN weed grow on the roadsides on the ditches and old walls.

Old people used in times gone by the Nettle as a herb: they cut nettles, boiled them and took them for their dinners like how we take the cabbage.

TRÚACH PÁDHRAIG, as the old people call Saint Patrick's Leaf, was used and is still used by some people as a cure for healing sores. The MALE FERN was also used as an herb for cattle.

BUACHALÁN: *ragweed or ragwort.*
SLÁNLESS: *slánlus, ribwort plantain.*
GÁRAWÓG: *this could be garbhóg gharraí, summer savory,*
or garbhógach, clubmoss.
FÚRÁN: *cow-parsley*
FORABAWN: *probably fearbán, buttercup.*
TRÚACH PÁDHRAIG: *probably Cuach Phádraig, greater plantain.*
MALE FERN: *a type of fern,* Dryopteris filix-mas.

These old cures

SCHOOL: *Newtownanner, Clonmel, Co. Tipperary*
TEACHER: *Proinnsias Ó Corcoráin*
COLLECTOR: *Maris Doyle, Clonmel, Co. Tipperary*
INFORMANT: *Mrs. Doyle, mother, Clonmel, Co. Tipperary*

My mother, Mrs Doyle, told me these old cures.

To use the water that the blacksmith cooled his irons in is supposed to be a cure for warts. A cure for measles is to meet a man with a white horse and ask him about it; whatever he says will cure it. There is a cure for whooping cough; it is to swing the person three times under an ass's stomach. Then there is a cure for a cold. It is to catch a mouse and boil it in milk. Then the person would drink the milk and it would cure the cold. There is a cure for a sore. It is to make a mixture of cow-dung and ashes, to rub it to the sore and it would cure it. They do this still in the west of Ireland.

A lot of local cures

SCHOOL: *Ballinakilla, Bere Island, Co. Cork*
TEACHER: *Donncha Ó Longaigh*
COLLECTOR: *Margaret P. Sullivan, Derrycreeveen, Co. Cork*
INFORMANT: *parent, Derrycreeveen, Co. Cork*

There are a lot of local cures for various diseases. The people in olden times never bought any cures. It is said that a dock leaf cures the sting of a nettle. The whites of eggs and turpentine and sugar of lead mixed will cure rheumatism. If you soaked seaweeds in water and keep it airtight, after a while the water will be like iodine and it will cure sores. The MEACAN AN TÁTHABHA that is found growing in the ground, if boiled, would cure boils. Boiled CARRIGEEN MOSS is very good for a person who would have the flu. Long ago the people used pick the yellow flowers off the furze and put them in a bottle with about a teaspoonful of whiskey and kept them airtight, and then gave them to the people when they would have pneumonia. The cure for a burn is to rub bread-soda to it and also soap. Long ago the people used gather sheep's droppings and boil them with milk and then give the milk to people who would have the measles.

MEACAN AN TÁTHABHA: *translated in different sources as root of hellebore, great common burdock, ragwort, or water hemlock.*
CARRIGEEN MOSS: *two types of seaweed,* Chondrus crispus *and* Mastocarpus stellatus, *share this name.*

I know some cures for ailments

SCHOOL: *Baile Mhodáin, Bandon, Co. Cork*
TEACHER: *Tomás Groves*
COLLECTOR: *Fred Wolfe, Kilbrogan, Bandon, Co. Cork*

In this world of ours, we suffer many diseases, very few of which are incurable. Of course, when we are affected by these diseases, our only wish is to be cured immediately if possible.

I know some cures for ailments. This is a sure remedy for chilblains. Mix together equal quantities of olive oil and turpentine and rub into chilblains twice or more daily. To heal a wart, get a lemon and cut it into little pieces. Rub the wart with one of the pieces, then throw the used piece of lemon away. Never use the same piece twice; repeat this frequently during the day, allowing the juice to dry on. Dandruff may be cured by rubbing lemon juice into the roots of the hair. When stung by a wasp, rub the affected part with honey. A raw onion is also good, and if rubbed on affected part will prevent swelling. To relieve a toothache, dip the piece of cotton wool with iodine and apply to the painful tooth. The iodine will deaden the pain, and leave patient in comparative comfort until the dentist's aid can be obtained. To relieve burns or scalds, rub the affected part with a raw potato; or bathe the injured part with cold tea, bandage carefully and keep moistening with cold tea until pain has gone. To cure a hiccough take a half teaspoonful of soft sugar in a teaspoonful of vinegar. This gives speedy relief. A good cure for corns is: soak some bread in vinegar for a few days, then put a small piece on the corn every night, binding with a piece of clean rag. Every third day, soak the feet in hot water and remove a layer of the corn. Continue treatment until corn vanishes. A sure cure for an earache: put a pinch of pepper into a piece of cotton-wool. Screw up into a ball, dip them into olive oil and insert into the ear. The oil breaks up the layer of pepper and causes a good heat. When seized with cramp in the legs in bed, the sufferer should press his heels into the bed as hard as possible and relief will be obtained.

There are two holy wells in the vicinity of Bandon town. One is at Ballinadee and the other in Kilbrogan Park. The one in Ballinadee is a surfeit well. Anyone that feeds himself too much and gets a surfeit goes there for a drink of the water, and many people have been cured. The well in Kilbrogan Park is at the edge of a stream and it is supposed to cure anyone that has sore eyes.

There are some herbs grown in the country and if managed properly will heal an ailment. A dockleaf if applied on a sting from a nettle will ease pain and swelling. For a cut or bruise, gather wild sage and boil it for twenty minutes, then strain off, and drink the juice of it.

Local cures

SCHOOL: *Slievenakilla, Co. Leitrim*
TEACHER: *Peadar Mac Fhlannchadha*
COLLECTOR: *Francie Browne, male*
INFORMANT: *Mrs. Susan Rynn, grandmother, Aughrim, Co. Leitrim*

A cold or chill

In former times the remedy for a cold or chill was to get a hot drink of buttermilk to which was added some cloves of garlic, while the patient was to remain in bed for at least forty-eight hours. This remedy, tried in time before any complications set in, was very successful.

Head fever

The cure for head-fever, e.g. such as a violent head-ache, was made by certain people by prayer. They first measured the head around the chin and up to the crown and then around from the back of the head to the centre of the forehead. If both measurements did not correspond, the difference between them showed an opening in the head on the crown, which had to be closed before the cure was completed. The patient had to go to the person possessed of the cure every Monday and Thursday, and each time the head was measured and the cure made until the two measurements of the head were found to correspond, after which the headache did not trouble the person any more, a complete cure having been effected. I have been cured myself in the way described by Miss Brigid Darcy of Graghnafarna, who has cured several others and still makes the cure.

Heart fever

This disease is cured by Francis Cairgan of Caintulla in the following way. He fills a cup of oatmeal and levels it very close on top around the brim. He places a silk handkerchief over the mouth of the cup and presses the cup opposite the patient's heart. He then says some prayers and removes the cup. If the meal is undisturbed and is as he left it, the patient has not the disease, but if the meal is hollowed in the centre and sunk down in the cup, the heart of the person is as much affected as the meal is in the cup. The cure is made then on each Monday and Thursday until the meal shows no further sign of being hollowed or of shrinking, and as the cure is being made the gnawing heart-ache gradually disappears and a complete cure is the result.

'The Evil'

The seventh son or daughter has a cure for a disease known as the evil. This is a parasite and affects any part of the human frame. There is what is known as a he and she evil. It starts by a swelling or discolouring of the skin, and the affected part generally takes the shape of the parasite which is forming inside. The seventh son or seventh daughter comes along and brings the patient outside and faces him against the wind and then blows their breath three times on the affected part, after which the parasite dies, and then the point of the sore comes to a 'head' and the parasite comes out dead. I have known several persons cured as I have described.

A mote in the eye

A mote in the eye was taken out by prayers. The performer of the cure prayed and afterwards took a mouthful of clean water and then let the water out of the mouth on a clean white plate. There in the water the mote was to be seen. I got cured by Mrs. Garret Forde of Demageer, who had this wonderful privilege. She has died (about 1917) and I know of no person who has the cure at the present time.

A persistent cough

There is an herb known as mountain sage which is pulled and harvested in August between the two Lady Days. When cured it is tied in bundles and kept in a cool place. This herb is brewed or boiled and a glassful each morning cures the most severe cough, no matter how longstanding.

Toothache

A frog rubbed on the gums three times is supposed to cure toothache.

The 'Smailcín'

An earthworm placed in the hand of a new-born child gives the cure of an eye disease known by the name of the smailcín. With this disease the eye gets inflamed and swollen. The cure is performed by three rubs of the hand into which the worm was put, repeating while rubbing the prayer 'In the name of the Father and of the Son and of the Holy Ghost'.

Second sight

The seventh son of the seventh son or the seventh daughter of the seventh daughter is reputed to have 'second sight', that is, they are subject to take a trance a certain number of times during life, in which is made known to them all their future life events and the events concerning that part of the world in which they live.

Whooping cough

A cure for whooping cough was to pass the patient in and out three times between the four legs of an ass foal.

Fever

A cure for fever was to take from the arm of the patient a certain quantity of blood by means of a lancet, thereby reducing the temperature, after which the patient was allowed only buttermilk whey for some days with no solid food, only flummery. This was a product taken from ground oats. The husk or covering was steeped in water and the water when fermented was boiled. The boiling formed it into a thick fluid resembling light gruel. When this cooled and sit it was very nice to eat and most appetising.

Cures of other diseases by visiting holy wells

The cures of various diseases are sought by visiting Holy Wells, particularly St Brigid's Well in Graghnafarna, Ballinaglera, and many cures are attributed to the intercession of the Saint by visiting her Holy Well.

Sprained limbs

The cure for sprained limbs is made by some form of prayer, which has to be said on a stone which is partly down in the earth and has never been stirred or removed. The person having the cure kneels on this stone with his knees bared of all cloth, and during the time of prayer he holds a thread in his hands which is made of flax. The thread is then worn on the sprained part until a cure is effected. The name given to the thread locally is a 'straining thread'.

Disordered stomach

A cure was affected by boiling an herb known by the name of ERRACH BHALLACH for a disordered stomach. The brew, given to the patient, caused a vomit from the stomach of all the acid and gastric formations, leaving it clean and healthy afterwards.

Sore or inflamed throat

A roast onion applied to a sore or inflamed throat produces immediate relief to the sufferer. When applied going to bed at night, a complete cure was often the result by next morning.

Disease of the heart

For disease of the heart a liberal supply of watercress, eaten in the morning before breakfast, is supposed to be the best remedy known for all heart trouble.

The disease known as 'the Rose'

This disease is cured by prayer. The disease attacks man or beast. The part affected becomes swollen and very painful. In some cases a piece of fresh butter is sent to the person having the cure. After the cure is made the butter is rubbed over the part affected.

Local cures

Cures by local people were numerous long ago, but of recent years they are less plentiful and doctors treat the diseases now. For their services those who have cures locally receive no fee except gifts of tea, sugar or tobacco and often food or sacks of potatoes. These gifts are called 'hansels'.

Heart weakness

One cure was with dandelion. This plant was gathered and bruised and pounded. Some water was added and the juice was drank. Sometimes it was taken as it was pulled with a grain of salt. There are two kinds of dandelion, namely male and female. The male plant was used for the heart.

Swellings

Chickenweed is a soft green plant which grows in cabbage plots and such places. It is used to reduce swellings by rubbing it to the swollen parts.

Sprains

'Goosesame' or fat of the goose was, and is still, used to cure sprains. When a person killed a goose the fat was kept safe and airtight, so that if anyone sprained his leg or arm or any other part it was rubbed to the sprained part.

Warts

There is a number of cures for warts. If you meet a stone unexpectedly with a small hole in it containing some water, the water is rubbed to the warts. Something is dropped into the hole such as a pin, a button, etc., and a promise is made.

Another cure for warts is to put a fasting spittle on them for nine mornings one after the other.

Another cure is to rub a black snail to the warts, making the sign of the cross. Then hang the snail on a whitethorn bush, pushing it well in on a thorn, and as the snail is withering the warts are withering also.

ERRACH BHALLACH: *probably odhrach bhallach, devil's-bit scabious.*

II

WEATHER

'Modern weather forecasting includes satellites, radars and radiosondes in its armoury, but many of us still rely on folk forecasting as our first port of call. A glance skywards or a sniff of the air will tell you a lot, and conditions change so often, we're never short of something to talk about.'

MET ÉIREANN WAS ESTABLISHED in 1936, just as the Irish Folklore Commission was preparing the ground for the Schools' Collection. Traditionalists might well have questioned the need for a meteorological service at all, particularly as the Irish were already well able to forecast their own weather, thank you very much. Centuries of observing the ever-changing patterns of sky, sea and animal behaviour had provided a real depth of knowledge.

Met Éireann's early warnings are vital, but they cannot stop the weather. In 2014, while filming *Creedon's Weather: Four Seasons in One Day*, I witnessed first-hand the anguish on the face of Mike O'Neill, a farmer in Knockanore, County Waterford, who lost 23 of his cattle in a storm. They had been sheltering under a tree when lightning struck. Surveying the devastation, a tearful Mike sighed, 'There are calves looking for their mothers and mothers looking for their calves. It's a horrible sight altogether.'

In neighbouring County Kilkenny, one hundred years earlier, another farmer, a Mr. Walsh of Cappa, near Thomastown, had the very same experience. He lost 17 cattle who had been standing in line when disaster struck. Our informant tells us, 'They were found in the morning by their owner, lying in a rank in the shelter of a high stone wall. The lightning burnt them to a cinder.' Losing any animal is always a source of upset to a farmer. But the scale of this horror is underlined by our collector, young Thomas Lyng, who reports that the local hurling team did the heavy lifting while a priest directed the burial.

Modern weather forecasting includes satellites, radars and radiosondes in its armoury, but many of us still rely on folk forecasting as our first port of call. A glance skywards or a sniff of the air will tell you a lot, and conditions change so often, we're never short of something to talk about. Even when passing someone on the street, many of us will say a brief hello by just acknowledging the prevailing weather. A simple 'Grand soft day' or 'Great drying out' is as good a greeting as any.

There's an entire language around amateur forecasting. Cormac O'Donovan of Ballydehob tells us of the *madra gaoithe* (wind dog), a band of light just above the horizon, which was regarded as a sure sign of an approaching hurricane. I'm sure many Irish people also remember 'the puff-down', whereby blustery weather outside would send a puff of sour turf smoke rolling across the kitchen. You can learn a lot sitting by the fire on a bad night. Several contributors to this collection tell us that if smoke goes straight up the chimney, you can expect calm weather. That makes perfect sense, as does the claim that twinkling stars are a sign of frost. Without cloud cover, land temperatures plummet after dark and the heavens put on a show.

Several children also tell us that soot falling from the chimney was considered a sign of rain. I can see why. Damp conditions will cause the black powder to congeal, become sticky and heavy, and fall away from the lining of the chimney, landing in the fireplace below. It's a simple but effective way of measuring humidity.

'Red sky at night, shepherd's delight' and other popular weather maxims are recorded here, but there are others that I haven't encountered before. For example, a number of contributors say 'if the cat sits with her back to the fire there will be rain', and 14-year-old Kathleen Cox of Rockhill, County Donegal includes the northern lights as part of her local weather forecasting kit.

These local variations underline the diversity of culture and language on such a small island, at a time when distances seemed great. Every time you turn a page you meet a new child with their own distinctive handwriting and personality. At times, you can hear the local *canúint* (the melody or accent of the area) in their writing and many of the children display a beautiful turn of phrase. One little boy from Carrenroe Upper, County Kilkenny, speaks of 'the heaviest thunder in the memory of man'. Now there's a storm of biblical proportions. Kathleen O'Leary of Glynn, County Wexford, assures us that rain is expected 'when the distant hills are looking nigh.' 'When Distant Hills Look Nigh' — what a beautiful title for a watercolour.

A terrible storm

SCHOOL: *Ballyhurst, Tipperary*
TEACHER: *Stás, Bean Uí Fhloinn*
COLLECTOR: *May Ryan, Comea, Co. Tipperary*
INFORMANT: *Tim Ryan, 47, Comea, Co. Tipperary*

About thirty-three [years] ago we had a terrible storm. It commenced at nightfall and continued all night until seven o'clock next morning. When people went out it was something terrible to look at the country-side. Trees were up-rooted and carried a long distance from where they stood. Houses were stripped of slates and were awful to look at. In one case a house covered with zinc was stripped and carried a half mile away before it touched the ground. Such a thing did not take place since. That house is very near our own and it is un-roofed since.

Houses were buried beneath the snow

SCHOOL: *The Rower, Inistioge, Co. Kilkenny*
TEACHER: *Risteárd Ó Cuirrín*
COLLECTOR: *Thomas Lyng, Carrenroe Upper, The Rower, Co. Kilkenny*
INFORMANT: *John Lyng, 54*

The Big Snow, as it is called, fell in the year 1917. It began to snow in January. The big fall was on the last Friday of January and it stayed freezing and snowing until the 10th of April. There was frightful misery and hardship among the people. The people had to go out to the fields with KISHES and pickaxes to dig potatoes and turnips. Houses were buried beneath the snow, and the people had to be dug out of the drifts.

In the year 1935, on the 25th and 26th of June, the heaviest thunder in the memory of man was heard, but no harm was done in our district.

In the year 1900, there was a very heavy storm of wind. It was in the Spring. It was blowing a gale all day but as night came on it grew stronger, and at midnight people were awakened in their sleep. In many places ricks of straw were swept away. Nearly all the roads were blocked by fallen trees.

A grove of valuable trees, which belonged to Mr. Bolger, Ballinabarna, was swept away. In a farmyard near Thomastown a cattle shed and fowl-house, the property of Mr. Walsh, were stripped of their iron roof. It was carried off by the wind and landed in his neighbour's yard.

There was heavy thunder and lightning the same night, and seventeen three-year old cattle, the property of Mr. Walsh, Cappa, Thomastown, were killed by lightning. They were found in the morning by their owner, lying in a rank in the shelter of a high stone wall. The lightning burnt them to a cinder. The following day was Sunday and the priest asked the people to go and help in the burying of the cattle. The hurlers of the district went and buried them.

KISHES: *wicker baskets, from ciseán.*

The biggest and strongest storm that ever came before

SCHOOL: *Kilgevrin, Milltown, Co. Galway*
TEACHER: *Proinsíos P. Ó Doláin*
COLLECTOR: *Kathleen Donelan*
INFORMANT: *Peter Donelan, 69, Kilgevrin, Milltown, Co. Galway*

In the year 1839 there was a big storm in Ireland. It was the biggest and strongest storm that ever came before. It was blowing very strong for one day and one night. The people called it the night of the big wind. It knocked houses and trees all over the country. There was a man in Kilgevrin at that time. He had a small house. There were no one living only himself and his mother. His mother was old and feeble. The wind began to blow the thatch of the house. The man thought it would knock the house. He began to bring out the things that was in the house. He brought out his mother. He tied her to a tree. He went in to bring more things. When he came out he could not see his mother or the tree. He never seen or heard anything about her untill the day he died.

There was another big storm in the year 1845. It was not as big as the storm in the year 1839. In September the storm came. That was the time the people was cutting the oat. In the middle of the night the storm started. When the people went out in the morning the oats was blowing every where. There was a lot of trees knocked across the road and in fields. There was one house knocked. The people build their houses down in hollows after the night of the big wind. They were not afraid of the storm then.

The sky was bright and wild-looking

SCHOOL: *Kiltormer, Co. Galway*
TEACHER: *Pádhraic Ó Muineacháin*
COLLECTOR: *Augustine Lyons, Ardranny More, Ballinasloe, Co. Galway*

The big storm arose at ten o'clock on 12th February in the year 1903. It blew from the South-East at first and then it changed to the West and it was then it did the harm. During the evening the sky was bright and wild-looking and then the wind arose very high and suddenly.

It did such destruction that the ruins of the houses which it blew down are still to be seen through the country. The horns were cut off the cattle by the slates which were blown from the houses, and some of the cattle were even killed. It knocked the dwelling houses. The trees were knocked across the road and they killed many people who were passing.

In some places where there were trees growing in the graveyard it blew them down, and their roots removed the corpses and blew them out of the graveyard. It uprooted the trees and brought the corpses on the roots of them. It blew the people before it, and dashed them to pieces against walls, trees or anything they met. It blew the water from the Shannon for miles around and filled the houses with water, and many children were drowned, and also men who were driven by the wind into the water.

It continued very strong from about 10 o'clock at night to 3 o'clock in the morning and then the big wind ceased.

A great thunderstorm and a big fall of rain

SCHOOL: *Killacrim, Co. Kerry*
TEACHER: *Micheál Óg Ó Catháin*
COLLECTOR: *Cáit Ní Dhuilleáin, Killacrim, Co. Kerry*
INFORMANT: *John Dillon, Ennismore, Listowel, Co. Kerry*

The big storm we had in Ireland some years ago blew down trees and wrecked houses and blew slates off many houses, and the thatch also. It sank ships and blew small boats into the land.

We had a great thunderstorm in 1908, and a big fall of rain that lasted about twenty hours. It drowned everywhere. The lightning we had about ten years ago killed a great number of cattle, and a great number of stalls were knocked, and a farmer's servant boy was nearly killed. He was standing near a water tank and the lightning struck the tank and he got an awful fright.

We had a big flood in 1926. It was raining for two days and two nights, and the flood caused people to leave their homes, and a great number of houses were knocked. The flood carried away Horgan's hay and knocked Horgan's house. It knocked Lynch's house too. It did a great lot of damage. Cattle and sheep were drowned. The railway was covered with water so that the train was held up for a couple of days.

We had a long period of dry weather in 1914. The heat was so great that several birds died of thirst. Wells, streams, and ponds were all dried up. The people had to go three or four miles for water. The heat was so severe that the grass in the fields was burnt and there was water nowhere.

The night of the big wind

SCHOOL: *Killacrim, Co. Kerry*
TEACHER: *Micheál Óg Ó Catháin*
COLLECTOR: *Pádraig Bairéad, Killacrim, Co. Kerry*
INFORMANT: *Michael Barrett, Gurtnaminch, Co. Kerry*

In the year 1839 there was a very severe storm. This night is now known as the 'night of the big wind'. It did an amount of damage; it took slates of every house in the town, and in the country it knocked a share of old thatched houses and stalls and ricks of hay and haysheds.

In the year 1898 a big storm arose. It swept ricks of hay and two haysheds in our surroundings.

In the year 1935 [...] a man named Patrick Kelly from Duagh was taking a bucket of water from a well when a flash came. He got a fright and ran in the shade of a bush when another flash came and he was killed immediately at the foot of the tree.

In the year 1926 a great flood came. It was raining for two days and one night. The water rose and overflowed the banks of the river. The water went into my house and many other houses in the district. It also destroyed the hay in the farmers; it was swept away by the flood. This occurred on June 10th 1926.

In the year 1875 a great fall of snow came. It was about three feet in height and it froze on top of it. Ten sheep and six lambs were covered with snow in John Dee's land and it was a dog that found them. Mr Dee and a few neighbours went looking for them, and in a field a dog which they took with them saw tiny holes in the snow.

A terrific storm

SCHOOL: *Tillystown, Shanganagh, Co. Dublin*
TEACHER: *Micheál Ó Heoghanáin*
COLLECTOR: *Niall Honan, Strand Road, Bray, Co. Wicklow*
INFORMANT: *Mr. William Mc Lellan, 75, occupation: gentleman, Victoria*
Avenue, Bray, Co. Wicklow

In the year 1933 there was a terrific storm over Bray. Houses were stripped of their slates, fences were blown down and houses were blown in. Then later on came heavy rain, which lasted for weeks. Every low-lying piece of land was submerged in water; the sea came in on the main road and flowed in on all low-lying ground.

In the early summer of 1934 a big thunderstorm occurred. Fork lightning slashed through the clouds and sky, tending to rip it up. A fireball fell and exploded, but did no damage.

His house was all snowbound

SCHOOL: *Tillystown, Shanganagh, Co. Dublin*
TEACHER: *Micheál Ó Heoghanáin*
COLLECTOR: *Thomas Byrne, Shankill, Co. Dublin*
INFORMANT: *Mr. Frank Byrne, 53, farm labourer, New Vale, Shankill, Co.*
Dublin

In the year 1935 a heavy storm swept over Ireland. In Shankill a crowd of people lost quite a share of property such as hay and straw. There haybarns were also blown away. Many trees were blown down all along the Dublin–Bray road. The electric wires were also down and many cattle were electrocuted.

In the year 1933 there was a heavy snowstorm in Shankill district. It was about two feet thick. There was a poor old man named James Doyle. He lived up on the hill. His house was all snowbound and he could not come out until somebody came to the house and dug the snow away.

'We are sure to have plenty of rain'

SCHOOL: *Glynn, Co. Wexford*
TEACHER: *Maighréad Ní Giolla Eoin*
COLLECTOR: *Josie Sexton*

Some of the old-time predictions still hold good. Of course they have various signs and tokens in different parts of the country, but here locally I have heard old people say that

When the soot falls down,
The spaniel sleeps,
The spider from its cobweb creeps,
Loud quack the ducks,
The peacocks cry.
The distant hills are looking nigh,
we are sure to have plenty of rain.

The most common signs of a storm coming on are foretold when the cows and horses seeks shelter in the ditches, or when the sheep and goats, if high on a hill, come down. So now, when you observe any of these signs, you shall know the coming weather.

When the distant hills are looking nigh

SCHOOL: *Glynn, Co. Wexford*
TEACHER: *Maighréad Ní Giolla Eoin*
COLLECTOR: *Kathleen O'Leary*

In this locality there are different signs with regard to the weather. A sure sign of rain is when a person is heard to say, my corns are going mad, the pain is dreadful, there is going to be plenty of rain.

Or when the soot falls down in showers from the wide chimneys, the old people get ready to receive the rain. When the distant hills are looking nigh we'll have plenty of rain. I was walking along the road the other day with an old man and as we were nearing the school he observed that the smoke was descending towards the ground. 'Do you know what that is the sign of?' he asked me, but of course I could not tell him. 'It is', he said, 'one of the surest signs of rain we have.'

A rainbow in the morning is a sailor's warning, while a rainbow at night is a sailor's delight.

A star near the moon

SCHOOL: *Ballydehob, Co. Cork*
TEACHER: *Ristéard Ó Lighin*
COLLECTOR: *Cormac O'Donovan, Ballydehob, Co. Cork*

When the seal is heard crying it is said that we are going to have bad weather. When the swallow flies low, and the dog eats grass, it is a sign that we are going to have rain. The MADRA GAOITHE in the sky is a sign of hurricane wind. When the clouds are flying fast in the sky it is a sign of a storm. When the dust is flying around in circles it is a sign that rain is approaching. It is said that when cows are GADDING, [rain] is not far off. When the sun sets with a reddish colour it is a sign of bad weather, and when sun rises with a reddish colour it is a sign of good weather. When there is a circle around the moon it is a sign of rain. A star near the moon is the sign of a storm. The stars winking is a sign of frosty weather. In this district the rain falls heaviest with the south west wind. Wind from the north is the sign of frosty weather, and wind from the east is the sign of hard dry weather, and wind from the south and west for good weather. Smoke from a chimney going in all directions is the sign of bad weather, and smoke going straight up is the sign of good weather.

MADRA GAOITHE: *a rainbow or light over the horizon that portends a storm.*
GADDING: *running around with their tails up, normally done to escape gadflies.*

The sign of bad weather

SCHOOL: *Lowtown, Galbally, Co. Limerick*
TEACHER: *Pádraig Ó Ceallacháin*
COLLECTOR: *Mícheál Ó Faoláin, Galbally, Co. Limerick*

To see the hen picking her feathers is the sign of bad weather. It is said if you see the robin coming into a house it is the sign of bad weather. It is also said that if you see the blackbird coming towards the house it is the sign of rain. If you see the sun coming out early it is the sign that the day will be dull or wet. If you see the smoke going up straight into the sky it is the sign of a clear in the weather. It is said if the wind is coming from the north it is the sign of snow. If you see the cat with its back to the fire it is the sign of frost. If you see wild geese going towards the lake (in the Galtees) it is the sign of bad weather. If you see the sun coming out late in the morning it is the sign of a good day.

It is said if you see a blue flame in the fire it is the sign of rain. If you see the kitchen 'weeping' it is the sign of wet weather. If you see small flies flying around it is the sign of good weather. If you see the sky red in the morning it is the sign of good weather. If you hear the crows singing early in the morning it is the sign of a fine day.

When the seagulls are whirling

SCHOOL: *Tillystown, Shanganagh, Co. Dublin*
TEACHER: *Micheál Ó Heoghanáin*
COLLECTOR: *Bridie O'Toole, Shankill, Co. Dublin*
INFORMANT: *Mr. Doyle, 44, farm labourer, New Vale, Shankill, Co. Dublin*

Some people believe that when the sky gets very dark and cloudy it is the sign of very heavy rain. They also say that if they look out at night and see no stars or moon it's a sign of a heavy snowstorm, or if they see a magpie passing the window it's a sign of rain. The people around our district believe that when the seagulls are whirling around the woods and fields it is the sign of a heavy snowstorm or else there is a great storm on the sea.

When the robin ceases singing

SCHOOL: *Rathanna, Borris, Co. Carlow*
TEACHER: *D. Eustace*
COLLECTOR: *Kevin McDonald, Killedmond, Borris, Co. Carlow*

The people of this district have certain beliefs with regards to the weather. They believe that a wet morning followed by a fine morning is a sign of rain. They also believe that a cat facing from the fire is a sign of rain; the same is expected when animals and birds seek shelter. A 'dull heavy' morning is a bad omen, or when a fog moves towards the left it is supposed to bring rain with it. Another dim belief as a sign for rain is the falling of soot from the chimney. A scarcity of water in the river is a sign of fine weather. When a fog moves towards the right it is a good sign.

They also possess weather foretellers which by certain movements are supposed to foretell the coming weather. Frost at night is a bad token but is even worse for anyone with young apple-trees. The North-Eastern winds bring rain while the North-Western ones bring snow, frost and sleet. The south wind is the warm wind in this district. There is a church bell in Ballymurphy and an old belief is 'If Ballymurphy bell can be heard from Rathanna it is a sure sign of rain.'

Swallows flying low is a sign of bad weather. Bats at night is a sign of fine weather. Thrushes keeping to the wood is a sign of storm. When the robin ceases singing it is a bad sign. When they see the first cuckoo they say, 'Summer is here at last.'

Weather lore

SCHOOL: *Ballymagrorty, Co. Donegal*
TEACHER: *Mícheál Ó Fiannaidhe*
COLLECTOR: *Kathleen Cox, 14, Rockhill, Co. Donegal*

If there is fog in the rivers there will be frost.
If the dog is seen eating grass, there will be bad weather.
If the cat sits with her back to the fire there will be rain.
If the smoke goes up straight there will be calm weather.
If a blue blaze is seen in the fire there will be frost.
If there is good heat from the fire there will be frost.
If a black frog is seen there will be bad weather.
If a yellow frog is seen there will be good weather.
If the black black-bird is seen about the farm-yard it is a sign of snow.
If there is a rainbow in the sky, in the evening, the next day will be good.
If the northern lights are seen in the sky there will be frost.
The hills appear nearer when rain is coming.
When rain is coming there will be snails on the road.

White frost is a sign of rain.
When there is a heavy mist on the mountains there will be rain.
If you hear the curlews whistling in the evening there will be rain.
When there is a cold wind there will be rain.
If the sky is red in the morning there will be wet weather.
A blue sky without any clouds is a sign of good weather.
If there is a ring around the moon a storm is coming soon.
If the stars are bright and twinkling it is freezing.
Sometimes a star shoots and it is said that the wind blows
from the direction that the star shoots.
If the seagulls fly inland there is going to be stormy weather.
The sea roars when there is going to be bad weather.
If the soot is falling it is a sign of rain.
When a crane is seen at a lake it is a sign of bad weather.

12

RELIGION

'While it's easy to scoff at the level of religiosity in old Ireland, my travels through many of the world's cultures have deepened my understanding of why people pray. Buddhist chimes, Hindu bells, the Angelus, and all the other calls to prayer serve as constant reminders to believers to keep one foot in the spiritual realm as they make their way in the world. In this regard, the Irish have rarely strayed too far from the spirit. We seem to have a prayer for everything.'

**OTHING WOULD LULL** my father to sleep like a good rosary with all the trimmings. He'd often be snoring before we'd get to the first 'Glory Be'. I was usually nominated to 'lead off'. 'John is a great man for the trimmings,' he'd boast to neighbours, with a wink. The trimmings were the added extras at the end of another marathon rosary. Just as the family had 'hit the wall' and were struggling towards the end of the final 'Sorrowful Mystery', I'd kick on with a 'Hail Holy Queen', an 'Angel of God my Guardian Dear', and an assortment of short prayers for sailors lost at sea, fallen women and the conversion of Russia. I now understand why my siblings were sighing and weeping in the valley of tears to which our kitchen had descended by the time I was finished.

It wasn't just my siblings who were sick of me. My best friend's mother constantly muttered comments at me under her breath. Things like 'God, forgive me my sins,' or 'Jesus, grant me patience.' I didn't know why she disliked me so much. Was it because I never stopped talking? Why couldn't she just come out with it? Her son recently explained to me that she was merely saying her 'aspirations', a series of whispered Christian mantras, and it had nothing at all to do with me. A bit late to be telling me now, after years of self-loathing and confessing that I was a blabbermouth.

In his beautiful book *Stillness Speaks*, Eckhart Tolle reminds us that while we have to make our way in the world, we should never lose ourselves in the world. In other words, a spiritual practice, like meditation, will still the ego, or 'the great troublemaker', as he calls it. While it's easy to scoff at the level of religiosity in old Ireland, my travels through many of the world's cultures have deepened my understanding of why people pray. Buddhist chimes, Hindu bells, the Angelus, and all the other calls to prayer serve as constant reminders to believers to keep one foot in the spiritual realm as they make their way in the world.

In this regard, the Irish have rarely strayed too far from the spirit. We seem to have a prayer for everything. Apart from obligations like Mass, Confession, Benediction, the Stations of the Cross and the Rosary, there was also the Morning Prayer, Evening Prayer, Grace Before Meals, Grace After Meals, a prayer when running late for Mass and even a prayer for a happy death.

Many Irish Catholic religious practices have their roots firmly planted in pre-Christian belief systems. Patrick Logan's *The Holy Wells of Ireland* traces the ancient reverence for water and wells. The well at Carbury, mentioned in the Schools' Collection as a Christian site, also features in pre-Christian mythology. Boann, the wife of Nechtan, enraged the well, causing it to overflow, and in doing so created the river which still bears her name, the Boyne.

It's easy to confuse the Irish-language terms *uisce beatha* (whiskey, lit. 'water of life') and *uisce beannaithe* (holy water, lit. 'blessed water'). And you can see why. Holy wells were not unlike today's micro-distilleries. They were everywhere and every connoisseur could read the nuanced qualities of one compared to another. As I recall, holy water from the local well was always respected, but a bottle brought back from Knock was a very welcome gift and Lourdes water was considered top shelf.

In these accounts we read traditional tales of prophecies and miracles, often linked closely to local geography. The Book of Prophecies of Colmcille is referenced many times in the Schools' Collection. All manner of minor local happenings are ascribed to the saint's remarkable vision. Brighidh Breathnach, a pupil at the Mercy Convent in Kinsale, tells us that locals once believed that a failed hotel development was predicted by Colmcille. However, our young folklorist raises an eyebrow to such a claim: 'Their descendants do not dwell so much upon these prophecies. And it is well, for many of these so-called prophecies are forgeries.'

Similarly, St Brigid's Convent in Mountrath, County Laois, provides us with a wonderful account of the priestly miracles of Fr Quigley, who is buried in Raheen. We're told that 'his grave is visited to this day for cures, and the earth has been removed and taken to every country under the Globe'. (Under the globe? I expect that there must be a particular devotion to Fr Quigley among the members of the Flat Earth Society.)

The Schools' Collection provides real insight to the syncretic mix of pre-Christian and Christian belief systems that evolved on this island. While there's no shortage of humour and wild claims amongst the entries, the collection also underlines the deep commitment of the Irish to matters of faith.

Beautiful prayers

SCHOOL: *Killavil, Co. Sligo*
TEACHER: *Seán Ó Conláin*
COLLECTOR: *Bridget Rafferty*
INFORMANT: *Michael Brennan, Killavil, Co. Sligo*

Long ago the old people had beautiful prayers. None of these prayers were ever seen in books or in Prayer books. The old people learned these prayers and they taught them to the younger ones. These are some of the old prayers.

This prayer is to be said when late for Mass. 'O My God I wish to be present at the adorable sacrifice of the Mass. If I cannot assist spiritually at all the Masses that are said through the whole world, I unite my intentions with Thy holy ministers in offering up the adorable sacrifice for the same intentions that Our Lord offered himself on Mt. Calvary. And with it too I offer all the works I am going to perform this day. Sanctify them, O Lord, and make them redound to Thy Glory, Sweet Jesus, Amen.'

This is a prayer which is to be said in the morning. 'O Almighty and most Gracious Lord, regard our prayers and deliver our hearts from the Temptation of Evil thoughts, That our souls may be made worthy habitations for the Holy Ghost, Through the same Christ Our Lord, Amen.'

This is another prayer which is said. 'The use of these ejaculations in Mary's honour is well calculated to bring us many blessings. Through Her, Through whom Our Lord came to us, I leave all to thee, My Sweet Mother. In the name of the Father, I leave all to Thee. In the name of the Son, I leave all to Thee. In the Name of the Holy Ghost, I leave all to Thee. In Thy known [Thine own] sweet Name, as God left all to Thee in Jesus.'

This is another prayer which is said. 'O My God, My only God, The Author of my life and my last end, offered in my heart praise and honour, Glory be to Thee now and for ever, Amen.'

This is another prayer which is said and it is about Good Friday. 'Welcome Good Friday, the day of Our Saviour being crucified, with the crown of thorns being plaited and pressed on Our Saviour's Head. When the temple began to bleed, the Jews came in with a sharp spear, and pierced Our Saviour through the heart, from heart to hand. With his blessed Mother being standing by, with a doleful heart and a mournful cry. Who will repeat these prayers three times by night and three times by day, he never shall die in mortal sin until the gates of hell been opened and never shall enter in. O Lord with the branch, O Lady with the flower, O Lord Jesus Christ this night and hour.'

All the lovely prayers are forgotten

SCHOOL: *Toberroe East, Co. Galway*
TEACHER: *Eibhlín, Bean Uí Mhuireagáin*

In olden times when the poor Irish people had no education and were not able to read prayer books, they had many beautiful old prayers which were probably made up by themselves or handed down. They had prayers for every time of the day, but since the Irish began to learn English all the lovely prayers are forgotten. The following are some of the prayers which were said on going to bed at night:

1. As I lay down on my right side,
    I pray to God to be my guide,
    If any evil comes to me,
    O, Lady Mary, waken me.
    There are four corners on my bed,
    There are four Angels on it spread,
    St. Matthew, Mark, Luke and John
    God bless this bed that I lay on.

2. As I lay on this bed to sleep,
   I give my soul up to the great God to keep,
   If I die before I wake
   I pray to God my soul to take.
   There are four corners, etc.,

3. God bless Good Friday and Friday too,
   The day our Saviour was crucified,
   His tender Mother standing by,
   With a heavy sigh and a mournful cry.
   God bless those who say this prayer,
   Three times by day and three times by night,
   The gates of hell shall never enter in.

4. Infant Jesus, meek and mild,
   Look on me, a little child,
   Pity mine and pity me,
   And suffer us to come to [thee].
   Heart of Jesus I adore,
   Heart of Mary I implore,
   Heart of Joseph meek and just,
   In those three Hearts I place my trust.

5. When sprinkling Holy Water: —
   O Lord, cleanse me of my sins,
   In the name of Father, etc.

6. O God the Father bless me,
   Jesus Christ, defend, and keep me, through the virtues of
   the Holy Ghost,
   Enlighten and sanctify me this night and forever. Amen.

7. My God I offer thee this day,
   All I shall do or think or say,
   Be nice with what was done
   On earth by Jesus Christ, Thy Son.

A little bread and a little fire

SCHOOL: *Presentation Convent, Lucan, Co. Dublin*
TEACHER: *Sr Gabriel*

The old people always said when blessing themselves with holy water,

> Sprinkle us oh Lord Jesus,
> Wash us and cleanse us,
> And make us pure and white as snow.

At every hour they said — 'Another hour of my life has passed, to thee sweet Jesus I commend the last.'

They had always a very great devotion to the Rosary. Every night the Rosary was said at 10.30. All the family had to be in for that, and anyone who was in the house visiting joined in. An old woman 80 years ago always said, 'Thank God for a little bread and a little fire.' No matter what happened she would say, 'Jesus, Mary and Joseph give me strength.'

'Never go anywhere without your Rosary beads'

SCHOOL: *Killimor, Co. Galway*
TEACHER: *Eilís Ní Domhnaill, Brighid Nic Chormaic*

There was a man living in a house in Killimor a good many years ago. He had a sister married in Ramore whom he visited every night; before he would come home he used to say the Rosary with them. He never carried his Rosary

beads around with him, although he had two of them, one at home in his own house and another in his sister's house.

One night he was coming home from his sister's house after saying the Rosary, and on the road he met a man who asked him to say the Rosary with him. He said he would and the two of them knelt down on the road. The stranger took out his Rosary beads and began the Rosary. When it was finished he asked the man had he no Rosary beads and he said he had two of them, one at his sister's house and one at home. 'Well,' said the stranger, 'never go anywhere without your Rosary beads.' He then disappeared and the man went home and never went anywhere again without his Rosary beads.

Many strange and startling prophecies

SCHOOL: *Clochar na Trócaire, Kinsale, Co. Cork*
TEACHER: *An tSr. Úna*
COLLECTOR: *Brighidh Breathnach*
INFORMANT: *Séamus Breathnach, uncle*

Some years ago there lived close to Clontead graveyard a brother and sister. DE MHUINTIR MHORCHADHA LÁIDIR A B'EADH AN BEIRT SEO. They were more commonly known as SÉAN LÁIDIR AND MÁIRE LÁIDIR. Some people called the man 'Jacky the Prophet' and how this nickname came into being is accounted for by the following story.

Before the railway from Kinsale to Ballinhassig was built, CARMEN from this town and neighbourhood were hired to carry military stores to other stations [when] the regiments were transferred. On one such occasion Séan Láidir was sent to Fermoy, and of course after such a long journey could not return immediately but had to sleep in the town 'that is ALL A WAN SIDE.' In the lodging house this carman found a book which was supposed to be a copy of the Prophecies of St. Columcille. Séan was so charmed with the book that he did not hesitate to slip it into his pocket when he set his horse trotting from the [home] of the salmon streams and old castles to his own place, of which the poet could say in those day's 'TÁ BÁD I GCIONN T-SÁILE MURA BÁDHADH Í.'

Soon after Seán's return the rumour spread – that Seán Láidir had one of the three existing copies of the Prophecies of St Columcille. He kept the book in a hiding place in the house so that nobody but himself had a chance of reading it, and every Sunday at Clontead Chapel the people, while awaiting the arrival of the priest, would gather around Jacky recounting many strange and startling Prophecies.

Two of these prophecies are believed to have been fulfilled. One was that children who were then looking at the railway being built would live to see the grass growing on it. This happened seventy years later. Another prediction was to the effect that the erection of a big house near Kinsale would be started but would never be finished. A company began the building of a hotel planned to be one of the largest in Ireland, at Scilly. It was a huge structure but when the walls rose high enough to have the roof put on, the work came to a sudden end. The reason for this was want of funds. The place where this ruin still stands is called Cham Locáin, and afterwards when any work was not prospering as well as it should, people used say, 'It will be like Coumlockin.'

If the saint made prophecies of this kind they would fill a book as big as Coumlockin Hotel. And of course he never troubled his head with such trifles. The reason why these so-called predictions were swallowed without hesitation was due to the condition of the country. The poor people were crushed so much by SEÁN BUIDHE and his garrison in Ireland that they encouraged one another to hope that some day a deliverer would suddenly appear and drive out the foreigners.

Their descendants do not dwell so much upon these prophecies. And it is well, for many of these so-called prophecies are forgeries.

DE MHUINTIR MHORCHADHA LÁIDIR A B'EADH AN BEIRT SEO: *These two were from the strong Morchadh family.*
SÉAN LÁIDIR AND MÁIRE LÁIDIR: *Strong Seán and Strong Máire.*

CARMEN: *cart drivers.*

ALL A WAN SIDE: *All to one side (Fermoy developed on one side of the River Blackwater).*

TÁ BÁD I GCIONN T-SÁILE MURA BÁDHADH Í: *There is a boat in Kinsale if it has not sunk.*

SEÁN BUIDHE: *literally Yellow John (a reference to William of Orange, but generically, the English).*

The sin of pride

SCHOOL: *Gneevgullia, Co. Kerry*
TEACHER: *Máire, Bean Uí Chróinín*
COLLECTOR: *Eily Moynihan, Gneevgullia, Co. Kerry*

There were only three saints in this district, one at the city, one at Cullen, another at Ballyvourney. The city is the most popular in this parish. There lived at the city a saint named CROB DEARG. There is a well dedicated to her still to be seen there. On the 1st of May a large number of people attend. They go and pay rounds and say prayers.

The most famous holy well is at Cullen. There was a saint there, and her name was St Lateran. Every day the saint used to go to the smith for a coal of fire, so this day she went and she was barefoot and the smith admired her feet, and said to her, 'What a lovely pair of feet you have,' and she looked down and so committed the sin of pride. As she was carrying the coal her apron took fire and she cursed the smith, and so no forge could be lit at Cullen ever since. The forge is about half a mile outside the village. The saint at Ballyvourney is another remarkable saint and people visit the well in Whit Sunday and pay rounds and say prayers.

CROB DEARG: *Crobh Dearg, literally 'Red Claw', a Celtic goddess later revered as a saint.*

The Mary of the Gael

SCHOOL: *Loughil, Co. Longford*
TEACHER: *P. Ó Corcora*
COLLECTOR: *Thomas Breaden*

Saint Brigid is the saint [connected] with this parish. There are stories connected with this saint. Here are two stories about her.

One day Saint Brigid was in Ardagh. A woman who lived there spoke ill of her. The woman went to Saint Mel to confession and the penance that he gave her was to carry a red coal from Ardagh to the Pound of Killin. She did so and threw the coal in to a lake near by. The lake dried out and is so to the present day.

One day Saint Patrick went to Saint Brigid in Ardagh for dinner. There was a shortage of water for them to drink. Saint Brigid went to a field and pulled up some rushes. All of a sudden water sprang up and it formed a well and is there to the present day. This well is called the 'Well of Saint Brigid'. I do not know of any miracles or cures. There are special prayers to be said at the well. If you want any cures you are supposed to walk around the well so many times and you will be cured.

Most of the people of this parish are called after her. On the feast of Saint Brigid, which is on the first of February, Saint Brigid's Crosses are made and are brought to the church to be blessed. Saint Brigid was buried with Saint Patrick at Downpatrick. She is called 'The Mary of the Gael'. The relics of Saint Brigid are preserved in Ardagh Church and the people who go to Mass on that day kiss the relic of Saint Brigid.

Patrick's Wells

SCHOOL: *Letterbrick, Co. Mayo*
TEACHER: *Seán Ó Grannacháin*
COLLECTOR: *Mary O'Boyle, Doonaroya, Co. Mayo*
INFORMANT: *Anthony O'Boyle, parent, Doonaroya, Co. Mayo*

There are two Holy Wells in this district. They are situated at the foot of Tristia, a small hill on the other side of Nephin mountain. The two wells are called Patrick's Wells. People visit those wells on Friday, and especially on the last Sunday in July, and that is Garland Sunday.

When doing a station we go to the big well first and say some prayers there and then we walk around it seven times and say the Our Father, Hail Mary, and Glory Be To The Father each time. Then we go to the rock and say more prayers there, and then we creep from there to the altar and say fifteen Our-Fathers and fifteen Hail Marys and Glory Be To Fathers at the altar. Then we creep to the big well and say more prayers there again. Then we go to the small well and say more prayers there, and then we go around it seven times saying Our Father, Hail Mary and Glory Be To The Father each time. Then we kneel at the small well again and say more prayers, and then we have the station finished. We drink some water from each well then, and wash ourselves with the water. Some people take some of the water home with them. It is an old custom to leave something on the altar after you.

Nothing only bog water

SCHOOL: *Edenderry, Co. Offaly*
TEACHER: *T. Mac an Fhrancaigh*
COLLECTOR: *Patrick Grey, Edenderry, Co. Offaly*

There are many holy wells around Edenderry. There is one out in Carbury called 'Trinity Well'. Every year on Trinity Sunday there is a pattern held out at Carbury, Co Kildare. Hundreds of people gather there and enjoy themselves each year. There are many games there each year. In the evening all the people go up to the well to get a drink before going home. If people take a drink that have sore throats it will cure them. It is on the side of a little hill beside an avenue going up to a big house.

There is another well out at the bottom of Carrick Hill on the right going out. It is about three miles from Edenderry and it is in a garden owned by a man called Mooney. It is called 'TOBAR NA CROICE NAOMTA'. It was used to cure people long ago but I never heard what it used to cure. It is neglected now and there are briars and weeds growing over it. It is not used for curing anything now. I do not know anything about the origin of this well.

There is another well out at Ballinakill and this is the story told about its origin. One day St. Columkill was walking out in Ballinakill, and he was very thirsty, and he went over to a house and he knocked at the door. A woman came out and he asked the woman for a drink, and she said she had nothing only bog water. He took the bog water and drank it, then he thanked the woman and he said she would never be without spring water. Then he stuck his heel in the ground and spring water came out, and ever since there is a spring water well there. Some years ago a man that owned the land tried to stop the well by filling it up with stones, but it sprang up in another place. I never heard about it curing anything.

TOBAR NA CROICE NAOMTA: *tobar na croiche naofa, well of the holy cross.*

A good sign if it roars and cries

SCHOOL: *Tiercahan, Co. Cavan*
TEACHER: *P. Ó Riain*

A baby was christened the next day after it was born. All the neighbours would be invited: every woman brought a couple of cakes of oaten bread (oat meal cake, for there was no flour then) and a MESSCAUN of butter. Every man brought a bottle of whiskey (it only cost a couple of shillings then). There was a big dinner and they ate and drank, and talked and argued till ten o'clock at night. The people nearly always went home at ten o'clock: it was not considered lucky to stop out after ten o'clock at night.

Patrick McGovern was brought in to be christened forty-nine years ago. The priest was away, and the sponsors were advised by the people of the village to wait till he did come, that it would be unlucky to bring him home unchristened. This they did, and the priest didn't come till long after night. He was in a rage at seeing them before him, but he baptised him.

The mother used to dress the baby to send it out to be baptised, and she was at her work as usual its second day. If she happened to go out of the house and lave [leave] the baby alone, she stuck a needle in its dress or else put the tongs over the cradle.

When the water was being poured on the child's head, it is a good sign if it roars and cries, as this is a sign that it will be a long liver. If it does not cry there is a danger that it will die early in life.

In olden times people did not like to see girl babies. They all wanted sons. Girls were supposed to be a burthen to their parents, and to be useless. This is all changed now in this district.

MESSCAUN: *meascán ime, a lump of butter.*

The station-house

SCHOOL: *Drung, Co. Donegal*
TEACHER: *Seán P. Mac Gabhann*
COLLECTOR: *Annie M. Harrigan, Drung, Quigley's Point, Co. Donegal*

Ireland, all through the ages, has been noted for its fidelity to the faith. In olden times, when there was a price on every priest's head, the people heard mass in caves in the hillsides. Their faith has not changed since then, as is seen by the attendance at the local 'stations', which are held twice yearly, in Lent and October.

About a month or six weeks before the 'stations', the priest announces in order to let the people know in what houses the 'stations' will be held, and also the dates. The inmates of those houses commence to clean their house from top to bottom, and to renovate them. They have the room specially cleaned, as that is where the priest says mass. The table, or some such article of furniture, is used as an altar, with flowers and two wax candles placed on it. A picture of the Sacred Heart, or of the Crucifixion, is hung above the 'altar'.

At about eight o'clock in the morning, the people of the district gather into the station house. The parish priest and one of the curates arrive at about half-past eight o'clock to hear the people's confessions, while the other curate goes to sick or disabled persons in the district, to attend to their spiritual welfare.

Mass, in the station-house, starts about half past nine o'clock, and ends about half past ten. After mass, the priest prays for the deceased members of the household, and for all deceased members of the parish. When the priest takes off the vestments, and puts them carefully into a large case, he collects the 'dues' or stipends. The people then disperse, when they have got some of the holy water, which is called 'station water', and which is blessed by the parish priest while the curate is saying mass.

The inmates of the house then commence to prepare the priests' breakfasts. In olden times, the priests remained in the station-house all day, but at present, they only wait for breakfast, after which they depart.

Two of the local school-boys carry the priest's case from one station-house to another, so as to save the priest any trouble. The boy who clerks the station-mass gets a shilling or one and sixpence from the 'head' of the station-house.

The piper and the bishop

SCHOOL: *Drumeela, Co. Leitrim*
TEACHER: *Ailbeard Mac an Ríogh*

Drumeela district is rich in folklore. An old rock not far from the school and lying in the townland of Corglass is still pointed out as the Mass Rock.

One tradition relates of a Confirmation ceremony carried out in the Penal Days. At the cross-roads just below the school the boys and girls had gathered and an open air dance was in full swing. Fun and frivolity were in the air as the piper with drone and skirl and bat's wing trill lent the wings of music to airy feet. Scouts were on the surrounding hills and all felt safe. Suddenly, the piper left aside his bagpipes and stepped up to a friendly thorn bush.

In a few minutes he had donned the robes of a bishop and was soon engaged in the ceremony of Confirmation. According to local belief, Confirmation was administered several times in the district in this manner. The bishop examined the children in doctrine through Irish as late as '48.

Father Quigley

SCHOOL: *St. Brigid's Convent, Mountrath, Co. Laois*
TEACHER: *Sr. Aquinas*

Father Quigley lived in a lane called Bannan's Lane with his mother during the Penal times. A price was on his head and in consequence he had to dress in disguise and travel on a mule. He was born in Clonkeen and was educated in Rome. There are several mysterious happenings related in connection with his life.

He was attached to the old chapel at the Hollow. This was a thatched edifice and existed up to the year 1886. It is now replaced by a pretty little chapel commenced by the late V. Rev. J. Phelan P.P. and finished by V. Rev. E. Brennan P.P.

Father Quigley ministered at the Hollow and Raheen. On Easter Sunday morning, as he was not turning up to celebrate Mass in Raheen at the usual hour, a messenger was sent to ascertain the cause and found Father Quigley dead in Bannan's Lane. (This lane is at the Pole Bridge over the railway line.) The mule was grazing by the ditch and the bridle-rein on the priest's arm. There was no evidence of foul play. When the messenger returned to the Parish Priest of Raheen, the Priest told the messenger that he had an inspiration that Father Quigley was dead, before [the messenger] had time to tell him.

He was buried in Raheen and the grave is visited to this day for cures, and the earth has been removed and taken to every country under the Globe. An apple tree marks the spot where he lived.

When he and his mother were evicted from their home in Cromorgan, Stradbally, LEIX, his mother felt very cold, and her son, taking compassion on her, made the sign of the cross on a pile of timber and it immediately lit up, warming her. On seeing this she said, 'Thank God I lived to see this day.' Father Quigley replied, 'I could do much more for you in heaven if I had died after baptism.'

On another occasion there was a man appointed to watch for him to pass, so that a party of them could do him harm. Friar Quigley passed without this man seeing him, and this man marvelled at the incident, and repaired to the priest's house that night in order to make his confession and become converted. Friar Quigley told him that, although he was a Protestant, that he knew that he had got private baptism in his infancy.

On another occasion he visited a house to administer the last Sacraments to a poor man in danger of death. A messenger came for him and led him to the house, and there he found everything in readiness for the man's reception of the Last Sacraments. The strange part is that the dying man sent no messenger, neither did he call in anyone to prepare him, and he lived alone. Many other such like stories could be related.

On his tomb in Raheen (a table-like tomb) is the inscription

Here lieth the body of Father Thomas Quigley who died on Easter Sunday 1805.
The seed of the Christian Religion which he planted in the hearts of Youth will live forever
as will also his matchless good nature.

LEIX: *co. laois.*

His silver riding whip

SCHOOL: *Corsallagh, Co. Sligo*
TEACHER: *Tomás Ó Ceallaigh*
COLLECTOR: *Mary J. Masterson, Tubbercurry, Co. Sligo*
INFORMANT: *Kevin Devine, Tobercurry, Co. Sligo*

There was once a priest and he was called on a sick call at night in Winter time up to the top of the mountain. He told the boy to saddle the mare and ÁS GO BRAC with the priest in the pitch black of the night. He had to cross

a stream on his way to the house. When he came to the ford the mare stood up as stiff as a stake and would not budge an inch. He coaxed him and patted him but one foot APASS the other the mare would not put. 'I will try another plan,' said the Priest to himself, drawing his silver riding whip and lashing the mare with it, but it was as well for him be throwing stones at his over coat. The Priest knew then that there was something on foot, so he blessed himself and threw his whip across the stream. With that the mare started and never stopped until she reached the sick man's house. The Priest attended him and came home again. In the morning he sent [...] for his riding whip, and when he got it he nearly FELL OUT HIS STANDING when he saw that the silver part was burned pure black, for he knew that he had hit the devil.

ÁS GO BRAC: *as go brách, off he went.*
APASS: *past.*
FELL OUT HIS STANDING: *fell over.*

13

HARD TIMES

*'While there's a universal tendency to look back
at childhood memories with a soft focus, our
contributors, when they open up about hard times,
also open up a deep wound that still aches in the Irish
psyche to this day.'*

HE TERM 'TRAUMA' has its origins in the Greek word for a wound. Ireland has endured centuries of trauma, often referred to as 'the 800 years'. This generic catch-all label understates the awful suffering of millions of individuals buried just beneath our feet.

The Norman invasion of 1169 was a gentle overture compared to the cacophony of battle and tears that followed. Cromwell arrived in 1649 to oversee the conquest of Ireland. 'To Hell or to Connacht!' was the battle-cry as ethnic cleansing was enforced on a grand scale. The Penal Laws were enacted to ensure the subjugation of all but the Established Church. The relentless regime of hangings, torture, displacement and debasement was described in the late 1700s by philosopher and statesman Edmund Burke as 'a machine as well fitted for the oppression, impoverishment and degradation of a people, as ever proceeded from the perverted ingenuity of man'. In simple terms, it was well-thought-out, systematic barbarity.

A failed rebellion by the United Irishmen — Protestants and Catholics — in 1798 drew merciless reprisals. One account here describes Wexford hero of the rebellion John Kelly thus: 'Seven feet was his height with some inches to spare... His gold curly hair hung down on his broad shoulders'. For all of Kelly's prowess, he was hunted, humiliated and hanged. His severed head was then rolled all the way to the door of his sister, who had sheltered him.

Patrick Gillen from Donegal refers to kind landlords, like Rev. Bishop Montgomery of Glenagivney, who watched out for his tenants' welfare. Patrick also tells us of Mr. Nickelson, a fair man who built a school for his tenants. Ireland's history includes several such stories, but for the most part, wealthy landowners remained indifferent to the suffering of the poor. Others returned to England when times got hard, leaving their tenants to the further exploitation of an agent. If 'To Hell or to Connacht' was the battle-cry that sounded the planters' advance, 'To Safety and to Society' seems to have sounded their retreat.

The Famine, or 'An Gorta Mór (literally 'The Big Hurt'), added another layer of trauma to a dispirited people. Millions starved to death or died while trying to flee. Again, the choice offered to the poor was bleak: to the workhouse or to the coffin ship.

The twentieth century brought little relief, as Ireland continued its quest for self-determination. The Easter Rising of 1916, followed by the War of Independence and the Civil War, saw atrocities and reprisals carried out on civilians as well as combatants.

To put this folk anthology into context, we must remind ourselves that the material was gathered in the 1930s, when Ireland's decoupling from England was still in its early stages. Remember, this was a full decade before the Republic of Ireland Act of 1948, when just 26 Irish counties finally became free of the British Commonwealth. All of the contributors and many of the collectors here were born under British rule. While there's a universal tendency to look back at childhood memories with a soft focus, our contributors, when they open up about hard times, also open up a deep wound that still aches in the Irish psyche to this day.

Numerous studies point to the transgenerational legacy of trauma. The American Psychiatric Association states, 'The psychological effects of forced relocation, assimilation and other traumas inflicted on indigenous peoples linger today.' There's no shortage of examples. The aboriginal peoples of Australia and North America and the victims of recent genocides in Europe and Africa show similar behaviours. Anger, addiction, low self-esteem and guilt are common to people who have been traumatised. Survivors of the genocide in Rwanda and the famine in Ethiopia have all spoken of the shame of not having the strength or wherewithal to give their dead a decent burial. This theme is also repeated here.

To witness injustice meted out to others is to be traumatised oneself. In one account, a John F. Sheehan of Banteer in Co. Cork speaks of the old piper running to alert the schoolmaster that an eviction was just starting: 'Permission was granted to the excited children, to view the "Red Coats" and the evictions from a height nearby. Many of them could see their own humble homes being entered, and their contents flung out …'

I have little doubt that scenes like these inform that deep desire for home ownership amongst the Irish. It's something you don't encounter in countries where security of tenure is a given. We also have a reputation for responding to crises in other countries with volunteers and donations. This compassion stems from an empathy born out of experience, I expect.

Mass emigration continues to be a crude economic safety valve for Ireland. Not only did my aunts and uncles leave Ireland in hard times, but so too did six of my siblings. Currently, three of my four children and five of my seven grandchildren live abroad. Those who did manage to maintain a toe-hold here displayed grim determination and ingenious survival strategies.

The Irish are often said to possess a gift for satire and a rapier-like wit. Why wouldn't they? When the only weapon you're entitled to carry is the tongue in your head, you'd best ensure it's kept razor sharp. Indeed, Fursey Clancy from Clifden, Co. Galway, outlines here the power of the widow's curse.

From Lyracrumpane, County Kerry, comes the story of an eviction and cattle seizure. In the confusion, a neighbour named Mrs Reidy manages to rescue one white heifer and hide it amongst her own herd, while another neighbour, Mrs Murphy, scalds the bailiff with boiling water.

The next time we hear someone dismiss the complaints of small farmers as 'The Poor Mouth', let us at least consider where the practice originates. For centuries any visible improvement to a farm holding would elicit a rent increase. I remember a teacher once telling us, 'Tax dodging is a national pastime for people who don't trust their government.'

Having one's story heard is key to healing past trauma. So, as Ireland's journey to recovery continues, I feel it's our duty to listen to the voices of our past.

They had no claim but the sword

SCHOOL: *Castlemaine, Co. Kerry*
TEACHER: *Máire, Bean an Chaomhánaigh*
COLLECTOR: *Peggie Sullivan, Ballinamona Lower, Co. Kerry*
INFORMANT: *William Hannafin, Laharn, Co. Kerry*

The great O'Connell, in his great aggregate meetings through this country, always concluded his speech by the remark 'This is a great day for Ireland,' but I think there was never a greater day came in this country than the day the Land Purchase Schemes were introduced and carried into effect. Landlordism was the after effects of the English conquest of Ireland. The favourites of the Lord [Deputies], or the Court, or those who distinguished themselves in the slaughter of the unarmed Irish, were granted huge tracks of land, to which they had no God-given right but the right of the strong man against the weak.

Thus we have Sir Edward Denny, granted 6,000 acres of splendid land all around the town of Tralee, from which the Irish peasant was driven to the mountains and bogs of the Dingle Peninsula. So also with the Herberts of Cahirnan, Muckross and Killeentierna. The Browns (Lord Kenmare), De Moleyns, and hundreds of others were granted thousands of acres of land, to which they had no claim but the sword. In fact one Lord Deputy was [perfecting] a scheme, which was to drive the Irish peasant out of the country altogether, and between the slaughter of the unfortunate people and the famine that would be created, there is hardly any doubt but he would succeed. But those large estates hung heavy in the hands of the spoilers. They had no one to work them, and there was no revenue coming of the thousands of acres of confiscated lands.

The new owners wanted money to spend in England, for they had little or no enjoyment in this country to suit them. So the Lord Deputy abandoned his scheme, and the Irish were enticed out of the bogs and glens of the mountains, and given portions of their own land, at an enormous rent fixed by the new landlord. The poor people were glad of any concession they could obtain, so they gladly went to work to try to make money for the landlord to spend in London and Paris. Anywhere from six to ten pounds per cow was reckoned a reasonable rent; and when more money was wanted, to recuperate the landlord, after the debauchery of London and Paris or Berlin. The order was sent home to raise the rent at once, and the next thing to occur was that the tenant had notice from the estate bailiff or driver, as he was then called, that the rent was raised, and to be prepared to meet it at once, as the landlord wanted money immediately.

The poor people, in order to meet these demands, were in a great many cases forced to live on potatoes and milk twice a day. They could not afford them the third time. Many of the people went away out of these lands at night, and carried with them what little effect they had. However, as one man said, the tenants died bravely trying to pay the rent, and some who were in a fairly prosperous position succeeded in doing so. England had nowhere to turn for food except to Ireland, and Irish butter, bacon and eggs were flooding the English markets.

Planters and robbers

SCHOOL: *Faugher, Co. Donegal*
TEACHER: *Bláthnaid Ní Fhannghaile*
COLLECTOR: *Brian Harkin, Ballymore Lower, Co. Donegal*
INFORMANT: *James Harkin, 58, Ballymore Lower, Co. Donegal*

There were Stewarts in Ards House. There were also Stewarts in Horn-Head and the Olpharts were in Falcarragh. The Stewarts were in Ards for almost two hundred years. The tenants always looked upon them as planters and robbers who took their lands by force, imposed rents on them and that they had no right in Ireland at all. There were plenty of evictions in the upper end of the parish. Most of all the evicted people left Ireland altogether and went to United States, but some of them went to live with friends.

The tithes

SCHOOL: *Castletown, Co. Meath*
TEACHER: *Owen Maguire*
COLLECTOR: *Paul Reid*
INFORMANT: *Mr. Michael Reid, 58, Knock, Co. Meath*

Long ago there was a landlord in this district called Mr Longfield. His family owned it for about two hundred years and they got it the time of the plantation. This man lived in Dublin and had a man named Tomas Donegan to collect the rent. They owned eight hundred acres. All the people had to pay tithes for the support of the Protestant clergy. The tithe proctor went round every October and the rent was about one pound per acre. This landlord had thirty tenants. The tenants got anywhere from a half an acre to one hundred and thirty. The tithes were collected up until 1829. There were never any evictions and they got from May till August to pay the rent. Anyone that did not pay the tithes got six months in jail. There was another landlord called Mr De Bath. He owned Knightstown, part of Ladyrath and Rathkenny. He had two thousand acres. There were five or six evictions. The rents were collected in May and December and the tithes in October. This man lived in Dundalk and had a man to collect the rent and he was the cause of the evictions. His name was Mr Bullock.

A fair landlord

SCHOOL: *Star of the Sea, Glennagiveny, Co. Donegal*
TEACHER: *Brian Mac Giolla Easbuic*
COLLECTOR: *Charles Gillen, Meenletterbale, Co. Donegal*
INFORMANT: *Patrick Gillen, father, 56, Meenletterbale, Co. Donegal*

About twenty-two years ago there was one landlord in this parish. He lived in Moville. In olden times there was a landlord for Glenagivney, another for Mossyglen, and another for Meenletterbale.

All the farmers of Ireland could hold their farms except for those who would not pay their rent.

Around this district there was no people evicted but in the year 1881 there was thirty-two families evicted between Carrowmeana and Drumaville. They went to their friends or neighbours and remained there until they got new houses built. This was called the 'Carrowmeana Eviction'. Those people were evicted because they would not pay their rent.

The landlords got the rents in olden times. Now the rent is paid to the Irish Land Commissioners, who live in Dublin. If we do not pay our rent nowadays, the 'Sheriff' would come and take the cattle off the land and sell them, and with this money the rent is paid.

Montgomery collected the rent for Glenagivney. Harvey was the Mossyglen landlord for a while but he was changed to Carrowmeana. After he left Nickelson came and took his place, then it was he that collected that rent. Nickelson was not liked by the people because he was very hard on them. The other two landlords were very much liked by the people. Harvey was never liked by the people; he never had any evictions in Mossyglen during his time there, but it was him that made the Carrowmeana Evictions. After the evictions the other inhabitants turned spiteful against him for being so cruel.

The Rev. Bishop Montgomery was the landlord of the town-land of Glenagivney. The tenants considered him to be a fair enough landlord. He would always give them a few extra months after the appointed day for paying the rents. He never evicted any of his tenants. He would allow them to divide their farms to suit the family. He visited his tenants almost on every summer and seemed to be anxious about their well-fare. He was very charitable. He was known to give the rents to people who had any misfortune, such as cattle dying or such.

Mr. Lepper was the landlord for Meenletterbale. The people of this district considered him to be a fair landlord. When the land was bought out, Lepper only owned the land that was under cultivation, and the mountain and bog belonged to the Earl of Shaffs Borragh [Shaftesbury]. Mr. Lepper bought the bog off him and made a present of it to the tenants of Meenletterbale, which leaves them with an everlasting supply of peat. Every year they are able to let moss to two or three other of their neighbouring town-lands. Mr. Lepper put a fixed rent on the farms which the tenants could easily pay. All the landlords before him had the farms so heavily rented that the people stayed on the land for a year and raised their yearly crops and then took a 'moonlight flitting' and left without paying any rent. This means that they left unknown to the Landlords.

Mr. Nickelson was the landlord for Mossyglen, Ballymagarhy, Breadaglen, and Falmore. He was a good man to his tenants and he never evicted any person. He gave an acre of land for Church property, and he also built a school in Falmore free of charge.

In olden times when the father of a house died his land was divided among his sons, no matter how small the farm was, and each one received an equal share. This is the reason there are so many small farms around this districts.

In olden times the people of this district had to pay for the upkeep of the Protestant Church. No one can tell how this was stopped or what tithe they used to pay. Over forty years ago the people of this district used to give the priests of this parish a few lumps of straw at the harvest. In those times every priest had a pony and trap of his own. Nowadays money is collected at the harvest instead of straw. Everyone left their straw at a certain place and then the priest appointed a few carts to leave it at his premises. The priest thought it was better to collect money because when there was a bad harvest the corn was destroyed before it reached them. One man valued the straw to be worth two shillings. Every one paid two shillings at the harvest instead of giving them straw until times got better. There is a man appointed for every town-land to go around the houses in the harvest to collect this money. Nowaday people pay from half a crown to ten shillings.

In olden times the people always gave their money to their landlords and whenever they wanted it they asked the landlords for it. Very often the landlords left the country whenever they got the money from the people and never gave it back. This was the money the people had left after they bought their goods every week. Any money that they had left they gave it to the landlords to keep for them. The people thought that the landlords were the safest to give it because when they came round every half year they could get the money from them if they wanted it. Montgomery and Leeper always gave back the money but Harvey kept most of it. Harvey was not liked by the people because he never gave back all the money to the people.

The grabber so quiet

SCHOOL: *Lyracrumpane, Co. Kerry*
TEACHER: *Pádraig Ó Súilleabháin*
COLLECTOR: *Siobhán Ní Mhaoldomhnaigh, Lyracrumpane, Co. Kerry*

The landlord in this district was Mr T. Hurley. He was very much disliked by the people and of course all of them were alike. They took him to be very bad. Evictions were very numerous by him. He turned households out on the roadsides but afterwards made agreements with them by getting another farm for them, but not half as good as the one they held previous possession of. They were fond of taking bribes and this led to a number of evictions. At the time the English owned all the lands and the landlords were appointed by them to collect the rent.

The farms were very often sold by auction as nobody would take possession of them when the evictions were made. Afterwards, in later years, the children of those who were evicted got several lands. Landlords had the privilege of travelling through every man's land, shooting and hunting as they pleased. They also gave the title of 'game keepers'. If other people, such as the common folk, were found on the lands shooting or hunting, he would impose a fine on them. The tithe war was also in force. This meant that the tenth of everything they had, had to be paid to the Protestants. The tithes were reduced to 25%. This was put on the landlord instead of the tenant. But the tenants had still to pay, for the landlords added the tithes to the rent.

During the time of the landlords the Carmody family was evicted at Ballyrobert. The farm was sold privately and it was bought by the O'Carneys. The moonlighters were then about and they fired shots at the Carneys — not wounding any of them at the time. A young boy of theirs died shortly afterwards from the shock. They were then boycotted and had police protection for several years.

Many fights were put up in them times. The [bailiffs] when they would come to the houses for cattle, would find the surrounding places barred against them, and a large army would be ready to meet them, and they would not stop a 'brace' until they would put flight on the whole of them.

> The grabber so quiet
> Because he got a great fright
> He doesn't know where he may fall.
> It is firm in my head
> That he will never die in his bed
> But be killed by an old mud wall.

A good man to some people and a bad man to some others

SCHOOL: *Lyracrumpane, Co. Kerry*
TEACHER: *Pádraig Ó Súilleabháin*
COLLECTOR: *Eilís Ní Churáin, Lyracrumpane, Co. Kerry*

John Joe Hurley was the last landlord of this district. He was in this district for about 32 years. He was a good man to some people and a bad man to some others. Daniel, Jack, and Robert Browne, Michael Quill, Din Scanlan, Mrs. Fitzgerald and Mrs. Murphy were evicted. Daniel and Jack Browne built little sod houses near their own fences and minded their farms. Robert Browne, Michael Quill, Din Scanlan, Mrs Fitzgerald and Mrs Murphy went dairying to some neighbour's house and took their cattle with them. After a time they were reinstated and came back to their own land, but some of their houses were torn down.

They were a branch belonging to the English and they made them landlords over so many districts. Lady Loclann was the first landlord, and she was not too bad to the people. Lady Thompson was next and she was hated by all the people, and when she died the Hurleys fell in, because he was an agent for her and she left him her property. When he died he left it to his son John. John Hurley was the last landlord. He went to England in 1903 and he died about four or five years ago. The Land Commission bought over his estate and the farmers purchased from them then. Some fathers divided their land between two children and it had to be revalued. Anyone that would 'grease their fists' with money in disguise got a good farm for a bad one and the people in the good farm had to go into the bad one. If you had not paid your rent up to the mark, your cattle would be taken away from you.

There was often a fight in the district between the people that were evicted and the bailiffs who were trying to carry off their cattle for the money, and they were often hunted.

James O'Sullivan had a fight with the bailiffs, trying to save his cattle. Only one was saved — a white heifer. It was Mrs Reidy that drove her in among her own cattle in the mountain.

Mrs Murphy threw boiling water at a bailiff and burned him and he could not go into her. The bailiffs were often burned with boiling water or boiling porridge.

This man was far more cruel

SCHOOL: *Abbeytown Convent N.S., Boyle, Co. Roscommon*
TEACHER: *Sr. M. Columbanus*
INFORMANT: *Mr. Patrick Kearns, Ballinashee, Geevagh, Co. Sligo*

The local landlord in Geevagh district was named Keogh. The Keogh family got possession of these lands during the reign of Queen Elizabeth. Philip Keogh was the last member of the family who lived in Geevagh. His grandson is still alive but he does not reside on the estate. In the year 1936 his lands were taken over by the Commissioners and divided among the poor of the parish.

There were several evictions during Keogh's reign; the ruins of some of the houses are still to be seen. On one farm, owned by a man named Pat Conlon, there were four evictions; on another farm owned by a man named Thomas John Conlon there were three evictions. Among the richer classes in this district it was customary to bribe the landlords to evict tenants and bestow the land on them. This is the reason that several large holdings are in the district to this present day.

To prevent this abuse a league was formed in the district, the principal leaders being John McLoughlin, Thomas Nangle and John Joe Curran. The league was proclaimed illegal, and the leaders were arrested and imprisoned for a considerable period.

The landlord never collected the rent himself, but he had a man named James Mullany employed to collect it. This man was far more cruel on the tenants than the landlord himself. After some time the landlord left the district and went to live in England, leaving his agent in charge of the estate. During the landlord's absence he treated the poor unfortunate tenants with greater cruelty than ever. A man named [...] who was living in the house where we now live tried to shoot him because he took his land, but he did not succeed.

Their own humble homes

SCHOOL: *Banteer, Co. Cork*
TEACHER: *Seán Ó Síothcháin*
COLLECTOR: *John F. Sheehan, Banteer, Co. Cork, and Jeremiah Connell, Fermoyle, Banteer*
INFORMANT: *James O'Connell, 55, Fermoyle, Co. Cork and P. C. Linehan, 62, Banteer.*

In the year 1882 evictions took place at Charlesfield, Banteer. The landlord, named Murphy, lived at Charleville at that time, and his agent, Connors, was from Abbeyfeale, Co Limerick. On June 4th 1882, this agent, protected by red-coated military, then stationed at Millstreet, proceeded to evict the tenants and easily succeeded in doing so. The late Very Rev. Canon Morrissey, just then appointed parish priest of Clonmeen, Banteer, was present at the evictions. A stone was thrown by a local woman, named Walsh, and narrowly missed the agent. A man in the crowd ran, and was immediately arrested. He was released, however, on the intervention of the agent, who assured the military that it was a woman who threw the stone.

The evicted tenants were then under the protection of the Irish National Land League. Wooden houses, covered with felt and containing three rooms, were built for them in the adjoining townlands, and they also got help from the League, which enabled them to exist. The local branch of the League used to hold their meetings at a house near Lyre Chapel, now occupied by John Sullivan. Canon Morrissey and his curate, Father O'Riordan, used to attend these meetings. The local farmers helped the evicted in tilling for them, etc. One farmer, however, refused, and as a result had his plough and some other farm implements smashed during the night. The evicted tenants lived on in the huts, dependent on the League and dependent on kind neighbours for some years. Many of them emigrated to America. Those at home gradually got back into the home places at very reduced rents. The farms were divided, however, between members of the families, the result being strife, and malice, which lasted for three generations.

On the day of the evictions, old Timothy Murphy, locally known as Tadhg a tSalainn, an old piper of Lyre, ran to Lyre Boys' School, where the children of the evicted and others were present. He spoke as follows from the school door – 'The evictions are on in Charlesfield today, Sir!' The late Jeremiah Sheehan was principal of that school at the time, and his monitor was John Dennehy, who afterwards taught in the Model Schools in Dublin, and who edited many books on drawing. Permission was granted to the excited children, to view the 'Red Coats' and the evictions from a height nearby. Many of them could see their own humble homes being entered, and their contents flung out, leaving an indelible memory on many of their minds to this day.

Bad, low and dirty houses

SCHOOL: *Scoil an Churnánaigh, Newcastle, Co. Limerick*
TEACHER: *Pr. Ó Fionnmhacháin*
COLLECTOR: *Patrick Aherne, Churchtown, Newcastle West, Co. Limerick*
INFORMANT: *Daniel Aherne, 78, Knocknaboha, Newcastle West, Co. Limerick*

Long ago all the people of the district had to pay rent to the landlords. The most of the landlords lived in England but they had agents going around collecting the rents. The agents were twice as cruel as the landlord himself.

Those agents used to raise the rent if the tenant improved his house or land without the landlord knowing it. When he would be paying the landlord he would keep the extra rent for himself.

The houses the people lived in were bad, low and dirty houses because they wanted to impress upon the landlord that they had no money. Sometimes when the people used not pay the rent there used to be evictions. The landlord used bring the police and all his men and evict the tenants. Sometimes the windows and doors would be barred. Then the landlord would get a long pointed pole and batter down the house and sometimes burn it. There used be great fights at evictions and people were often killed. There were a number of people evicted in Glensharrold; all the [families] were thrown out on the roadside. The farmers build houses for them. The houses were called campaigns. The people would lend a horse or a cart or go and help to put it up. There are a great many of those in the country yet.

They sold everything except the potatoes

SCHOOL: *Ballaghnagearn, Co. Monaghan*
TEACHER: *T. Finnegan*
COLLECTOR: *Mary Freeman, Corlea, Kingscourt, Co. Cavan*

Until 1908 this district was ruled by Major Shirley. He was not so hard on the poor people but [his] agents were even worse than he. There was one time Major Shirley would not allow the people in the estate to keep a goat. Shirley was a servant in England and he got that estate as a gift for something he did.

Eviction took place very often in the district and the evicted people had to go to the work house. At an eviction the houses would be knocked or burned. The rent was so high that the people had to sell all they had to pay it. This happened in 1846 when they sold everything except the potatoes, which rotted, and the people had to starve. Major Shirley built houses for tradesmen in the district. He also built schools and it was he who appointed teachers.

Major Pratt was the landlord who ruled our district. He was not too hard on the people and therefore he was liked fairly well. Evictions took place very often but there were not many planting.

When a man was not able to pay the rent, which amounted to about £1-10-0 an acre, he was evicted. The landlord sent his bailiff and the crow-bar brigade to evict the people and to knock down the house. Some people went to America when they were evicted. Everyone who was a tenant of the landlord had to salute him when he met him. If they did not, he would either evict them or raise the rent.

Tithes were collected in this district. Each farmer had to give 1/10 of each of his crops to the landlord. The people were not willing to do this as it was for the support of the Protestant religion. Then the tithes were stopped, but there were more evictions than ever. This continued for a long time until the Irishman fought for freedom.

Cruel tyrannical powers

SCHOOL: *Templetuohy, Co. Tipperary*
TEACHER: *Seán Ó Meadhra*
COLLECTOR: *Tim Geehan, Tullow, Co. Tipperary*
INFORMANT: *John Fogarty, 25, Tullow, Co. Tipperary*

Before Tenants-right was accomplished, landlords held all tenants under sway, and many evictions were recorded by their cruel tyrannical powers. Whether tenants paid their rent or not, the landlords or agents cast the people out of their homes, to roam where they liked. Evictions took place in the district just the same as everyplace else. People named Quinlans were evicted by Captain French's agent for not paying the rent. The people lived in Tullow, in the parish of Templetuohy. When the morning of the eviction came, a cruel force of armed police, on horse-back and on foot, came to the cabin where these people lived. They craved and begged for another [lease], and they would pay the rent as soon as possible. This request was refused, so the eviction commenced. The agent first declared them [evicted], and then every article in the house was thrown out on the wayside. Even old china mugs and jars were thrown out, so that the [four] walls of the cabin was all that was left standing.

After this the people had to refuge with neighbours, by the name Gleesons, until they got another house under another landlord named Lord Orkney.

Now for another eviction in this parish of Templetuohy, at Lisanure. People by the name of Brynes were evicted for nonpayment of rent. These people were evicted twice and now I will give you a detail of the evictions. The first eviction was for only a short duration, but the second was more severe. After the first eviction they were allowed to come back, but only for a short time. When the morning of the eviction came, a large crowd of police was drawn up outside the door. When they got the notice to quit, [they] removed up all articles they possibly could to Bradshaws in Ballyknockane, where they stayed for a short time before they sailed for England.

The widow's curse

SCHOOL: *Clifden, Co. Galway*
TEACHER: *An Br. Angelo Mac Shámhais*
COLLECTOR: *Fursey Clancy (male)*
INFORMANT: *Mr. Keely, 78, Roundstone, Co. Galway*

In Roundstone there lived a landlord called Toole and he was a noted tyrant. Up in the hills there lived a widow and her family and she had an old shack rented from this landlord. The widow paid the rent weekly and, like many others, found it very hard to scrape up the money. But at last the widow's store of money was exhausted and she told the landlord so and begged for time to pay the rent.

'No,' said the landlord, and he evicted her and her family at once without an atom of consideration.

Then the widow put the widow's curse on him and she said, 'The devil will haunt you in the shape of a calf this very day.' The landlord jumped on his horse and, laughing with scorn, rode home.

As he was passing a place called Letterdive he noticed a calf floating in the air on one side of him and the most peculiar thing about it was it had no legs whatsoever. The landlord got off his horse with fear and he entered a house near by as though for a drink. The 'BEAN AN TIGE' was inside and she noticed the cold sweat on his face. She asked him what was the matter with him but he made no reply whatsoever. He left for his horse again but he was not gone far when the calf without the legs appeared once more. He made the horse gallop, but the calf still kept at his side, and when he stopped the calf stopped also.

At last with the dint of fright he beat his horse and closed his eyes until he arrived at his own house. Then he jumped off his mount and he ran to his bedroom. When he entered his bedroom he fell into a dead faint from which he never recovered. In the morning he was found dead with a print of a hoof on his chest. After he was buried a calf was seen in his room and around his house. That man paid dearly for evicting the poor widow and her family.

BEAN AN TIGE: *bean an tí, woman of the house.*

They saw it was no good fighting

SCHOOL: *Moneyduff, Co. Leitrim*
TEACHER: *Pádhraic Ó Heádhra*
COLLECTOR: *John Fowley, Kilmore, Fivemilebourne, Co. Sligo*
INFORMANT: *Lawrence Fowley, 46, Kilmore, Fivemilebourne, Co. Sligo*

The local landlord was the name of Whyte, a native of Fivemilebourne, the Parish of Drumlease and barony of Dromahair, the Electoral division of Snamore. Colonel Whyte was not a bad landlord but his agent was far worse – Mr Palmer, [Sheriff]. Whyte lived in England. He used to come round once a year; he was not hard on the tenants but his agents used to put on a pound if they made any improvements on their farms. There were evictions in the Fivemilebourne and the people turned out on the roadside, because the landlord wanted the land for a sheep farm. He levelled the ditches and made it into a big sheep ranch. The people went out quietly, as they saw it was no good fighting. Plantings did not take place in my district. The people that were evicted, any of them that were able to go to America went, and the others died on the side of the road.

Before the people left the house they were evicted out of, they put down a fire of stones so that the people who went into the house would have bad luck there. Colonel Whyte got the land around the Newtownmanor because the Protestants were backed by England, and they turned out the Catholics and gave over the land to Whyte and he became landlord. In a kind of a way the land was not divided under the landlord's power. But a few men started the Land League; their names were Charles Steward [Stewart] Parnell and

Michael Davitt. Then the people joined also, and they used to drive the grazing cattle off the lands, then they boycotted the lands. So the landlords was able to make no profit on the lands. This property fell into debt and was sold in Judge Rosse's court. He used to put so much money on the lands that time and if the land fell into debt he could get the lands sold.

The lands then were bought over by the Congested District Board and they divided it again among the tenants and made economic farms of it. If a farmer had six children and when they were getting married he divided his farm equally among them and by doing so there was no emigration. The landlord had special powers over his tenants in voting. The voting was public and if the people did not vote for the landlord he evicted them the next day. There were certain townlands for keeping up the Protestants' Church. The rents of these townlands went to the up keep of the Church and [they] were called the Glebe lands. In this area the townlands were Killenna and Kinara and in the Dromahair area Corrudda and Conaghil, but there was no such collections for the Catholics; all went to the Protestants.

A fire of stones

SCHOOL: *Dernakesh, Co. Cavan*
TEACHER: *T. Ó Curry*
INFORMANT: *Charles Shalvey, Dernakesh, Co. Cavan*

George Bernard Shaw was our landlord and an officer in the old police force of Ireland. He married Miss Nixon, who owned Dernakesh and Ralaghan, and lost the property when she died. He himself died about the year 1898 at his residence in Bray.

He was considered a very hard man on his tenants as he carried out a very cruel eviction on Mrs. White, Ralaghan, about the year 1894; and his bailiff, James McEntire, Corrogarry, drove off her cattle and destroyed the furniture.

Anyone who took part in the eviction would be cursed by the evicted party. A fire of stones would be lighted and some 'prayers' said backwards. If the fire burned the curse was sure to be effected.

Incidents of the Land War

SCHOOL: *Rathnure Upper, Co. Wexford*
TEACHER: *Cáit Ní Bholguidhir*
INFORMANT: *Patrick Bolger, parent, male, principal, Rathnure Upper,*
Co. Wexford

The following incidents of the Land War were often related by my Father, Patrick Bolger, Principal Teacher of the Rathnure Boys' School, who lived in the district during that time. [...]

The landlords themselves chiefly lived in England, and came to spend the Summer in Ireland. The agent, Mr. Ruttledge, did all the work, and collected the rents from the farmers. He was very severe on the Catholics, and cared not how many he would evict if they could not pay their rents, so as to seize on their homes and farms to give them to Protestants. The landlords were rack-renting the tenants, and when the farmer was unable to pay the exorbitant rent that the landlord tried to extract from him he was evicted.

About sixty years ago Michael Davitt, who began the Land War, founded the great Land League for the redress of the many wrongs of the Irish tenant farmers. The Land League spread like wildfire through every district in Ireland. Charles Stewart Parnell joined Michael Davitt in the agitation, as well as other Irish members of Parliament.

There were several meetings held here, in Rathnure, at the Chapel Gate on Sundays after Mass. There were speeches made by the leading farmers in the district: Peter Whelan, James Forrestal, Richard Forrestal, John and Daniel

Quigley, James Johnson, and James Hughes. They taught the people of the district to resist the unjust landlords and refuse to pay unjust rents, and resolve no longer to be ground into the earth by the heel of landlordism. They had one powerful weapon which was 'boycotting'.

'Boycotting' took its name from Captain Boycott, a harsh land-agent in Mayo, whom the people ostracised. They refused to work for him, to speak to him, to buy anything from him, to sell anything to him, to let anyone serve or help him, and by this means they drove him out of the country.

These speeches from the platforms on Sundays stirred up the people of the parish, and were successful in frightening both the landlords and the landgrabbers.

Peter Whelan, a prominent farmer who lived in Grange, was one of the first who refused to pay the rent. He had a large farm of land, and spent a great deal of money improving his land, manuring it and building new houses on it, and according as he was making all these improvements, the landlord kept on increasing the rent. In the end he refused to pay it when the time came. He was then threatened with eviction. A certain day was named for this.

The people of the parish knew about it, and they all congregated together at the house of Mr Peter Whelan to stop it. They were armed with pikes, SPRONGS, spades, shovels, fire irons, stones, and any weapons they could seize. They brought two male goats with them, led by a long rope, and on their horns hung the bold sign 'Pay no Rent'.

The bailiff, supported by police from Killanne and Enniscorthy, arrived. They were faced by a strong body of men, with their weapons. The goats were let loose amongst them, and they were chased back again, some of them being severely wounded. The police were armed with guns, but did not fire a single shot. They took flight as hard as they could.

Another farmer, named John O'Leary, had a nice snug farm in Rathnure. He lived happily with his poor aged mother. John was unable to pay the high rent, and was threatened with eviction. The people gathered together the eviction day, and opposed the bailiff who was supported by armed police, so they withdrew, fearing the same thing might happen as at Peter Whelan's.

About a fortnight later when matters cooled, the bailiff and police came secretly to John O'Leary's house, and seized on all his stock, his farm implements, and entered the house, stamped out the fire, threw out the bed and bedclothes, and the furniture. They put out John and his mother then. They took refuge in a neighbour's house.

John's farm was taken by the landlord and given to a Protestant, named Richard Binions. This land-grabber was boycotted by all the people of the district. No one would speak to him, work for him, buy from him, sell to him, serve or help him. Still he stuck on to the farm, as he had his own family to work and help him. If a person attempted to speak to him, or a shop in the locality buy from him, or sell provisions to him, they were instantly boycotted.

The Land League, by means of a collection which they made, were able to erect a Land League Hut in Ballybawn for John O'Leary and his aged mother; so they lived in it, until John purchased a small farm in Kiltealy. John is still living but his mother is dead.

SPRONGS: *manure forks.*

The beautiful crucifix

SCHOOL: *Clochar N. Muire, Wexford, Co. Wexford*
TEACHER: *Sr. Breandán*
COLLECTOR: *Anna Whitmore, Bishop's Water Hill, Co. Wexford*

When Cromwell had conquered the town of Wexford and slaughtered the people there, he turned his attention to Lady's Island, a village which is situated some miles outside Wexford.

The inhabitants, hearing of his coming and knowing his murderous nature, abandoned the place immediately. But one little boy, in his hurried flight, thought of the beautiful crucifix which hung on the altar of the little chapel and which was cherished by the people. He knew that if Cromwell's soldiers saw him no mercy would be shown to him; but nevertheless he turned back to the little church which was now empty and lonely.

He got the crucifix and silently and slowly stole out of the church with the relic clasped reverently to his breast. He was seen by a Cromwellian soldier, who at once noticed the crucifix. He took careful aim and shot the little boy, who when falling flung the crucifix into a lake.

The crucifix was recovered some years afterwards by a fisherman. Today it can be seen hanging on the altar in the church at Lady's Island.

A leaf never grew on this branch after

SCHOOL: *Tullyallen, Drogheda, Co. Louth*
TEACHER: *Bean Uí Chonchobhair*

On the hill of Coolfore, which is in the parish of Mellifont, can still be seen, after many hundred years, the remains of an old Catholic Church. At the time when our Irish priests were persecuted and dare not celebrate Mass in any chapel, there was a close watch kept by the British soldiers on Coolfore Chapel.

Sometime about Christmas, the good priest was offering Mass in the very early hours of a dark Winter's morning. All the Catholics in the parish attended Mass.

A widow, living near the chapel, left her son, aged ten, in charge of a pot of dumplings, while she attended the Mass. During the Mass, the dumplings began to bubble loudly and this was the sign for the removal of the pot. The innocent child got a lantern and rushed to the chapel (where the Mass was being celebrated) for his mother. The sight of the lantern attracted the attention of the soldiers, who were, as usual, on the watch some distance away. They surrounded the chapel and seized the good priest, brought him about a quarter of a mile away, and hanged him on a branch of an ash tree.

A leaf never grew on this branch after. Sometime after, a woman took this branch for firewood, and she died in a short time.

There is a mound round the tree, and it is said that the people of that time held it in so much respect that they buried their children under it at the time of the Famine.

This tree still stands about a mile from Tullyallen in the district of Begrath.

His new dress

SCHOOL: *Gortagarry, Co. Tipperary*
TEACHER: *Seán Ó Donnabháin*
INFORMANT: *Thomas Ryan, 50, merchant, Stook, Co. Tipperary*

During the Penal Times, a priest dressed in ordinary clothes used to visit a house in this part of the country very frequently. He was very fond of the children and they were very fond of him. He used to bring them toys occasionally.

This day when he was in the house, he was playing with the children and one of them took his crucifix from his pocket without his knowledge. In a short time the house was entered by soldiers who were priest hunting. They searched the priest but, not discovering any religious object on his person, they let him off.

When the soldiers were gone the little girl brought back the crucifix, which she had covered with a tiny dress, and remarked to the priest, 'Doesn't he look lovely in his new dress?' Then he knew that it was the action of the child who took and dressed the crucifix, believing it to be another toy, that saved his life.

The Mass rock

SCHOOL: *Ballybay, Co. Monaghan*
TEACHER: *Miss Hargaden*
INFORMANT: *James Prunty, 53, farmer, Laragh, Ballybay, Co. Monaghan*

During the time the Catholic priests were hunted out of this country, the hunted priests in those days said mass in secret places and used a rock as an altar. There is a Mass Rock three miles from my home. It is situated in Caraga in the townland of Cornanure. The priests said mass at this rock and the Catholic people assembled round the rock to hear mass. The Catholics arranged that one of their number should keep guard and give the alarm if they saw any sign of the English spying on them. The priests often said mass before the break of day.

One Easter Sunday morning, while a priest was saying mass there, a party of English soldiers attacked them and killed the priest. To this day the stains of his blood can be seen on the stones of the rock where he was killed. It is said that who ever would rise early on an Easter Sunday morning and go to the rock at Coranure fasting would see the priest kneeling on the stones where he was killed.

Helmets and skeletons

SCHOOL: *Kiltycreevagh, Drumlish, Co. Longford*
TEACHER: *S. Ó Murchadha*
COLLECTOR: *Katie Cassidy, Fardromin, Ballinamuck, Co. Longford*
INFORMANT: *Paddy Dolan, 85, Kiltycreevagh, Ballinamuck, Co. Longford*

The Irish and French stood to fight the battle on Shanmullagh Hill. The British army went up a narrow lane by Felix Gormley and went round about a quarter of a mile that lane until they turned up a hill to the right and got in range of the Irish Army. They opened fire on them, and cut them down. All of them they didn't kill retreated and went to the bogs. They fired after them and killed many of them. They pursued them and took them prisoners all that they got, and sent them on to Dublin to be hanged. The battle lasted about three hours. Some of the French fought in the whole battle and some of them retreated when they saw there was no success, some of the French were killed and some of them retreated [...]. When the battle was over the Croppies had to hide in the bogs till English army went away. The Croppies that were captured were brought to Dublin and hung.

Gunner MacGee fired on the English army and killed hundreds of them. His cannon could be got all around the place and also his helmets and skeletons could be got at Kiltycreevagh crossroads. There were about 700 Irish killed, 300 French, and about 700 English in the battle. The Irish and French were buried in Shanmullagh Hill and all around Ballinamuck. How you would know the graves is that there are bushes growing on them and also heaped up in heaps. There are boxes buried around the crossroads with helmets and skeletons in them from the remains of the battle.

One man's head at the other man's feet

SCHOOL: *Kilgraney, Moneybeg, Co. Carlow*
TEACHER: *Mary Baker*
COLLECTOR: *Peggie O'Neill, Kilgraney, Co. Carlow*

Last August, while excavating sand for Borris Tile Factory, my father found skeletons in our sand pit in Kilgreany. There were twelve skeletons of men found in the sand. They had been buried in rows with one man's head at the other man's feet. It is believed that they are there since the Battle of Kilcomney. This was a battle fought at Kilcomney in 1798. The Irish rebels were guarding the ford across the Barrow at Goresbridge. They were attacked by English soldiers who came from Kilkenny. They retreated to Kilcomney, where a battle was fought. The old road from Goresbridge to Kilcomney passed by our house and through the sand pit where the skeletons were found. A number of Irish rebels were killed on the way and they were thrown along in trenches in the sand. They were buried about 2½ feet under the surface. About 14 years ago my father was ploughing this same field and he found two roughly hewn stones placed in the ground about 2 feet under the surface. They are believed to mark the burial place of some of the Irish rebels of 1798.

The fateful year of 1798

SCHOOL: *Clochar na Toirbhirte, Wexford, Co. Wexford*
TEACHER: *An tSr. Bearnard*
COLLECTOR: *A. Cullimore, Wexford, Co. Wexford*

Wexford had many brave men who went to save Ireland from the Yeomen in the year 1798. John Kelly was one of the heroes of '98. He was born in Killane in the year 1772, the son of a farmer and merchant. In the year 1798 he was 25 years of age. 'Seven feet was his height with some inches to spare and he looked like a king in command.' His gold curly hair hung down on his broad shoulders.

The yeomen were very cruel to the Irish people and they hanged any Irish person that came their way. John Kelly got some able-bodied Irishmen and drilled them and they were prepared to go to war against the yeomen. Wexford did not rise until May 25th. Although in the [muster] roll of United-Irishmen drawn up by Lord Edward Fitzgerald in March 1798, the number at the beginning of the Rising exceeded 300 men.

So little did the British think that Wexford would rebel that at the beginning of the Rising the only regular force in the country was the North Cork militia numbering 600 men, of whom two thirds were Catholic. The Country Yeomen were nearly all Protestants, the Catholics among them having been shot. The Three Bullet Gate was guarded by the yeomen, and John Kelly was ordered to force his way through, and he defeated the yeomen; but at the moment of victory, sad to say, John Kelly received a ball in the thigh and he fell from his horse and lay motionless on the ground. He was nursed by a Miss Hickey.

He was brought to his sister in Cornmarket, who tended his wound. The yeomen were looking for him, and when they came to his sister's house they dragged him out of bed to Court Martial. He was arrested, and the executioners brought him in a car to the place of execution on the bridge, and he was hanged. His head was severed from his body and they rolled his head along the street until they came to his sister's house; there they threw his head up in front of the window. His head was stuck on a pike outside the gaol by Captain Kehoe. Ninety-eight will ever be remembered for the brave heroes who died for Ireland in the fateful year of 1798.

For fear of the Yeomen

SCHOOL: *St. Brigid's, Wexford, Co. Wexford*
TEACHER: *M. Gúld*
COLLECTOR: *Thomas Goff*
INFORMANT: *father, name not given*

In the year 1798 the United Irishmen stayed up in the rocks in Wexford for fear of the Yeomen. Their hiding place was a cave in Maiden Tower. They had a tunnel going down to the bay. Every time they could get a chance they would go down to the town and kill the Yeomen. They used to wait outside the town and ambush the Yeomen or Redcoats and kill them. The Government would send down a regiment of soldiers to capture the United Irishmen but the United Irishmen would escape through the fields and get away.

The blood of this unfortunate priest

SCHOOL: *Carlanstown, Co. Meath*
TEACHER: *Séamus Ó Gérbheannaigh*

Father Michael Murphy came from Wexford into Meath with a band of croppies in 1798. They were surrounded at Tara by [Yeomen] and British

soldiers and brutally murdered, all except Fr. Murphy and a few more, and these fled northwards until they came to Raffan in the parish of Castletown. Here there were met by another band of yeomanry and a fierce battle was fought. All the croppies were killed, I believe, but Fr. Murphy made his escape. They buried the 'dirty croppies' in shallow graves and in the fall of the year the wheat which they had in their pockets, and which was all they had to eat on the journey from Wexford, sprung up through the thin earth which covered them and ripened in the sun.

Father Murphy sought refuge with the Protestant Minister of Castletown, who was a good man and in sympathy with the downtrodden Catholics. For a few days he remained in hiding there, for that was the last place on earth his persecutors would think of searching for him. But, still, the poor man was troubled in mind. What if he should be found; wouldn't his friend the minister get into trouble too? So, in spite of all protests, Father Murphy set out one night on his journey home to Wexford.

He was crossing a stile at Drakestown Bridge when three Yomen, Corbally, Naulty and Smith, rushed upon him and foully murdered him. It was a terrible, never-to-be-forgotten deed, for these devils in human form were Catholics too, in the pay of the British.

The blood of this unfortunate priest can be seen to his day on the stones of Drakestown Bridge and on one stone is rudely cut out – ''98' – nothing more but quite enough, I say. I have seen it myself and the place where the poor croppies were buried too.

Black '46 and '47

SCHOOL: *Abbeytown Convent N.S., Boyle, Co. Roscommon*
TEACHER: *Sr. M. Columbanus*
COLLECTOR: *Dell Kivlehan, Ballinameen, Co. Roscommon*
INFORMANT: *Mr. Pat Carney, Granny, Ballinameen, Co. Roscommon*

The Famine times were during the years 1846 and '47. 'Black '46 and '47' they were called. They affected my district very much, and many people died. Before that time, there was a good population in the district, but after it, between some of the people dying and more of them emigrating to America, there were hardly any people left in it.

The start of the Famine was the failure of the potato crop in '46. Some of the people did not lose heart when they saw that, because they had enough of potato seed for the following year. They put their whole hearts into the crop of '47, but great was their dismay when they saw that crop failing before their eyes. At that time there was no mention of blue-stone and washing-soda in the country, which would prevent blight, and the people knew nothing about them. When the crop failed, the poor people were faced with starvation.

During those times, the people had to work very hard, by tilling their bits of land, and sowing crops of oats, which they had to sell to the English at a very low price. With this money the people had to pay the rent, which was very high, with the result that they had very little money left to buy food for themselves.

People died in great numbers in those times, and the only way they were buried was by digging holes in the ground, and putting the corpses into them, without any coffin and in most cases without the rites of the church.

There was one family named O'Beirne, who lived in Tartan — a district about two miles from the village of Ballinameen — and they were faced with starvation. There were ten of them in it altogether, and the youngest was only about six months. Three of the young fellows in the house got work, from some of the rich people in the district. In return the payment they got was plenty of food and drink, so that the household had plenty to eat for about a week. They were overjoyed when they saw all the food, and they sat down to eat a good meal, for the first time in many months. The poor people were weak from hunger, but still they ate a good meal. Alas! on the next day, the father and mother of the house were dead, and every day for about a week after that, the young people of the house were dying, until they were all dead. They were so weak with hunger, that when they had eaten such a good meal, they got kind of choked and smothered, and they were not able to live. All that family were wiped out during those years, and many more families besides.

The worst result of the Famine times in my district was emigration to America. The people went in small boats, and some of them died with fever on the way, and they were thrown into the sea, which was the only grave they could get, out in the middle of the ocean.

A little pet dog

SCHOOL: *Ballycallan, Co. Kilkenny*
TEACHER: *P.J. O'Hara*
INFORMANT: *Mrs. Kelly, Riesk, Kilmanagh, Co. Kilkenny*

There was a family living in Ballycallan during the Famine years and they had a little baby. One day, when the father was going out to work, he told his wife to have the child killed and cooked for him when he came home. The woman was out on the road crying and a gentleman was passing. He asked her why she was crying, and when she told him, he killed a little pet dog he had with him and gave it to her.

Black with fresh graves

SCHOOL: *Cloonmackon, Listowel, Co. Kerry*
TEACHER: *Liam Ó Catháin*
INFORMANT: *Dan Twomey, 50, Dromin, Listowel, Co. Kerry*

About a hundred years ago the Irish people were very badly off. They were treated cruelly under English laws and had to pay very high rents to the landlords and heavy taxes. They were scarcely able to live owing to the way they were crushed and could not afford to buy proper food or clothing. At that time there were no such foodstuffs as flour or tea and sugar, such as we use now, and people had to depend on the potato crop for their food. They had to eat potatoes with milk for their three meals.

In the year 1847 the potato crop failed and as they were depending on this crop for food they had nothing to eat. A great number of people died of hunger. Some people tried to live on boiled mangolds. The people who had the mangolds had to stay up all night watching them and those who had not any used to go out at night and steal a few to eat. Martin Kennelly of Dromin states that people used to make bread out of boiled turnips and mangolds minced with meal, but few people could get the meal, and the very poor people who had not much land had no mangolds or turnips set and had nothing to eat. These people used to go along streams and dykes and pick water cress, which they ate. He also says that several people were found dead from hunger in dykes where they used go picking the water cress.

Owing to the hunger and the sort of things people had to eat several diseases broke out and a large number also died from these diseases. He says that in one case a man was found dead in a field with grass in his mouth. The number of deaths was so high that all the grave yards were black with fresh graves, and this is one of the reasons why the year of the Famine is called Black Forty-seven.

The road was leading nowhere

SCHOOL: *Balla, Co. Mayo*
TEACHER: *P. Ó Maolanaigh*
COLLECTOR: *P. Ó Maolanaigh*

In this district the Famine came and the people suffered very much. The old people everywhere heard their grandfathers tell of the sufferings of the people. The blight came one day and the big stalks got black and withered in field after field in one day. The potatoes got soft and rotten straight away. They were unfit to eat after that day. Some people had meal enough for themselves but others had not. From the villages around the people flocked into the town. Some died on the way in. In Walshe's in Craggagh there were sacks of meal in the kitchen stacked up to the roof. People used to come for meal to there to buy it, or beg it if they had no money. Two men died there, one after getting some meal and milk, the other was dead just when he reached the garden. Both were buried beside a beech tree, which is still pointed out.

People ate rabbits, birds and hares. Some even ate docks and weeds and raw turnips. The people before this were fairly comfortable around Balla. The landlord was friendly and they were able to pay the rents by selling oats. They also set some wheat, kept some pigs and cattle and sheep. After the first year of the Famine all these were gone and very little relief came. A road was started through Nallys' farm at Leanagh. Nallys were the agents for the landlord. The road was leading really nowhere in particular. It may be easily traced at the present time. Then evictions came and whole families went to U.S.A. The landlord paid some of the passages, it is said. Traces of old houses that were knocked down can still be seen in the Ardboley, Ballymakergh, Prizon and Drumara districts around Balla.

People were buried in the field near the doctor's house and down in Drimadoon also. I heard one man, John Dockery, aged 71, say he heard of two who died and their bodies swelled up and turned black with the plague. No one would go near their house until soldiers came and buried them. They lived in Tavanagh na Bó, about three miles from Balla.

A pitiable state

SCHOOL: *An Clochar, Kilrush, Co. Clare*
TEACHER: *An tSr. Pól*

There are numerous tales of the Famine years, as they were called, in 1846 and 1847. In those years the potato crop failed and the potatoes, which were then the staple food in the country, blackened in the ground and were diseased and unfit for food. Then, owing to the shortage of food, the Government distributed meals through local agents. In some cases next was starvation and it is recorded that a man travelled thirty miles to Kilrush and was in such a pitiable state that he put his hand into a large boiler in which turnips were [being] boiled to get a turnip to eat, having scalded his hands.

There was an epidemic of cholera and the people died in large numbers. There was a case of a man in Kilrush who was [being] buried when he kicked at the cover of the coffin. He was released, his health was restored, and he afterwards went to Australia. The population decreased and a good many old habitations are landmarks of the Famine years.

14

FEAST DAYS AND CELEBRATIONS

'The Schools' Collection is a wonderful repository of information about Ireland's feast days. While some have faded or taken on new meaning with the passing of the years, I'm struck by how many have survived centuries of cultural shifts from the arrival of Christianity, the Vikings, the Normans, penal times and, more recently, the television and internet age.'

 HOSE OF A CERTAIN AGE will remember 'Holy Days of Obligation', feast days when Catholics were obliged to attend Mass and refrain from unnecessary work. Christmas Day, All Saints' Day, the Feast of the Immaculate Conception and St Patrick's Day were amongst the most important here in Ireland. However, with the decline in religious practice and the cultural slide from the sacred to the secular, the religious significance of the dates has waned. Some might argue that church attendance has been superseded by pub attendance. The term 'bank holiday' underlines the level of shift from the spiritual, although society has reclaimed the branding rights for what we now increasingly call 'public holidays'.

The history of most of Ireland's feast days is shrouded in the mists of time and it's hard to see their origins through the haze. Many of them are pre-Christian; others were transplanted from Rome, England and beyond. Even the names of the days of the week have their origins in Ancient Greece. Old Irish took the names from Latin, which itself had drawn on the Greek system of naming each of the seven days after the sun, moon and planets. The English names show Hebrew and Christian references, along with Germanic deities who had become part of Norse mythology. Wednesday is named after Woden, Thursday after Woden's son Thor, and Friday honours Woden's wife Frigga. So now, separate that lot!

There's a popular theory that St Patrick (d. 460 AD) landed on the east coast of Ireland and travelled up the Boyne to the Hill of Slane. It being Easter, he decided to light a Paschal flame at the top. In doing so, he upstaged King Laoire (Lóegaire, d. 462 AD), whose privilege it was to light the first fire, on the nearby Hill of Tara, as a symbol of his dominion over the land and its people. By all accounts, the King sent his druids to investigate and to remonstrate with the usurper. However, they returned to the King with 'the Good News', as Patrick might have described the Christian message. The King accepted Patrick and the rest, as they say, is history. Some cynics say the story is fanciful, as the two hills are 15km apart as the crow flies. Well, on our TV series *Creedon's Epic East*, we put the theory to the test. With the help of historian Mickey Dillon and the local community, we lit a huge fire on the Hill of Slane. We travelled the 21km by road to Tara, climbed to the top and pointed ourselves towards Slane. Lo and behold, just like King Laoire of old, we saw the light!

Given our weather, it's easy to understand why the ancient peoples of Northern Europe celebrated the passing of midwinter. Evergreen plants were considered special. Holly and ivy were brought indoors to ward off evil and as a symbol that life endured, even when much of nature was dead or dormant. I expect it's no coincidence that the modern-day Christmas tree is also an evergreen. The druids regarded mistletoe, which flowers in winter, as a symbol of life and fertility. The tradition of kissing under the mistletoe is another nod to reproduction. Soon spring would emerge and the sap would rise again.

However, the spread of Christianity through the Roman Empire, and eventually to Ireland, saw ancient ways reconstituted as 'Christian'. In 336 AD, Constantine, the first Roman emperor to embrace the teachings of Jesus, designated 25 December as the date of Christ's birth, in an attempt to upstage the existing pagan midwinter celebrations. Many other dates in the calendar went the same way. A case of 'If you can't beat 'em, join 'em, or at least meet 'em half-way.'

Turning to the Schools' Collection, Mr. P. Mc Gennis of Coragh, County Cavan, tells it straight and informs us that the Irish held bonfires on every hill long before the Christians arrived. He speaks of scores of girls and pagan youths spending long nights of mirth and carousing. St Patrick introduced rival midsummer feast days dedicated to St John and also Saints Peter and Paul, as Mr Mc Gennis puts it 'to prevent his converts from intercourse with the Pagans'. I can't help but see Fr Ted and Fr Dougal protesting outside the pagan bonfire with their 'Down With This Sort of Thing' placard.

St John's Night was known in my part of Cork City as 'Bonna Night'. Little did we know that we were upholding an ancient tradition that is rooted in the *tine chnámh* (lit. bone fire) and the practice of human sacrifice, or at least the burning of animal bones to fertilise the land. Nor did we care that our Easter eggs were a pagan celebration of fertility that somehow made its way into the passion and resurrection of Christ. We always referred to St Stephen's Day as 'Wran Day' and our little song went

> Knock at the knocker,
> Ring at the bell.
> Please gi's a copper
> for singing so well.

But there are some lovely local variations in the Collection. Many of these accounts also mention Shrove Tuesday. Apart from its religious significance,

Shrove Tuesday was a deadline for marriage, as weddings were not held during the 40 days of Lent. Bachelors and unwed young women would be publicly teased without mercy if they hadn't tied the knot by Shrove Tuesday. My friend and UCC folklorist Shane Lehane explained to me that there was one loophole available to such couples and it was to be found off the coast of West Kerry.

You see, Ireland finally adopted the Gregorian calendar in 1752. Incredibly, that year, Wednesday 2 September was followed by Thursday 14 September! However, the monastic settlement at Skellig Michael, like the Greek Orthodox Church, stuck by the older Julian calendar, meaning Easter fell later in the year. Many couples availed of what became known as 'Skelliging Day' to beat the Shrove Tuesday deadline!

The Schools' Collection is a wonderful repository of information about Ireland's feast days. While some have faded or taken on new meaning with the passing of the years, I'm struck by how many have survived centuries of cultural shifts, from the arrival of Christianity, the Vikings, the Normans, penal times and, more recently, the television and internet age. Much of the credit goes to the parents who supervise midsummer bonfires and the generations of teachers who have patiently helped little hands to shape a Brigid's Cross or to cut out and colour in shamrock badges for the St Patrick's Day Parade.

Brat Brigde

SCHOOL: *Ballyduff West, Co. Waterford*
TEACHER: *Caitlín Madders*

A very common custom in this part of the country is the hanging out of a ribbon or a piece of cloth on the night before St. Brigid's Day.

It is said that St. Brigid comes along and blesses it on that night. This ribbon or piece of cloth is supposed to be a cure for headache and sorethroat. It was usually titled by the old people as the 'BRAT BRIGDE'.

Another custom long ago was spreading freshly cut rushes out side the door for St. Brigid to walk upon when she was entering the house.

BRAT BRIGDE: *brat Bríde, Brigid's cloth or cloak.*

Drowning the shamrock

SCHOOL: *Garrafine, Co. Galway*
TEACHER: *Bean Uí Mhuirgheasa*
COLLECTOR: *Seán Morrissey, Garrafine, Co. Galway*
INFORMANT: *Mrs Tierney, grandmother, Esker, Co. Galway*

On St. Patrick's Day everyone is decorated with a shamrock, for it was with this plant that our patron saint taught the pagan Irish the mystery of the Blessed Trinity. In olden times the men used to get drunk; this was called drowning the shamrock.

On Twelfth Night, that is on the eve of January 6th, twelve candles are lighted and every member of the household chooses one. It is believed that the person who owns the candle that quenches first will die before the others in the house, and that whoever owns the candle that lasts the longest will live the longest. Long ago, instead of candles, the people used twelve rushes dipped in tallow, and up to about thirty years ago they made a cake of cow-dung and ashes in which they stuck the lighted rushes.

A great day in Ireland

SCHOOL: *Newmarket on Fergus, Co. Clare*
TEACHER: *P. Mac Conmara*
COLLECTOR: *Padraig Mac an Ultaig, 14, Latoon, Newmarket on Fergus, Co. Clare*

The feast day that I am going to talk about is called St. Patrick's Day. It is a great day in Ireland; the feast is held on the 17th of March. The people wear a piece of shamrock on that day. The shamrock does not grow in any other [country] but Ireland.

The people of Ireland at the time of Patrick were pagans. He went to every county town and village in Ireland except to Co. Clare. He blessed Clare from Knock Patrick, which is across the Shannon.

The people of Clare, especially from west Clare, went across the Shannon to hear him.

The sun and moon dancing

SCHOOL: *Edennagully, Co. Cavan*
TEACHER: *S. Ó Cléirigh, C. Ó Baoighealláin*
INFORMANT: *Bridget Claire, Moyer, Kingscourt, Co. Cavan*

There are still some Easter customs left in this district. On Easter Sunday morning most people eat two eggs for their breakfast. On that evening children gather together and light a fire outside in the fields. This fire is called CLÚDÓG. Another custom is that a few days before Easter the poor people send their children around through the country gathering eggs for Easter. This fire is lighted in honour of Saint Patrick lighting his fire on the Hill of Slain [Slane] on Easter Saturday. Also the lighting of the fire on Easter Sunday is held in honour of the Resurrection of our Lord from the dead.

Easter always comes in April or May. It is a great feast day in all countries. On the night before Easter severals of the people do not go to bed, the way they would be able to see the sun and moon dancing.

CLÚDÓG: *this term can mean a gift of eggs at Easter, or the tradition of cooking those eggs over an outdoor fire.*

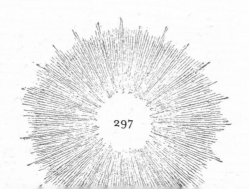

The May bush

SCHOOL: *Duleek, Co. Meath*
TEACHER: *Micheál Ó Braonáin*
COLLECTOR: *Seán Ó Conchubhair, Commons, Co. Meath*
INFORMANT: *Ristéard Ó Conchubhair, grandparent, 76, Commons, Co. Meath*

Long ago in Duleek on May Eve the boys would go away through the field for a May bush. When they would cut down the bush, they would trim it and bring it home.

When they would reach home the girls would have a good heap of flowers tied in little bunches. When the girls would hang all the flowers on the bush they would all go for sticks and furze. When they would come back with the sticks they would build a ring of stones round the May bush, with one stone in the middle. Then some of them would tie butts of candles on the May bush, while the rest of them would set the fire. Then some of the boys would stay at the May bush and mind it while the rest of them would go home for their supper. When they would come back the boys who were minding the May bush would go home for their supper.

When they would all be ready they would send someone round for the people. Then they would send for the fiddler, and he would sit on the stone under the May bush while the old people would sit on the stones round the May bush. Then the fiddler would start playing the fiddle while the people would dance. It would be a beautiful sight to look at the bush with all the candles in it.

The great fire they had to the memory of Baal

SCHOOL: *Lattoon, Co. Cavan*
TEACHER: *P. Ó Hiorraí*
COLLECTOR: *Brigid Coyle, Coragh, Ballyjamesduff, Co. Cavan*
INFORMANT: *Mr P. Mc Gennis, Coragh, Ballyjamesduff, Co. Cavan*

Bonfires were very common until 30 years ago and they are now completely wiped out. The chief cause of the decay of bonfires is due in part to lack of firewood and another cause is the decrease of the population of youngsters. In the olden times there was a bonfire on every hill, but in parts of the locality there was a special bonfire and young men and some old people too walked a considerable distance to one of these given out bonfires. There would be fiddlers and all kinds of musicians, tambouring and fires. Young girls were there by the score and if the night was good and dry they sang and danced until the small hours of the morning, and this custom was continued from the time of St. Patrick.

When he came to convert the Irish people they had their great bonfires, especially the great fire they had to the memory of Baal, their chief god. Young men frequented these bonfires which were held on the 1st of May. They had various games and athletic fetes and other games, mirth and carousing, and the Pagan youth watched and waited eagerly for May Eve. So as St. Patrick went through Ireland converting young and old he found it difficult to keep the young men converted to his faith (and idols) from patronising the great Pagan bonfire. The saint and wise man, as he was, thought the best and only means to prevent his converts from intercourse with the Pagans and their fires was to have a bonfire in memory of St. Peter and St. Paul on the eve of the 23rd of June and on St John's eve. So that is how the first bonfires started and continued to be held, but alas they are gone, never to return.

The bone-fire

SCHOOL: *Ballyburke, Co. Mayo*
TEACHER: *Micheál Ó Cheallaigh*
COLLECTOR: *James Ludden, Ballyburke, Ayle, Westport, Co. Mayo*
INFORMANT: *Maggie Ludden, Ballyburke, Ayle, Westport, Co. Mayo*

There was a man long ago and he used to be at every BONE-FIRE. As soon as he had finished with one bone-fire he would go off to another one. St John's eve falls on the twenty third of June every year. It [is] a custom to throw a bone into the middle of the fire. There is a bone-fire on the top of every hill because the first fire was lit on the top of a hill. It is a custom to have a fire every year on the top of a hill. All the children bring a load or two of turf. The fire is lit early in the evening. When the people are going home they bring a coal with them and they throw it into the crop because the people say that it makes the crop grow better. The bone-fire lasts a long time. It is going on until two or three o'clock in the morning. They say prayers at the bone-fire. They get six or seven small BEBBLES and every time they go around the fire they throw a bebble into the fire. There does be all kinds of fun and sport at the bone-fire.

BONE-FIRE: *tine chnámh, bonfire.*
BEBBLES: *pebbles.*

November night

SCHOOL: *Ballindereen, Co. Galway*
TEACHER: *Treasa Bean Uí Bheirn*
COLLECTOR: *Kathleen Flannery*
INFORMANT: *Michael Fahy, 78, Cartron, Co. Galway, and John Flannery, 48, Ballindereen, Co. Galway*

November night is generally called 'Halloween' in this district. On that night several games are played by the young children. Long ago the young and old people used to take parts in the games but nowadays the games are played by the youngsters.

First the household and the neighbours, if there is any into visit, have a big feast. After the feast the children play the games such as the Blind Man's Buff, Snap Apple, and divining in water for money.

Then they leave down three saucers of water with a ring in the first saucer, a thimble in the second and a sixpence in the third saucer. It is then the fun begins. A buff is put around one person's face and he walks to the place where the saucers are placed. It is said if the person puts his hand into the saucer where the ring is he will be married the soonest, and if he puts into the saucer where the thimble is he will never get married. If he puts his hand into the saucer where the sixpence is he will be rich forever.

Then three more saucers are left down. Water is put in to the first saucer, clay into the second saucer and a bead in the third saucer. If the person puts his hand into the saucer where the clay is [he] will be the soonest to die and if he puts his hand into the saucer where the water is he will cross the water. If he puts his hand into the saucer where the bead is he or she will be a priest or a nun.

Old customs about Saint Martin's Day

SCHOOL: *Ballindine, Co. Mayo*
TEACHER: *Séamus P. Ó Gríobhtha*
COLLECTOR: *James Cleary, Cloonmore, Co. Mayo*
INFORMANT: *John Cleary, 45, Cloonmore, Co. Mayo*

Saint Martin's Day is on the eleventh of November. They used to kill a cock and a goose and they used to sprinkle the blood on the four corners of the house and on the door steps. That was the superstition they had. They thought that it would keep away evil and misfortune for the year. The old people used not spin wool or work a spinning wheel. They would not work a grinding mill because they said that when Saint Martin was killed he was grinded under a wheel.

The old customs about Saint Martin's Day are observed yet. They used to cook the goose on Saint Martin's night. They used to cook the cock on the evening of Saint Martin's Day. That was the custom they had of cooking the fowl. Some people used not kill a goose for Saint Martin's Day.

Christmas Day

SCHOOL: *Cloncarneel, Co. Meath*
TEACHER: *Máire, Bean Uí Bhreacáin*
COLLECTOR: *Phyllis Boylan, Moyfeigher, Kildalkey, Co. Meath*

On Christmas Eve the people are very busy decorating the house. First it is white-washed and painted. Then holly, ivy, and mistletoe are put on the walls and behind the pictures.

The children go to bed early that night. They hang up their stockings for Santa Claus to put toys in them. In the morning they are overjoyed to see the toys.

The people have a turkey or a goose for the dinner on Christmas Day. They also have a plum-pudding.

All the shopkeepers give a Christmas-Box to all their customers. The children play all day with their toys. People send cards to one another at Christmas.

People buy a very large candle at Christmas. It is lit and put in the window. Some people leave the door open as a sign of welcome to any poor travellers who maybe out that night. On that night they think of the way Joseph and Mary were treated in Bethlehem, when all the doors were shut on them, and they do not want to treat travellers in the same unwelcome manner.

Festival customs

SCHOOL: *Páirc Árd (High Park), Carrowgilhooly, Co. Sligo*
TEACHER: *Eoghan Ó Conaill*
COLLECTOR: *Kathleen Diamond, Tubberunane, Skreen, Co. Sligo*
INFORMANT: *Mrs Dooney, 45, Tubberunane, Skreen, Co. Sligo, and Mrs Diamond, 50, Tubberunane, Skreen, Co. Sligo*

Saint Martin's Day

It is said that it is not right to put a wheel of [machinery] round on that day. One memorable instant happened near ourselves, when Ballisodare Mills went on fire on St Martin's Day and when there were a lot of lives lost, and that happened about seventy years ago. It is supposed that if they had not put the wheel round that day, the mills would not be burnt or the lives would not be burnt either. It is said that the fox knows St Martin's Day as he kills fowl on that day or else the night and he sheds their blood also.

May Day

It is supposed when you are milking on May Day and if a person crosses your field that time, it is said you will never have a bit of butter that year again. It is also said that when you go out milking on May morning or evening you should give the first few streams of milk to the fairies and that you will have luck during the rest of the year when you will leave the first few streams of milk on the grass for the fairies.

Good Friday

On Good Friday people sow seeds in the ground as it is said it is a very lucky day for sowing seed. It is also said any eggs that are laid on Good Friday, if you watch them and keep them safe, they will keep fresh for a year.

Whit Sunday

It is said if you get a cut on your finger on Whit Sunday that it will never get better and that there will be always a mark on it.

Shrove Tuesday

Any house you would see a flock of geese around that wasn't eaten at Xmas it is said that there was surely a young girl there long ago, on the look out of a young man, and they kept on the fowl so that there would be a fowl for the dinner on Shrove Tuesday for the wedding; and Shrove long ago was a great time for marriages.

Michaelmas Day

An old time custom is a roast goose on Michaelmas day for the dinner and people that have them always try to kill one for the dinner that day as it is said from that day on they are fit for killing.

Little Xmas

At Little Xmas some people get twelve rushes, name twelve if they are in the house, and if they are not, name as many as are in the house. Then take the rushes, peel them, dry them, and grease them, then light them on Little Xmas night; and it is said which ever of the rushes burns out first, it is supposed they are first to die in the house, and which ever of them keeps lit the longest are supposed to live the longest in the house.

Xmas Day there's full and plenty,
New Year's Day is very scanty,
And the twelfth Day
the bag is empty.
We will wash our face in a cabbage bowl,
And dry it in a silken towel,
And go up to Heaven to School,
On Easter Sunday morning.

Some people say on Easter Sunday morning just at sunrise they see the sun dancing and it is said with that dancing it cuts the image of a cross in the sky.

Many feasts are followed in some special way

SCHOOL: *Milltown, Newbridge, Co. Kildare*
TEACHER: *S. P. Ó Donnchadha*
COLLECTOR : *Nell Maguire, Hawkfield, Newbridge, Co. Kildare*

In most districts many feasts are followed in some special way as they occur each year. On St Stephen's Day, boys and in some places grown up men gather together in small bands and go around from house to house, singing the wren song; they have a decorated bush, with a wren on it, and sometimes they only have an imitation of a wren on it. The song sung is:

The wren, the wren, the king of all birds.
St Stephen's Day, she was caught in the furze
Although she is little her family is great.
Rise up land-lady, and give us a 'TRATE'.
Up with the kettle, and down with the pan
Give us a 'trate' and let us be gone.

On Shrove Tuesday most people make pan-cakes, and eat them with their tea that evening. Many people in my locality say it is lucky to get married on Shrove Tuesday.

On Easter Sunday it is a custom for all people to eat many eggs on that day, and the children eat chocolate eggs, and sometimes boys and girls, and sometimes grown-up men, come out to the country from the towns, looking for Easter eggs. The eggs that are laid on Good Friday are marked with a pencil, and are eaten on Easter Sunday.

In most places a May bush is decorated and placed outside the door during May Day. If the wind is coming from the north early on May morning, it is the sign of a good summer.

On Hallow E'en the boys and girls of this locality dress up in queer old clothes and put VIZARDS on their faces and go from house to house, singing and dancing, and they get money and nuts and apples. In almost all homes, there are games played by the children, such as 'snap apple' diving for apples, nuts, and money in a bath of water; most people have a barm brack for Hallowe'en. On Christmas Eve in most places a big candle is lit and put in the window, because it is said that the Blessed Virgin and Saint Joseph pass by every house that night, and put a special blessing on the house where the candle is lighting to show them light.

TRATE: *a treat.*
VIZARDS: *masks.*

A very enjoyable time of the year

SCHOOL: *Clochar na Trócaire, Ballymahon, Co. Longford*
TEACHER: *Sr. M. Clement*
COLLECTOR: *Nora Walsh, 12, Toome, Ballymahon, Co. Longford*
INFORMANT: *Joe Walsh, brother, Toome, Ballymahon, Co. Longford*

Christmas Day

Christmas is a very enjoyable time of the year. The people are always very busy preparing for it. About a fortnight beforehand they whitewash the walls, and a few days before Christmas they decorate the walls with holly and ivy. They also hang up Christmas decorations. A couple of days before Christmas my mother makes a plum-pudding, and cakes and other kinds of puddings. Then there is midnight Mass on Christmas Eve and all the people attend it.

The children go to bed early and hang up their stockings on the end of their beds for Santa Clause to put presents into them. Next morning they awake very early and jump up to see what they have in their stockings. On Christmas Day they keep playing with their toys. The dinner is very late on Christmas Day as my mother has to cook the goose.

On Christmas Eve the people light candles because they think that Our Blessed Lady would be going about and the light would show her the way. There are five Masses said in our Parish Church on Christmas Day.

St. Stephen's Day

St. Stephen's Day falls on the twenty-sixth of December. St Stephen was the first martyr who shed his blood for Our Lord, for he was stoned to death. We all look forward to St. Stephen's Day. Some people call it the wren-day, because on that day the boys go out to hunt the wren.

They all dress themselves very queer and they put on false faces. Then they go from house to house dancing and one of them plays music. The people of the house give them money. They carry big sticks and one of them carries a dead wren. [...]

The Mummers' Day

The Mummers' Day always falls on the first of January. It is nearly like the wren-day. On that day the boys all dress up the same as on St. Stephen's Day. They put on queer clothes and false faces. The boys wear girls' clothes, and the men wear women's clothes.

Then they go from house to house dancing and singing. One of them plays music and the others all dance. Sometimes they dress up an ass with ribbons, bells and holly. Then one boy rides the ass, and another boy leads him from house to house. When the ass would walk the ribbons would fly in the air, and the bells would shake.

On that day the children divide the money between themselves, and the big people buy drink. Any person who goes out to hunt the mummers has to get leave from the guards first. I like the mummer's day.

Shrove

Shrove is the time between Christmas and Ash Wednesday. During that time the people make matches and get married. On Shrove Tuesday night my mother makes pancakes and it is called pancake night. The next day is Ash Wednesday and from Ash Wednesday to Easter Sunday the people never get married.

St. Patrick's Day

St. Patrick's Day always falls on the seventeenth of March. On that day all the people wear shamrocks in honour of St. Patrick. The girls wear green harps, and green dresses, and green bands on their hair on that day. The band goes up and down the street playing 'Hail Glorious Saint Patrick' and 'The Rising of the Moon'. On St. Patrick's Day the children are always merry. The big people have dances on that night because they have no dances during the rest of Lent. Everyone likes that day.

Easter Sunday

Easter Sunday is a movable feast. On the first Easter Sunday Our Lord rose from the dead. The old people say that the sun dances in the sky on that morning. The people always look forward to that day because whatever they give up for lent they can enjoy on Easter Sunday.

On that morning some people sell Easter lilies and they also wear them. Some people call Easter Sunday the 'Sunday of the eggs'. It is so called because the people used not eat any eggs during Lent, and on that morning the children would have a competition to see which of them would eat the most.

The people have a great feast for their dinner that day. They always have roast beef. Then they have some kind of a pudding and jelly for dessert after their dinner. Everyone likes Easter Sunday.

May Day

May Day is the first of Summer. The people observe many customs about that day. Some people never change to a new job on May Day as they think it very unlucky. Other people never go to a new house on that day, as they think that the fairies have possession of the house, and they think that they would never have a day's luck in it. Then some people never churn on that day as they think that the fairies would run away with the butter.

If a poor person or a neighbour went to a house for a drink of milk, some people would not give it to them, as they consider it very unlucky to give away anything on May Day. They say that if you give away things on May Day that you will be giving them away all the year. Some of the people never sell milk on that day as they think that the people to whom they sell it would steal the butter. If the people did sell milk they would put a grain of salt in it, in order that the person to whom they sold it could not steal the butter.

The night before, the children gather cowslips and they throw them at the door and some people make a may-bush. If you washed your hands in the dew on that morning you could open any knot that would come before you that year.

St. John's Eve

St John's Eve always falls on the twenty-first of June. A couple of days before that day the boys go around collecting turf and sticks. Then they get more turf in the bog. They also get rubber and straw. Then they settle a place to light a bon-fire and they bring the turf and all the other things to that place. Then they light the fire and they sing and dance around it till about eleven o'clock. They go to a certain house and they dance there till the next morning. The people say that it is the longest day and the shortest night of the year.

Special things to hang up

SCHOOL: *Naomh Nioclás, an Cladach, Townparks, Co. Galway*
TEACHER: *P.S. Ó Neachtain*
COLLECTOR: *Patrick Doyle*
INFORMANT: *Mrs Doyle, 39, New Docks, Co. Galway*

Sometimes the people have special things to hang up in honour of some feasts in their houses. For one example there is Saint Patrick's cross. This is usually made of straw and is shaped like a cross. It is hung up some time before Saint Patrick's Day. The usual place is over the door of the house.

Next is Saint Brigid's Cross. It is shaped more or less like a diamond and it is also made of straw. The straw is placed bit by bit and is woven tightly. The most usual place one can see one of these is in a country house some time around the feast-days.

Herbs and branches: – The people usually hang up a branch covered with leaves called May-bush on May Eve. They say that this is to bring luck. Nettles are boiled for young ducks and are used for hunting flies out of a house. Cuckoo saddle grows in fields and has a salty taste, and the leaves are small with long stems.

Woven articles: – The young people in this district make hats out of reeds. They are pointed at the top and there is a space of an inch or so between each reed.

Pieces of cloth: – The people have an old custom of collecting pieces of cloth such as those worn by saints. They say that there is a cure in these by believing in the power of God.

Holy water from blessed wells: – The last Sunday in July is the usual day for visiting St Augustine's Well in this district. The people take a small amount of holy water home and they have great faith in its cures. Easter Saturday we go to the chapels and take holy water home.

Acknowledgements

A little encouragement never goes astray, and neither does a little gratitude. I would like to thank everyone who assisted in the making of this book:

Deirdre Nolan, who paved the way for the project to move beyond the 'what a lovely idea' stage.

Críostóir Mac Cárthaigh of the National Folklore Collection at University College Dublin for trusting me with the key to this priceless archive.

Josephine Weatherford for investing so much of her time in the work and for brilliantly guiding me through the huge volume of material.

Again, I salute the wonderfully supportive team at Gill Books, who ensured a safe delivery: Aoibheann Molumby, Teresa Daly, Fiona Murphy and Paul Neilan.

I'm also hugely grateful to Esther Ní Dhonnacha, and to Brian Gallagher for his brilliantly evocative illustrations.

I also wish to acknowledge the assistance of the staff at the Royal Irish Academy; An Roinn Béaloideas at University College Cork; the Heritage Council; the Office of Public Works; and Cork City Library.

Míle buíochas do Cristín Ní Chonchubhair as Ionad na Gaeilge Labhartha at UCC, who is hugely missed. Cristín's classes had as tight a weave of good humour and love of Irish as a good súgan. Suaimhneas síoraí dá hanam.

I'd like to acknowledge all the publications that have fed my understanding of the subject matter here, including Patrick Logan's *Holy Wells of Ireland*, Seán Ó Súilleabháin's *Handbook of Irish Folklore*, and *The Cork Anthology* by Seán Dunne.

I'd also like to thank the numerous other writers and folklorists whose passion for the people fuels my own love of folklore. Amongst them are Eddie Lenihan of Brosna, Co. Kerry; Shane Lehane from the Department of Folklore and Ethnology at UCC; and before him, his father Tadgh Lehane, whose illustrations in the *Evening Echo* ignited my boyhood sense of wonder.

I am forever grateful to Peter Woods, Elizabeth Laragy, Colm Crowley, Séan Mac Giolla Phádraig, Ann-Marie Power, Jim Jennings, Margaret Newport, Martina McGlynn and numerous other colleagues in RTÉ for their ongoing encouragement and faith in me.

In particular, I salute the Irish Folklore Commission, for initiating the Schools' Collection back in 1937, and the Department of Education and the teachers of the INTO for facilitating this remarkable meitheal.

Huge credit is also due to Dúchas for overseeing the digitisation of this wonderful hive of information.

But above all else, I salute the worker bees: the children.